Praise for Brett Battles
And the Jonathan Quinn series

THE CLEANER

"Brett Battles makes a grand entrance into the thriller scene with this **unputdownable** spy novel. *The Cleaner* has it all: exotic locales, James Bondian derring-do, and ingenious plot twists that will keep you sweating all the way till the end."
—TESS GERRITSEN, *New York Times* bestselling author

"This book is a pure delight. Protagonist Jonathan Quinn is a unique and welcome addition to the world of crime fiction. *The Cleaner* is a brilliant and **heart-pounding** thriller; I'm on the edge of my seat, awaiting future installments of Quinn's adventures."
—JEFFERY DEAVER, *New York Times* bestselling author

"An emotionally tense tale of espionage and betrayal from a new author who writes with assurance and sophistication, *The Cleaner*'s **teeth-gritting action** is an auspicious debut for the talented Brett Battles."
—PERRI O'SHAUGHNESSY,
New York Times bestselling author

"Hypnotically gripping, *The Cleaner* moves with the speed of an assassin's unerring bullet. From Colorado to Vietnam and Germany, this **ripping-good read** will leave anyone who loves suspense not only happily satisfied but eager for Battles's next thriller."
—GAYLE LYNDS, *New York Times* bestselling author

"Brett Battles is a compelling new voice in the thriller genre. *The Cleaner* combines the best elements of Lee Child, John le Carré and Robert Ludlum. Deftly plotted, perfectly paced and expertly executed . . . Jonathan Quinn is a character worth rooting for. Battles is a **master storyteller.** Find a comfortable chair and plan to stay up late. You won't be able to put it down. A stellar debut."

—SHELDON SIEGEL, *New York Times* bestselling author

"*The Cleaner* is a terrific novel. It features a compelling plot, **thrilling action** and an unforgettable cast of characters. This debut novel is a powerful read."

—ROBERT K. TANENBAUM,
New York Times bestselling author

"Globetrotting suspense, intriguing characters and a plot that ricochets like a bullet, Battles's first novel is definitely in the running for **best thriller debut of the year.**" —*Daily Record* (UK)

"A page-turner . . . Quinn [is] a **compelling** protagonist. . . . Admirers of quality espionage fiction can look forward to a new series worth following."—*Publishers Weekly*

"Battles hits for extra bases in his first novel. *The Cleaner* is **a tightly written page-turner,** filled with tradecraft and offering as much action as a James Bond film . . . a wild ride." —*Booklist*

SHADOW OF BETRAYAL

"Battles has established himself as **one of today's best thriller writers,** right up there with Lee Child, Barry Eisler and Thomas Perry. His writing is smooth and perfectly paced. His 'cleaner' is eminently believable as well

as a hero worth caring about. I look forward to many more years of Brett Battles's books on my nightstand."
—*Deadly Pleasures*

"As in [Battles's] previous two Jonathan Quinn novels, **the action is heart-pounding**, gripping, and always engaging."
—*Tucson Citizen*

"An absolute pleasure to read. Battles has a true gift for writing thrillers and this book should put him on everyone's list. . . . From page one this is **a perfect summer read**."
—*Crimespree* magazine

"[A] plot so **downright clever** it's a wonder somebody hasn't tried something similar in real life. Start *Shadow of Betrayal* early in the day, or be prepared for a later-than-usual bedtime."
—*BookPage*

"Battles **keeps the reader hooked** to the last sentence. *Shadow of Betrayal* is a wonderful thriller."
—www.iloveamystery.com

THE DECEIVED

"Breakneck pacing, colorful locales, and **dizzying plot twists** make the Quinn series a welcome addition to the political thriller genre."
—*Publishers Weekly*

"Plenty of **globetrotting nonstop action**, plot twists, tight writing, whiz-bang high-tech devices . . . Derring-do will always find an audience."
—*Booklist*

"A successful sequel to *The Cleaner*. **Highly recommended.**"
—*Library Journal* (starred review)

"**Complex and believable.**"
—*Deadly Pleasures*

NO RETURN

A NOVEL

BRETT BATTLES

DELL
NEW YORK

A Dell Mass Market Original

Copyright © 2012 by Brett Battles

All rights reserved.

Published in the United States by Dell, an imprint of The Random House Publishing Group, a division of Random House, Inc., New York.

DELL is a registered trademark of Random House, Inc., and the colophon is a trademark of Random House, Inc.

ISBN 978-0-440-24562-9
eBook ISBN 978-0-345-53219-0

Cover design: Jerry Todd

Printed in the United States of America

www.bantamdell.com

9 8 7 6 5 4 3 2 1

Dell mass market edition: February 2012

There are two people
I'd like to dedicate this novel to—
Gunnar, the best friend the teenage me
could have ever had,
and Lieutenant Commander Theodore Faller,
a true hero

NO
RETURN

CHAPTER
1

A DISTANT BOOM ECHOED FAINTLY ACROSS THE hills.

Wes Stewart peered at the sky. He recognized the sound, but it was one he hadn't heard in years.

"What the hell was that?" Danny DeLeon asked. He was holding the second camera.

"Sonic boom."

Danny still looked confused, so Wes added, "You know, when a jet breaks the sound barrier."

"Really?"

Wes squinted toward the western horizon, then raised his arm and pointed. "There. See him?"

Danny shaded his eyes. "I don't see anything."

"Flying south, just a little bit above the mountains." Wes's finger tracked the movement of the jet.

"No, I don't. . . . Wait. It's like a white dot."

Wes nodded. "Yep."

"That thing's moving *fast*."

"It's a fighter jet, Danny. That's what they do."

"Damn."

While it was novel to Danny, for Wes it was a reminder of a time when he would have barely noticed a sky full of jets.

"You guys set?" Dione Li, their producer/director, asked from behind them. She was leading a group of three others over to the base of the rock formation. The look on her face was pure Dione: ten percent annoyed, fifteen percent pissed, and one hundred percent determined. "We got a lot to do today, and I don't want to mess around."

"Same speech, different city," Danny said through the side of his mouth.

"I'm sweating," Monroe Banks announced, more an accusation than a statement.

"On it," Anna Mendes called out. She whipped out a couple of Kleenex from the makeup utility belt around her waist and dabbed at a line of perspiration that had formed on Monroe's forehead.

"Is it going to be this hot every day?" Monroe whined as she fanned herself with her hand.

Wes rolled his eyes. The last he'd checked, the temperature had been hovering around ninety-two degrees, not so bad for mid-day in the high Mojave Desert. Of course, that was because it was October—not August, or July, or September, or June, or even May, when it seldom dipped below one hundred while the sun was out.

Donning her faux, producer-mode smile, Dione stepped over to the spot she'd picked out earlier, then turned back to the others. "So, Monroe, we'll have you stand right here for the intro shot. Behind you we'll see the empty desert, then, as you finish, look to your right and follow the rock up. Wes will mimic your movement with the camera. Danny, I want you to get a wide shot from down the slope. Try to get as many of the formations—"

"Pinnacles," Wes corrected her.

"As many *pinnacles*," Dione said, smirking, "as you can into the frame."

Danny gave her a nod. "Will do." He shuffle-stepped down the small slope into position.

Their location was the Trona Pinnacles, a group of tufa deposits that stretched in an east–west line across the dry bed of Searles Lake. It was a few hours north of Los Angeles, and twenty miles from Wes's hometown of Ridgecrest, California. The Pinnacles had been formed by an ancient sea, and the best way Wes had ever heard them described was as a bunch of giant, caveless stalagmites.

Alison Pringle, the tallest member of the crew, slipped behind Wes. "Where do you want me so I'm not in your way?" she asked.

Wes pointed at a spot a few feet behind his position. "There should be good."

She touched his arm just below his shoulder. "Thanks." She smiled, then moved off.

While Monroe moved into position, Dione glanced at Alison. "Are we good with sound?"

"Monroe, can you give me a level?" Alison wore a pair of headphones that allowed her to monitor both Monroe's voice and any ambient noises the host's mic might pick up.

"One. Two. Three."

"We're fine," Alison said.

"Four," Monroe finished.

Dione turned her attention to Wes. "Set?"

Wes nodded.

She leaned toward him, and in a low voice asked, "You all right?"

"Yeah, I'm fine."

"You're awfully quiet."

Wes frowned. "No I'm not."

"Whatever you want to think, but, yeah, you are." She did a quick check of the rest of the crew, then said, "All right, Monroe. Whenever you're ready."

Monroe closed her eyes for a second. When she opened them again, an entirely different person emerged. The less-than-pleasant Monroe the crew had been subjected to since they'd arrived in Ridgecrest the night before had been replaced by the bright, friendly version the 1.3 million viewers of *Close to Home* were used to seeing.

"All right," Dione said. "Here we go. And . . . Monroe."

Monroe gave it a beat, then, "A vast nothingness. Brown for as far as the eye can see. A wasteland. A place no one would willingly visit, right?" Another beat. "If you believed that, then you'd be missing out on some of the most interesting and beautiful parts of the Mojave Desert north of Los Angeles. Hi, I'm Monroe Banks, and welcome to another episode of *Close to*—"

"Hold on," Alison called out.

Dione groaned. "Seriously? She almost had it in one take."

Alison had a hand pressing one side of her headphones tight against her skull. "I'm picking up a hum."

"Electrical?" Wes asked.

Alison shook her head. "Don't think so."

"I don't hear anything," Dione said.

"It's getting loud—"

"I think I hear something," Wes said. It wasn't so much a hum as a rumbling whine.

"I hear it, too," Monroe said, cocking her head.

A second later it was loud enough for everyone to hear.

Dione frowned. "What the hell is—"

"Oh, God!" Danny cried out from the bottom of the slope.

He was staring off to the east.

Whatever he'd seen was hidden from the others by the massive pinnacle at their side. Wes half ran, half slid down the slope toward his fellow cameraman.

"Where are you going?" Dione shouted after him. "I want to get this shot off."

She hadn't seen the look on Danny's face. Wes had. Danny was terrified.

As Wes skidded to a stop he turned his head to follow Danny's gaze, but it took a moment for his mind to actually figure out what he was seeing.

A military jet. A fighter.

Only instead of being a white dot in the distance, this one was a mass of gray ripping through the sky no more than five hundred feet above the ground. And its trajectory was taking it lower, not higher.

Wes's first thought was that it was going to crash. His second was, *It's going to crash into us.*

"What?" Danny said, alarmed.

Wes hadn't realized he'd spoken aloud.

"Up the slope. Behind the rock," he yelled.

Not having to be told twice, Danny took off running for the questionable safety of the pinnacle.

Wes scrambled to follow, but slipped on the loose dirt and fell to his knees. The ground began to shake as the roar of the aircraft intensified. He looked back quickly and saw there was no way he was going to make it to shelter in time.

He was going to die.

He started to turn away, but a flash of light from the back of the jet stopped him. For half a second it seemed as if nothing had changed, then the nose of the aircraft inched upward a few feet, and the jet veered to the left, away from the pinnacle.

He saw me, Wes thought. *He saw me and did something to miss me.*

But whatever the pilot had done was only enough to change his path, not his fate. Wes watched as the plane began dropping lower and lower—its new target the emptiness south of the crew's position.

Wes pushed himself up and began sprinting toward the crew's vehicles. He'd only made it a dozen feet when—

Whomp.

He skidded to a stop, mesmerized as the plane plowed into the desert floor.

He had expected the jet to flip and roll, breaking into a million pieces seconds after it smashed into the ground. Instead, the multimillion-dollar aircraft barreled through the earth, throwing up dirt and plants and rocks, but remaining intact. Then, just before it stopped, it twisted sideways, enveloping itself in a cloud of dust.

Wes jerked out of his trance and raced the rest of the way to the green Ford Escape he'd been in charge of driving out to the location that morning.

As he started to drive off, he glanced back and saw some of the shoot crew running toward the other vehicle, a Toyota Highlander. Dione was in the lead and waving frantically for Wes to stop.

But stopping wasn't an option. He jammed the accelerator to the floor and sped into the open desert.

CHAPTER 2

WITH NO ROAD OR PATH TO FOLLOW, WES
pushed the Escape faster than he should, bouncing over
dirt and rocks and avoiding what vegetation he could.
Soon he was surrounded by sagebrush set ablaze by the
crash.

Thump.

Sparks flew out from the side of the car as he smashed
over a clump of burning brush.

Immediately he heard a rumble. *The axle?* Had he
damaged it?

Just then a fighter streaked across the sky, a mere hundred feet above his roof.

Jerking back in surprise, Wes nearly swerved the truck
into the gouge created by the crash. But he quickly regained control and shoved the accelerator back to the
floor.

It took him four and a half minutes to get from the
pinnacles to the plane. Four and a half minutes that felt
like a year.

Slamming to a stop, he jumped out of the SUV and
ran toward the aircraft. The fighter that had buzzed by

moments before had been joined by another, both circling helplessly a few hundred feet above the wreck of their friend.

The dust cloud from the crash was still dissipating as Wes weaved around the small pockets of fire where the groundcover was burning.

The aircraft was pointed almost toward him, so he could see into the cockpit. The glass canopy was gone. He had no idea when that had happened, or where it was for that matter. It certainly had been in place when the plane had swept past him before it had hit the ground.

Wes looked around anxiously, thinking that maybe the pilot had been able to eject. But then he spotted a person still in the cockpit, slumped to the side, unmoving.

Unmoving didn't mean dead, though.

Wes ran around the plane looking for the easiest way up. But the brush next to the aircraft was more densely packed, pushed together by the crash, and all of it on fire. He continued searching until he spotted a narrow gap.

I can make that, he thought.

Somewhere behind him doors opened, then slammed shut.

"Wes!" It was Dione. "Get back!"

He ignored her as he sprinted toward the gap, then leapt up onto the wing at the last second. But he landed hard, his knees slamming into metal and sending him sliding backward. Groaning, he clutched at the wing to keep from falling off. Once he'd stopped moving, he shoved himself to his feet and lurched toward the fuselage.

"Wes!" Dione yelled. "That thing could explode!"

Wes reached the fuselage, then shimmied down a lip that ran from the wing to the cockpit. He could see the back of the pilot's head now, tilted to one side, still motionless.

He grabbed the back of the cockpit opening and threw himself forward, aiming his feet for the lip just outside the pilot area. But his toes barely touched the edge before slipping off. Immediately he clamped his hands tight to the rim of the cockpit to keep from falling to the ground. Below his dangling feet, he could feel heat from the burning brush.

"Wes!" a different voice—Anna, it sounded like—called out.

He heaved himself upward, scrambling with his legs until one of his feet found the lip. Ten seconds later he was exactly where he'd been trying to get, only now sporting a long scratch down the inside of his left arm.

He leaned into the cockpit and pressed two fingers against the man's neck. A pulse. Strong.

"Can you hear me?" Wes said.

No response.

He quickly scanned the man's dark green flight suit for any blood. When he saw none, he probed lightly down the man's arm, across his ribs, then down his thighs.

He was pretty sure the pilot's left leg was broken, and possibly two of the ribs. But there were no other obvious injuries.

"Hey," he said again.

The pilot remained motionless.

He was about to give the man a shake when he noticed something that should have registered right away. The pilot was holding his helmet under his left arm.

Holding his helmet. No way he'd been flying like that.

"Hey," Wes said, moving the man's face side to side. "Hey, wake up!"

There was a moan, but nothing more.

"Come on, buddy. Wake up!"

This time the man's head rolled forward, then slowly tilted up.

"Good, good," Wes said. "We got to get you out of this thing."

Wes grabbed the buckle of the harness holding the man to the chair and tried to pop it open, but it didn't budge.

"Is there some kind of safety lock on this?" Wes asked.

The man moaned again. "See the ground . . . trying . . . it's not . . . it's not. . . ."

Wes slapped the pilot's face. "You've gotta wake up." This time the man's eyes blinked several times, then opened all the way. "I'm trying to get you out of here, but I can't undo your harness. Help me. What am I doing wrong?"

The pilot jerked his head right, then left, his consciousness returning. He focused on Wes. "What happened?"

"You put your plane down in the middle of the desert," Wes told him. "And if you help me, you'll actually walk away."

"The crash," the man said. "Oh, God. Tried to eject . . . followed protocols but . . . the display . . . the electrical . . . everything just . . . something . . ."

"Yeah, okay. We can talk about that later," Wes told him. He yanked on the harness, but it didn't give. "Help me get this open."

The man looked down at his chest, staring for a moment.

"Jammed," he said. "Already tried. Wouldn't open." His head lolled back. "Must have blacked out."

Wes stared at the buckle. If it was jammed, how was he going to get the guy out? There had to be some way. His eyes moved from the buckle to—

The straps! He could cut through them.

He turned and looked out at the others. Dione and Anna were standing back by the SUVs, looking worried.

"I need a knife!" Wes yelled.

Dione pointed to her ear and shook her head.

"Dammit," he cursed under his breath.

Just then something off to his right caught his attention. Danny. He was toward the front of the plane, holding his camera and shooting the wreck.

"You have a knife?" Wes yelled.

Danny moved his eye away from the viewfinder.

"No," he yelled back, shaking his head.

Wes turned to the pilot. "Just hang on. I'll be right back."

The pilot nodded, gritting his teeth. "I'm not going . . . anywhere."

Wes leapt from the plane and landed just beyond the edge of the burning brush. His knee howled in pain, but he ignored it and sprinted toward the SUVs.

"A knife!" he called out. "There's one in the Escape."

Anna shot to the back of the truck and threw open the rear hatch. As Wes neared, she popped back around and ran up to him.

"Here." She held out a utility knife, blade retracted.

"Thanks," Wes said as he grabbed it and turned.

Anna didn't let it go right away. Her fingers strayed against his palm, her face full of concern.

Wes looked back. "I'm going to be okay."

With a reluctant nod, she let go, and Wes started toward the plane.

"Wait," Dione said, reaching out and grabbing his arm. "You're not going back there."

"He's stuck! The only way to free him is to cut his straps."

"I don't care. It's not safe."

He shrugged out of her grasp and began running.

This time he angled himself so that he didn't have to stop as he jumped onto the wing. Again his knees smashed against the surface, but he anticipated it this time and didn't slip.

When he stood up, he could see the pilot straining to look over his shoulder. Wes raised the knife. The pilot started to smile, then suddenly he craned his neck, as if he was trying to look behind his seat.

The man's eyes went wide. He started to yell at Wes. "Get ba—"

Whoosh.

An explosive burst of flames engulfed the cockpit.

"No!" Wes yelled.

He started to charge forward, hoping he could still get to the pilot.

"Wes! Stop!" Anna screamed.

He made it to the middle of the wing before the heat of the new blaze forced him to throw his arms up in front of his face. He staggered backward a few steps before the wing disappeared from under him.

He hit the ground hard, knocking the air out of his lungs. Gasping, he rolled out of the burning brush.

Hands grabbed him, pulling him farther away as he sucked in air, trying to fill his lungs again.

"We've got you," Anna said, her voice raised so she could be heard over the roar of the fire.

Danny showed up a few seconds later and helped them lift Wes to his feet and half walk, half carry him farther back.

Wes tried to turn back. "The pilot!"

"It's too late," Anna shouted. "There's nothing you can do for him."

Wes looked toward the cockpit. It was completely engulfed in flames. He sagged against his friends.

"It's all right. We've got you," Danny said.

Together the three crew members dragged Wes away from the heat of the fire into the cooler heat of the desert, finding shelter on the other side of the vehicles.

Once Wes finally caught his breath, Dione asked, "Are you okay?"

"Yeah . . . Fine."

"Here." Anna handed him a bottle of water.

Wes took a sip, paused, then took another. "Thanks."

"What the hell were you—"

"We've got company," Danny said, cutting Dione off.

Wes's eyes, stinging from the smoke, were having a hard time focusing on anything. But before he could ask Danny what he'd seen, a not-so-distant thumping answered his question.

Helicopters. A whole mess of them.

CHAPTER 3

"YOU'RE LUCKY." THE SEARCH-AND-RESCUE paramedic applied ointment to Wes's forearm. "A little singed hair, first-degree burn, a few bruises, and that scrape on your arm. Could have been a lot worse."

Wes owed two people for his life that day: the pilot for changing his plane's course, and Dione for delaying him. Those few critical seconds she'd blocked him from running back to the jet had kept him from being caught in the flames.

He stared at the wreckage while the medic continued to work on him. The fire was out now, and several members of the naval rescue team were working to remove the pilot's body, while others were moving around the plane, some taking photographs, others searching for God knew what.

"Excuse me, Mr. Stewart?" Wes pulled his gaze away from the wreckage. Standing a few feet away was a naval officer. He was wearing a khaki uniform, not the olive green jumpsuits of the rescue team. "I'm Lieutenant Miller. When you're through, there are a couple of questions we'd like to ask you."

"Of course," Wes said.

The medic taped a piece of gauze over Wes's burn, then stood up. "He's good to go."

"Please," the lieutenant said, "if you'll follow me."

He led Wes to the helicopter farthest from the plane. A canopy had been set up beside it, and several portable stools were scattered about underneath. The other members of the *Close to Home* crew were all there, even Alison and Monroe, who'd been left back at the Pinnacles when the others had followed Wes to the crash site.

The moment they saw him, those who weren't already standing jumped to their feet and ran over.

Anna was the first to reach him. She looked at the gauze bandage on his right arm and grimaced. "Are you all right?"

"Yeah," Wes said. "I'm fine. Nothing major."

"Jesus, Wes, you could have been killed," Dione said, not for the first time.

Wes shrugged, but didn't reply.

Danny gave him a lopsided grin. "You going to be able to hold your camera up with that?"

"Danny, seriously," Anna scolded.

"I was just joking," Danny said.

Alison glared at him. "Now might not be the right time."

The lieutenant put his hand on Wes's back. "Sir, if you'll please step into the helicopter."

"Are you taking me somewhere?"

"No, sir. Just more privacy inside."

"They just want to know what you saw," Dione said. "They've talked to the rest of us already. The guy inside said once they finish with you, we can get out of here."

The lieutenant stopped at the open door of the helicopter and motioned for Wes to pass through.

Inside, another man sat on the bench seat that ran along the back of the passenger space, glancing at the top page of a notepad. He, too, was dressed in khakis, but he was older than the lieutenant, probably in his mid-forties. On the collar of his uniform were the silver leaves denoting a commander.

The commander set the pad down as he rose from the bench, his back hunched slightly to compensate for the limited space. "Hello, Mr. Stewart. My name is Thomas Forman."

Wes shook his hand. "Good to meet you, sir."

"Have a seat." Forman settled back on the bench, motioning to a spot near him. As Wes sat, the commander glanced toward the door. "That'll be all for the moment, Lieutenant."

Lieutenant Miller saluted, then closed the helicopter door, leaving the two of them alone.

Forman gave Wes a smile. "First of all, I want to thank you for reacting as quickly as you did. Your colleagues told me you didn't hesitate to rush to the scene. Not many people would do that."

Wes shook his head dismissively. "I don't know about that, Commander. It didn't end up helping, anyway."

"I think you're undervaluing your efforts, Mr. Stewart." Forman picked up his notepad. "As much as I wish it wasn't, my job is to investigate this accident, and try to find out what happened. Part of that means interviewing witnesses such as yourself and your colleagues."

"I'll help however I can," Wes said.

"Thank you, I'm sure you will." Forman smiled briefly, then turned serious. "As you can imagine, what you witnessed here is an event we consider very sensitive. It's always a matter of national security when one of our planes goes down, but today we've also lost a member of our family."

"Of course," Wes said. "I understand completely."

"Thank you. I promise I won't take up much of your time. Just a couple of questions and you can go." The commander glanced down at his pad. "Mr. Stewart, why don't you start by describing what you saw?"

"You can call me Wes, sir."

"All right." Forman paused, his eyes seeming to assess Wes anew. "You're a Navy brat, aren't you?"

Wes looked surprised. "Yes, sir. How'd you know?"

"You called me Commander. Then the 'sir,'" Forman said. "One of your colleagues, Miss Li, I believe, mentioned you're actually from around here."

"That's right," Wes said. "I grew up on the base, then moved to Ridgecrest during high school."

"Hell of a homecoming," Forman said.

"You can say that again."

"Were your parents in the Navy?"

"My dad made lieutenant commander." Wes hesitated. "Retired when I was fourteen and took a job with one of the defense contractors in town."

"Was he a pilot?"

Wes shook his head. "No. He did something out at the airfield, I think, but he never really talked about it."

"He still in town?"

"He's dead," Wes said matter-of-factly.

"I'm sorry," Forman said.

"Thanks. It . . . happened a long time ago."

Forman gave him a sympathetic nod, then said, "The crash. Tell me about it."

With a deep breath, Wes did just that, telling the commander about the noise, Danny's initial reaction, running down the hill to see what was happening, then the realization that the plane was heading right for them.

"You're sure about that?"

"I'm not an expert," Wes said, "but I think he must have seen us."

"How do you mean?"

"Well, it seemed like at first he was going to hit us, then I'm pretty sure the engine flared, and he pushed past us and angled out here. At least that's what it looked like to me."

The commander took this in for a moment. "And then what happened?"

"I knew he was going down, so I ran for the car. But he hit before I got there. He skidded across the ground, then I took off to see if there was anything I could do to save him."

"I applaud your courage, Wes," Commander Forman said. "Your father would be proud of you. But you should know the chances of surviving a crash like that are basically zero. There was little you could have done. The pilot most likely died the moment he hit the ground."

"Actually, that's not true, sir," Wes said.

"I'm sorry?"

"The pilot wasn't dead. When I reached the cockpit, he was still alive. But his harness was stuck, so I went to get a knife. Before I could get back to him, the cockpit caught fire."

The commander stared at him for a moment. "Was he conscious?"

Wes shook his head. "Not when I first got there. But he had a pulse, so I did what I could to bring him around, and he eventually came to."

"Did he say anything?"

Wes struggled to remember. "Told me his harness was

jammed. Then he was muttered some other things, but nothing clear."

"He was alive," the commander said. Not really a question.

"Yes," Wes said. "I think Danny even recorded it."

"Recorded what?" The commander checked his notebook. "Danny DeLeon?"

"Yeah. He's our second cameraman. He shot everything."

The commander leaned back, his head nearly touching the wall of the helicopter as he stared past Wes. Then he suddenly sat forward again.

"It would be a huge benefit to me and my team if we could see what was shot."

"Of course," Wes said. "That shouldn't be a problem."

The commander stood up. "Maybe we should take care of that now."

"Sure. No problem."

Forman opened the door, then let Wes exit first. Once they were both outside, the commander motioned to Lieutenant Miller. "Come with us."

Wes and the two officers headed toward the far corner of the awning, where Danny was standing with Dione and Alison.

"Mr. DeLeon?" the commander asked.

"Yes?"

"Your colleague tells me you have footage of the plane from right after the crash."

"Um, yeah," Danny said. "I've . . . uh . . . also got some from while it was still in the air, too."

"We'd really like to see that," Forman said. "It could help the investigation."

"I can show it to you if you want," Danny offered.

"I was hoping we could take it with us," Forman said. "I'd like some of our experts to take a look at it and see if it might help determine what went wrong."

Danny looked uncertain. "We don't have any way to make you a copy right now. We could do it on one of the laptops back at the hotel."

"Copying's not a problem. If you'll just give *us* the tapes, we could—"

"Digital card," Danny interjected.

Forman smiled. "Digital card, then. We can make the copies back on the base."

Dione took a quick step forward. "Hold on. That footage belongs to the Quest Network. It's not leaving our hands. If you'd like a copy, you can send someone to pick it up at the hotel."

"Miss Li, I totally understand your reluctance," the commander said, his voice calm and accommodating. "I promise you, we will return your original as soon as possible."

"Oh, no. No one's giving anything to anyone," Dione told him. "There's a certain thing called freedom of the press."

"Again, I understand your reluctance," the commander said patiently. "But this isn't a matter of press freedom. It's a matter of finding out why one of our men is dead, and trying to prevent it from happening to someone else. All I'm asking for is your help."

Before Dione could say anything else, Wes jumped in. "Sure," he said. "No problem. We can get you the card."

Dione glanced quickly at Wes, her jaw clenched. "This isn't your responsibility. It's mine." She turned her attention back to the commander. "That footage is network property."

Wes locked eyes with her. "They said they'd give it back as soon as they can. You know it's the right thing to do."

She held his gaze for a moment before finally turning away. "Fine," she whispered.

Wes turned to Forman. "Danny can get you the digital card."

"But we want it back tomorrow," Dione demanded.

"We'll do what we can," Forman said.

She frowned, then gave Danny a single terse nod.

"Please give it to Lieutenant Miller," Forman said.

Danny led the lieutenant over to the SUVs.

"I'm going to lodge a formal complaint," Dione said.

The commander smiled sympathetically. "If you feel that's necessary, then by all means do so."

She pulled away from them and marched off to where the others were gathered.

"Sorry," Wes said as he stood waiting with Forman.

"It's okay," the commander told him. "She's just doing her job. That I can understand."

A few moments later, Danny and Lieutenant Miller returned. In the lieutenant's hand was a digital card.

"Thank you," the commander said. "If we need to speak to you further, we'll be in touch. But you're free to go now."

He started walking back toward his helicopter, Lieutenant Miller falling in step behind him.

"Excuse me," Dione said.

The commander looked back. "Yes, Ms. Li?"

"Don't you need to know where we're staying? So you know where to return the card when you're done?" There was more than a little accusation in her question.

"Of course. I'm so sorry. Sometimes I get too focused on the task at hand. Where *are* you staying?"

"At the Desert Rose Motel on China Lake Boulevard," Wes said.

"Thank you. We'll get the card back to you as quickly as possible."

"We appreciate that."

"Again, thank you all for your help."

As the crew climbed back in the SUVs, Wes took a final look at the mangled remains of the plane. He was trying to think of something more he could have done, but he knew deep down there was nothing. He got behind the wheel, then headed back to Ridgecrest.

"I can't believe you did that," Dione said to Wes once they'd reached the highway.

Wes remained silent.

"They had no right to take our footage."

"I don't know if they had a right or not," Wes said. "But it wasn't worth arguing about. We watched someone die out there today, remember?"

She took a deep breath. "I realize that. It's just I don't like being taken advantage of."

"So you're taking the moral high ground on this?"

"Damn right I am."

"You thought it was perfectly fine to have Danny shooting footage of the trapped pilot?"

"Don't get righteous on me, Wes. News teams shoot that kind of stuff all the time."

"Last I checked, we weren't a news team."

"It doesn't matter that we're not a news team," she said, getting heated. "We witnessed a news event, and were the *only* people on the scene."

"So it was our obligation," Wes said.

"Absolutely."

Wes caught Danny's eyes in the mirror and shook his

head. Danny arched an eyebrow, but gave a slight nod and remained silent.

The truth was, they *did* have the footage. Wes had gotten the auto-backup system working that morning before they'd left the hotel. It was set up to wirelessly transfer everything from the cameras to a flash hard drive in the back of the Escape at fifteen-minute intervals without the operators needing to do anything.

They'd tell Dione in a few days. But not now. If she knew they had the shots, she would have Wes send them to L.A., and they would be on all the networks within an hour.

But that wasn't really what made Wes keep his mouth shut.

He had been right beside the pilot, had actually talked to him. He'd had the chance to save the man's life and failed.

This wasn't news to Wes.

This was far more personal than that.

CHAPTER 4

THE BIG BROWN, THAT'S WHAT ONE OF WES'S old friends used to call the desert. And that's exactly what it was. Vast and tan. The dirt, the bushes, the birds, the rocks, everything variations on the theme.

Wes had never intended on seeing it again. Not in person, anyway.

But time had a way of changing things, and when the assignment for the "High Desert" episode had come up, Wes had realized it would be his opportunity to do something he should have done a long time ago.

When they'd arrived the night before, they had entered the valley high on the western edge, driving along the base of the Sierra Nevada Mountains. Below them, the eastern half of the valley had been lit up like a squashed ball of Christmas lights, a glowing oasis in an otherwise dark landscape. At night the city of Ridgecrest was indistinguishable from the adjacent Navy base at China Lake.

The moment Wes had seen those lights, his chest muscles had begun constricting tightly across his ribs as if they were trying to crush him. In his ears, blood had thundered past, sounding like the rapids of the Kern River. He'd glanced around to see if anyone had picked up on his distress, but the others had been either staring out the window or half-asleep.

The next morning the town had looked somewhat diminished. There was just no way to hide all the brown from the sun. And while Wes's tension had mellowed, it hadn't gone away, becoming a low simmer he was unable to shake off.

"You grew up here?" Danny had asked incredulously as they'd driven through town that morning on their way out to the Pinnacles.

"It's got its good points," Wes had replied.

"Name three."

"The people are nice. Air-conditioning is a given. And you always know someone who has a swimming pool."

Danny had snorted.

"I don't know," Alison had said from the back. "I kind of like it. Looks homey."

"It was," Wes had said. *For a while, anyway.*

Now that the sun had set on a day none of them could have ever expected nor would ever forget, Wes wondered if there was any way he could just return to Los Angeles. Not even back in his hometown for twenty-four hours, and a fighter jet—an F-18, he'd learned from the medic who'd patched him up—nearly killed him.

If that wasn't an omen, he didn't know what was.

He had just stepped into the shower when someone pounded on the door to his room. He tried ignoring it, but whoever it was wasn't giving up.

"I'm coming!" he hollered as he climbed back out and threw a towel around his waist.

He pulled the door open. Danny was standing there, his arm in the air ready to knock again.

"What?" Wes asked, pissed.

"Uh . . . hey. Just wanted to let you know we're all meeting at the cars in ten. Going to grab something to eat."

Wes stared at him, saying nothing.

"I . . . uh . . . I thought you'd like the heads-up. Maybe we can get a drink, too. Don't know about you, but I could sure use a beer or three."

Wes shook his head and shut the door without replying.

"Does that mean you're coming or not?" Danny called through the door.

Wes got back into the shower, letting the hot water stream over his head. He knew the others were going to want to know what he'd seen. They'd want to hear details. And if it didn't happen tonight, it would happen tomorrow.

Better to get it over with now.

He finished his shower, pulled on some clothes, and was at the SUVs only a few minutes late. With the exception of Monroe, everyone was already there. But that wasn't surprising. She seldom joined the crew after hours.

Dione looked at Wes. "So, where should we go?"

"What do you mean?"

"To eat," she said as if he were dense as a brick.

He shrugged. "Hell if I know."

"Come on, Wes, we're starving," Tony Hall, the crew's production assistant, said. Dione had kept him running errands all day, so he'd missed all the fun at the Pinnacles.

"It's been seventeen years since I've been here," Wes said. But no one in the group seemed very sympathetic.

He dug deep into his memory. "Uh . . . if it's still there, John's Pizza's not too far away."

"John's it is," Dione said.

John's was still there. Unfortunately, though, the beer and the pizza didn't last long enough for Wes to finish telling them about the crash. So, at Danny's suggestion, they stopped off at a bar within walking distance of the motel named Delta Sierra.

"That booth's empty," Alison said, pointing across the room.

Danny laughed as they sat down. "Check this out." He pointed at the table. It was glass topped, and underneath was a large piece of paper with the words PILOT LINGO in bold on top. Term number one, printed larger than the others, read:

DELTA SIERRA—Dumb Shit

The aviation theme didn't end there. The walls were covered with framed pictures of pilots and planes and hangars. And prominent on the list of drinks were a Bogey Shot, a Flattop Martini, and something called a Hornet in a Cage.

Alison touched Wes on the arm. "Maybe we should have gone somewhere else."

"Why?" Danny asked. "This place is great."

"That's because it was obviously named after you," she scoffed. "I was just thinking that after the day we've had, maybe someplace a little less *aircraft* oriented might be better."

Anna smiled at Wes. "We don't have to stay."

"Don't worry about it," he said. "It's fine. Besides, Danny's buying."

Laughter all around.

Danny grinned. "I don't believe I actually promised that."

"I don't care if you promised or not, it's what's going to happen."

More laughter.

When things settled down again, Danny said, "I'll tell you what surprised me most out there today. I thought that plane was part of the Air Force, then all of a sudden we were surrounded by all these Navy people . . . sailors . . . whatever you call them. Since when is the Navy in the middle of the desert?"

"China Lake's a naval base, Danny," Alison said.

"Yeah, but where's the water? Correct me if I'm wrong, but isn't the Navy's thing boats?"

"The Navy needs a place to test its planes and weapons," Wes said. "So they set up out here a long time ago. Nothing better than the empty desert to drop a bomb in. And it's 'ships,' not 'boats.'"

"Seriously, Danny," Dione said. "It was all in the episode brief."

"Like I'm the only one who never reads those." He looked around the table for support, but everyone stared back at him like he was an idiot. "Okay, fine. Sorry."

"I think it's time for that first round?" Dione suggested.

"Right." Danny climbed out of the booth.

"Take Tony with you," Alison said. "So they won't card you."

"Ha-ha," Danny said, glaring at her. Though he was twenty-seven, he had one of those baby faces that made him look like he was barely out of high school. By comparison, Tony, a couple of years younger, actually looked like he was in his late twenties. As Danny turned for the bar, he motioned Tony to join him. "You can help me carry the drinks."

As soon as they were gone, Alison and Anna decided to make a pre-drink trip to the ladies' room, leaving Dione and Wes the only ones still at the table.

"Don't spread this around yet," Dione said, "but the office wants us to try to make up the time without adding a day."

"Did you expect anything less?"

"I was looking at the schedule, and I think if we cram two of Tuesday's interviews into Monday, we'll be able to do it." She gave Wes a hopeful look. "Might mean working an extra hour, though."

Wes shrugged. "I could always use the overtime."

"It's just an hour."

"Easy to say with your cushy staff job. Freelancer rule number one: Get paid for every hour you work."

She gave him her best puppy-dog eyes, which only caused him to sneer. With a chuckle she shrugged. "Hey, it was worth a try. I guess it'll be cheaper than shooting an extra day. I really should charge the Navy for the lost time."

"Seriously, Dione. We saw someone die today."

"I know, I know. I don't really mean it. It's just that officer taking our footage pissed me off."

"He didn't *take* it. He asked for it, and we gave it to him."

"Ha! If we hadn't, I'll bet he would have taken it." She looked around. "Get this. I talked to the office, expecting them to be as upset as I was, but they were all like it was no big deal, and that we'd done the right thing handing it over. Come on. Doesn't anyone have any journalistic integrity?"

Wes stared at her, smirking. "Uh, not sure you know

this, but we shoot vacation spots. We're squeezed between a show called *Quest for the Perfect Cocktail* and *Tanya Takes a Trip*. Where, exactly, does journalistic integrity fit in there?"

As Dione scoffed, Danny and Tony returned carrying several drinks. They weren't alone, either. Behind them were two men wearing jeans and button-down shirts, but giving off the obvious vibe of military.

"This is Lieutenant Wasserman," Danny said, nodding his chin at the man closest to him. "And this is Lieutenant . . . uh . . ."

"Jenks," the other man said. He held out his hand to Wes. "Just call me Ken."

"And I'm Reid," Wasserman added, also shaking Wes's hand.

"I overheard these two guys talking about the crash, and told them we were there," Danny explained. "They wanted to meet us. Well, you specifically, Wes."

"Danny mentioned that you tried to get the guy out," Tony said, then mouthed behind Danny's back, "Sorry."

Wes cringed inside.

"Your friend here told us you actually got up next to the cockpit," Jenks said. "Is that true?"

Wes nodded.

"Said you were trying to get him out."

"His harness was jammed. If I had a knife, maybe. But . . ." Wes just let it hang, not knowing how to finish.

"Did you talk to him?" Wasserman asked.

"Briefly. Sort of. He wasn't in much condition to talk."

Jenks nodded knowingly. "I don't doubt that. What did he say?"

Wes adjusted uncomfortably in his seat. "Nothing much. He was in a lot of pain."

"Did he tell you what happened?" Jenks persisted.

"Look," Wes said. "I don't know what to tell you. He basically only acknowledged that he was conscious. I was too busy trying to free him to get into a conversation."

"Of course." Jenks leaned back. "Sorry. I didn't mean to push."

"Thank you for trying to help him," Wasserman said. "That means a lot to all of us."

"We won't bother you any longer," Jenks added. "But we do want you to know your tab's on us tonight. I mean all of you."

"You don't need to do that," Wes said.

"We insist." Lieutenant Jenks held up a hand, indicating further protest was unnecessary.

"Thanks," Wes said.

They gave Wes a nod, then turned and left.

"For a second there I thought they were going to salute you," Danny said as he sat back down.

"Well, that was . . . interesting," Anna said. She and Alison had returned in the middle of the conversation, but had hung back until the two Navy men had left.

Danny took a swig of his beer, then said, "When I started talking to them at the bar, a couple of the women came over. They were even more interested than our Navy friends." He leaned toward Wes. "Man, if you play this right, you're not going to have to sleep alone the whole time we're here."

"Danny," Alison and Anna chided almost in unison.

"So not cool," Tony said.

Wes shook his head. "Okay, I've had enough."

He motioned for Dione and Alison to get out of his way, then scooted out of the booth.

"I'll see you all in the morning." He tossed Alison the keys to the Escape and started across the room.

"Sorry, man. I didn't mean anything. . . ."

If Danny said anything more, Wes didn't hear it.

He weaved through the crowd and headed for the door. As he pushed it open a voice called out, "Wes, hold up."

Looking over his shoulder, he spotted Tony moving around a small group of people standing just inside the entrance.

"Mind if I tag along?" Tony asked.

"Be my guest. But you're missing free drinks."

Tony let out a halfhearted laugh. "Sorry about the thing with those guys in the bar. That was all Danny."

Wes smiled. "Don't worry about it. I know how Danny is."

"A deadly combination of harmless and clueless."

Wes laughed. "Exactly right."

They walked in silence for a few minutes, the whole time Wes sensing that Tony had something he wanted to say. Finally the production assistant worked up the nerve and asked, "You think we'll have time to do a little training this trip?"

Over the past couple of assignments, Wes had been tutoring Tony on camera techniques during downtime. "I don't see why not. That is, if you don't drop the ball like you did today."

"Drop the ball?" Tony looked confused.

"What is it I like to have in my hand when I'm drinking my coffee in the morning?"

Tony looked momentarily baffled, then he laughed to himself. "Poppy seed muffin."

"And what was missing from my hand this morning?"

"A poppy seed muffin," Tony said. "Sorry. Completely my fault."

"You want to learn to be a good cameraman, then the first rule is take care of the one teaching you. I'd hate to forget some critical piece of information because I hadn't had a proper breakfast."

"I'll do my best."

"I know you will."

Once Wes was back in his room at the motel, he lay in bed unable to sleep. At just after 11 p.m., someone knocked on the door.

"Just a minute," he called out as he pulled on his jeans and T-shirt.

When he opened the door, he found Anna standing outside.

"Hey," she said.

"Hey," he replied, mellowing.

He pushed the door open wide enough so that she could slip in, then shut it behind her. A few seconds later they had their arms wrapped around each other and were in the middle of a deep, long kiss.

"I've been wanting to do that all day," Anna said when they finally pulled apart.

"I've been needing that all day."

"What you've been needing is a slap upside the head," she said. "I nearly had a heart attack when I saw you running toward the plane."

"Don't get all Dione on me," he said.

She considered him for a moment. "Fine. But if that happens again, and I'm around, you'd better run the other way, or I will personally kill you."

"I bet you would, wouldn't you?"

At five foot four, she was a good half foot shorter than Wes. She arched her head upward and kissed him again, her long brown hair falling down her back. She then put her hand in his and led him toward the bed.

"Danny was right about one thing."

"What's that?"

"You're not going to sleep alone the whole time we're here."

CHAPTER
5

COMMANDER THOMAS FORMAN WAS STILL SIT-
ting at his desk as the clock ticked past midnight.

It was the crash, of course. Since the moment the
plane had gone down, he'd been on the move putting
things into motion, making sure every base was covered.
He knew he should go home soon and try to get a little
sleep, but until the call came through, he couldn't go
anywhere.

The phone finally rang at 12:09.

"Sir," the voice on the other end said. "They've all
returned for the night."

"Any suspicious contact?" Forman asked.

"No, sir."

"Phones?"

"The ones in their rooms were taken care of while
they were out, and their cellphones are being monitored."

Forman exhaled. It was all just precaution, but when
it came to national security you didn't take chances.
"Have someone continue monitoring, and dismiss everyone else," he ordered. "But first hint of trouble, everyone's back on. I want this sealed tight."

CHAPTER
6

WES'S ALARM WENT OFF AT SIX. ANNA GAVE HIM a kiss, rolled out of bed, and slipped quietly out the front door. He was pretty sure he mumbled a goodbye, but it could have been a dream. A second alarm woke him a half hour later. With a groan, he hobbled on sore knees into the bathroom to take a shower. The reflection that greeted him in the mirror was bruised and scratched.

"Awesome," he said with zero feeling. The day ahead had to be better than the one he'd just gone through.

But before he could even get the water started, his cellphone rang. The name on the display read CASEY.

"Hey," Wes said into the phone.

"You can't be serious," Casey said.

"Way too early for cryptic. What are you talking about?"

"The plane crash yesterday. You were there?"

"How did you know that?"

"I never reveal my sources."

Casey Dake worked as one of the top researchers at the Quest Network. His job was information. He assisted producers and writers in gathering any facts and other data they might need for future shows.

Casey and Wes had been friends since college, meeting in the television/film department while working together on such collegiate classics as *Drive-Thru Confessions* and *The Man from La Mirada*. After graduation they'd stayed close. Casey had helped Wes get his gig at Quest. And when Casey had broken up with his longtime girlfriend, Wes had offered up the guest bedroom in his Santa Monica townhouse. They'd roomed together ever since.

"No. Really. How did you find that out?"

"Racquel over in HR. She just sent me an email to see if I'd heard from you. Apparently a couple military guys in uniform came to the office yesterday afternoon and asked about you."

"Seriously?"

"Yeah. Racquel said they were making sure you worked for the company."

It kind of made sense. The Navy would want to confirm Wes and the crew were who they said they were. But a phone call should have been enough to take care of that.

"So what happened?" Casey asked.

Wes gave him a condensed version of events, then asked his friend to keep him posted if any other gossip surfaced at the office.

"Sure," Casey said. "And you try to stay out of trouble today, huh?"

"Don't worry. I plan on it."

Wes soaked in the shower, letting the heat work out some of the soreness in his muscles. Once he was finished, he dried off, shaved, brushed his teeth, and got dressed, marginally more awake than before. That's when he noticed that the red message light on the motel phone was lit. He followed the message retrieval instructions, heard a beep, then:

"I'm calling for Wes Stewart," a male voice said. "Wes . . . em . . . it's Lars . . . Lars Andersen. From high school? I just found out you were in town. Look, why don't you give me a call when you get this. I was thinking maybe we could get together. Here's my number. . . ."

Wes wrote it down, deleted the message, then stared at the piece of paper.

Lars Andersen. *Wow.* He hadn't thought of him in years.

Wes looked at the clock on the nightstand. He still had twenty minutes before he had to meet the others.

What the hell?

He grabbed his cellphone and punched in Lars's number.

"Lieutenant Commander Andersen," a voice answered.

"Lars?"

A pause. "Wes?"

"You're in the *Navy?*"

After growing up with him on and around the China Lake naval base, Wes thought Lars had been as anxious as he had been to do anything but join the service.

"You think I'd be back here if I weren't?" Lars said with a laugh.

"Good point."

"How are you?"

"I'm fine," Wes said. "But surprised, I guess. How did you know I was here?"

"You haven't seen the paper this morning?"

"No. Why?"

"There's a front-page article about yesterday's F-18 crash. It mentions you and your colleagues were nearby and witnessed it."

"How did they get my name?"

"I don't know, but if they hadn't included you, I wouldn't have known you were here."

"Of course." Wes paused. "So . . . uh . . . how are you?"

"I'm good, thanks. Busy. But that's normal. Hey, listen. I can't really talk too long right now, but why don't we meet up for lunch? It would be great to see you again."

"Hold on," Wes said. He grabbed the shoot schedule off the dresser and scanned his day ahead. "Looks like I can probably break free around noon for about forty-five minutes."

"Perfect," Lars said. "I know exactly where we should go."

"Where?"

"Tacos."

Wes smiled. "Don't tell me. La Sonora."

"Yes, my friend. La Sonora."

"They're still around?"

"I know. Surprising, huh?"

"Is Hannibal Lecter still running the register?"

"Still there."

Wes laughed. "I would have sworn she'd have been dead by now."

"It's possible. Could be they're just propping her up."

CHAPTER 7

THE CREW OF *CLOSE TO HOME* DROVE UP THE slope on the south side of the valley to Cero Coso Community College. When Wes lived there, people called it Harvard-on-the-Hill or Tumbleweed Tech. On the schedule were interviews with a geology professor and an area historian. Dione always liked shooting experts in an academic setting. Said it made the show look more important.

By nine-thirty, the professor was already done and gone, a whole half hour ahead of schedule. While the crew waited for the historian to show up, Tony set out a box of pastries and a bag of fruit in the open back of the Escape.

Monroe pulled a banana out of the bag, then grimaced. "Who taught you how to pick produce?" Before Tony could say anything, she tossed the banana back in the bag and said, "I can't eat that." Then walked off.

Tony glanced at Wes, a look of genuine concern on his face.

"Don't worry about it," Wes said. "She won't starve."

Tony looked only partially relieved. Then he brightened. "Your muffin's in the box."

Wes glanced inside and smiled. "You just earned yourself an after-lunch lesson."

He grabbed the muffin and headed over to where Alison was leaning against the grille of the Escape, a newspaper spread out in front of her on the hood.

"That the local paper?" he asked.

"Yeah," Alison replied, eyes not leaving the paper.

"Today's?"

"Yeah again."

"Can I take a look at it?"

She glanced at him, a mock smirk of annoyed superiority pushing up the left side of her mouth.

"When you're done, I mean," he said.

"That's what I thought." She flipped the page. "Ah, the comics. This might take a while."

Wes rolled his eyes and started to turn away.

"Fine," she said, folding the paper and holding it out to him. "Here. There's no *Dilbert,* so what does it matter?"

Wes set his muffin on the car and took the newspaper from her. "Thanks."

She leaned close and said softly into his ear, "If you're looking for the mention of you, it's in the article on the front page."

Wes put on a smile as he took a casual step back.

"Dione made it, too, but no one else," Alison continued in a normal voice. "Well, except for Monroe. They even have her quoted about how horrible it was. If I recall correctly, she was with me, nowhere near the crash for most of the time. Whatever." She gave Wes an exaggerated shrug. "Are there any chocolate old-fashioneds?"

"One left, last I saw."

"You checked? Isn't that sweet."

"Just happened to notice."

"Right." She winked, then called out, "Hey, the old-fashioned's mine," and made her way to the back of the Escape.

Wes watched her go, then picked up his muffin and unfolded the paper.

A picture of the crash site took up nearly half the space above the fold. It had been shot not too far from where Wes and the others had been when the plane had flown past. There were at least a half dozen more helicopters than Wes remembered being there. The gray distant lump that had been the F-18 seemed to be swarming with people. Wes guessed the photo had been taken after Commander Forman released them.

JET CRASHES NEAR TRONA PINNACLES

Wes started reading. The pilot's name was Lieutenant Lawrence Adair, age twenty-seven, native of Michigan. According to the article, the plane had experienced a catastrophic but unknown problem during a routine training mission. After a moment Wes reached the part Alison had mentioned:

> The incident was witnessed by a crew of the cable show Close to Home, who were at the Pinnacles filming a segment for an upcoming episode.
>
> "I've never been so scared," Monroe Banks, host of Close to Home, said. "For a few seconds I thought it was actually going to crash right in front of us. Thankfully that didn't happen, but that doesn't take away from the tragedy."
>
> Banks said she and the other members of the pro-

duction team could only watch as the disabled jet plowed into the earth, creating a scar across the ground at least a quarter mile long.

"One of the people in our crew was closer to our vehicles than the rest of us," Monroe said. "I yelled at him to do what he could."

That person, identified as former China Lake and Ridgecrest resident Wesley Stewart, raced out to where the plane had come to rest. Soon he was joined by other members of the crew, including show producer and director Dione Li. But they were too late.

An unnamed source tells the High Desert Tribune that Lieutenant Adair had most likely died on impact. He—

Not true, Wes thought. But he got why the paper had been told the pilot was already dead. The public didn't really need to know the gory details. The article did clear up one thing, though. Monroe must have been the one who had given the paper his name.

He flipped the front page over so he could read the rest of the story, but his attention was drawn to a picture next to the text. It was a head shot of a young man in a naval uniform.

Wes read the caption below the picture:

Lieutenant Lawrence Adair, killed in a crash at the Trona Pinnacles, twenty miles southeast of Ridgecrest.

Wes looked at the picture again, then reread the copy beneath. Confused, he flipped through the paper, searching for any more pictures that went with the article. But there were no others.

He returned to the photo on the front page.

No matter how hard he stared at it, the image of the pilot didn't change. Whether he was Lieutenant Lawrence Adair or someone else, Wes knew one thing for sure.

He was not the man Wes had tried to rescue from the cockpit.

CHAPTER
8

"MAYBE IT'S AN OLD PHOTO," DIONE SAID.

She, Danny, Tony, and Alison were standing with Wes at the back of the Escape. Anna was touching up Monroe's makeup inside the college.

"I'm telling you, this isn't the guy," Wes said. "Can't you tell?"

"You're the only one who got close enough to see him," Dione said. "But if you're saying it's not him, okay, I believe you. It's not him. Maybe the paper just ran the wrong picture."

Wes paused. That possibility hadn't crossed his mind.

"Wouldn't be the first time that's happened," Alison remarked.

Wes chewed at the inside of his lip. "Okay, you're probably right. Just an error. Sorry. Guess this thing's got me more worked up than I thought."

"Of course it has, but you gotta give yourself a break. You did everything possible," Dione told him. "In fact, you did more than most people would have."

"I'd have never jumped up there," Danny said.

"Yeah, you would have," Wes told him.

"If it helps," Alison said, "I woke up dreaming about it in the middle of the night. I think it's pretty much affected all of us. Well, except for Monroe. Unless you count seeing it as a PR opportunity."

They all shared a laugh. Even Wes.

He gave them a smile. "Sorry."

"Don't sweat it," Dione told him. "Now come on. Let's finish setting up. The next talent should be here any minute."

As Wes headed back to the cameras, he tossed the paper in a garbage can.

Just a mistake. That has to be it.

CHAPTER 9

THEY RAN A LITTLE OVER WITH THE HISTORIAN.
She'd gone on and on about alluvial fans and ancient lake beds.

"We're never gonna use this," Wes muttered to Dione.

"Let her talk. Maybe there'll be a nugget buried in there somewhere."

When Wes finally got to La Sonora to meet Lars, it was closer to twelve-fifteen than twelve o'clock. He went inside and looked around, hoping he'd recognize his friend after seventeen years. But Lars wasn't there.

As Wes got into line, he couldn't help but let out a little laugh. La Sonora hadn't changed at all since the last time he'd eaten there: the brown-tiled counter, the kitchen, the wall-mounted menu—all the same. And sure enough, sitting on a stool behind the cash register was Hannibal Lecter. It was Mandy who had given the cashier the nickname. Maybe the woman had a few more wrinkles than she used to have, but her uncanny resemblance to Sir Anthony Hopkins remained intact.

The glass door opened behind Wes, and before he could turn around he heard Lars's voice.

"Wes Stewart!"

Lars, dressed in a pressed khaki uniform, strode up smiling broadly, his hand extended. "Good God. Almost twenty years and you don't look a damn day older."

Wes sneered as he shook his friend's hand. "Then you've gone blind, and the Navy needs to think about getting rid of you."

Lars laughed.

"You've certainly changed," Wes observed.

Lars patted his lean stomach. "Navy prefers its pilots to be a little less rotund than I used to be."

"You're a pilot?"

"Now we come back to the vision thing. Wanted to be, but I inherited Mom's eyes. Forced to stick to the ground. But I liked how I felt after I dropped the pounds." He smiled. "Sorry I'm late."

They ordered their food from Dr. Lecter and, once it was ready, grabbed a shaded table on the patio.

As Lars began unwrapping his taco, he said, "So. Hollywood. How the hell did that happen?"

"Honestly?"

"Absolutely."

"A girl I liked when I was a freshman in college."

Lars snorted. "This should be good."

"She was a film major, so I thought it would be cool to take some production classes. You know, show her we had similar interests. Would have worked, too, if she'd actually noticed me. But what I did realize was that I kind of had a talent for the production stuff."

"What exactly do you do now?" Lars asked.

"Depends. I mostly do both camera and editing. I've directed a few of my own shorts, too. But the only place you can see those is on YouTube."

"So do you do both for this show you're here for?"

"Kind of. I shoot during the day, then, when we have enough footage, I put together a rough cut on my laptop. They got another guy back at the network who does the final edit."

"That's so cool."

"Yeah, well . . ." Wes took a bite of his taco. "And you? I distinctly remember both of us saying we couldn't imagine joining the service."

"We did, didn't we?" Lars said with a laugh. "But there's this little thing called tuition. My parents couldn't spring for it, and I sure as hell wasn't going to work my way through school."

"So you joined the Navy because you were lazy?"

"Ha. Ha. You would think that, wouldn't you? No, not lazy. Not that can be proven, anyway. The summer after you . . . left, my brother got me out onto Armitage Field. I got to actually sit in some of the aircraft. That was enough to hook me. Of course, then I thought I'd be flying."

"So if you're not flying, what do they have you doing?"

"Operations. Mission planning, that kind of thing. For some reason the Navy got the idea that I'm smart."

"That makes me have *so* much more confidence in them," Wes joked.

When Wes was washing down his last bite with some water, Lars said, "So, yesterday. That must have been pretty intense."

Wes swallowed, then nodded. "I swear, Lars, I thought he was going to hit us. But then the plane veered off at the last moment. That guy saved our lives."

Lars stared at his food for a second, then blinked and looked at Wes. "I'm sorry, what?"

"I said he saved our lives."

"You think he saw you?"

"I don't see any other explanation."

"That wasn't in the paper."

"I never talked to anyone from the paper. Only one of your guys, Commander Forman. You know him?"

Lars nodded. "He's in charge of VX-53. They're the Flying Hammers. Air test and evaluation squadron. There are three different ones that fly out of the base."

"The pilot who was killed yesterday, was he part of the Flying Hammers?"

Lars nodded, his eyes drifting off for a moment. "Lieutenant Adair, a new transfer."

"You knew him?" Wes asked.

"Hadn't met him yet."

Wes leaned back. "Today must not be a very good day at the office."

"Truthfully, that's why I wanted to have lunch with you. I knew it wasn't going to be pleasant, and having a prearranged getaway seemed like a good idea. I did really want to see you, too."

"Nice save," Wes said, but could only imagine what was going through the minds of Adair's colleagues. "I'll bet the article in the paper today didn't help."

Lars cocked his head. "I'm sorry?"

"The picture?"

Lars scrunched his eyes together.

"They ran the wrong picture," Wes said as if it should have been obvious.

"Which picture?"

"The picture in the paper?"

When Lars still didn't look like he understood, Wes did a quick glance around and spotted a newspaper rack on the sidewalk right outside the restaurant. "Be right back."

A few moments later he returned with a copy of the paper and laid it on the table. He pointed at the photo. "That one. Whoever this guy is, he probably doesn't think it's funny they're saying he's dead."

Lars looked at Wes, his brow even more furrowed than before. "Okay. You've completely lost me. What are you talking about?"

Wes wondered if he was suddenly speaking a foreign language. "That's not Lieutenant Adair."

"Of course it is," Lars said. "It's the same picture that's in the initial incident report."

Wes stared at his friend for half a second. "No. You must be mistaken."

"No mistake. I read the report this morning. That's the picture in the file. What's the problem?"

Wes felt the skin on his arms tighten. "You're saying this was the man who was supposed to be flying the plane yesterday?"

"What do you mean 'supposed to be'?"

Wes leaned toward Lars. "What I mean is this wasn't the man I found sitting in the cockpit."

CHAPTER
10

"THAT'S NOT FUNNY."

"I'm *not* being funny, Lars. I'm serious. This isn't the same guy."

Lars looked down at the paper. After a moment he said, "You're the one who must have made the mistake. It's easy to misidentify someone, especially from a distance."

"What do you know about the crash besides what was in the newspaper?" Wes asked.

Lars hesitated. "Just what was in the preliminary report. But there wasn't much."

"Did it say anything about me?"

"You?"

"My involvement."

"Just that you were first on scene. But there was a fire and you couldn't do anything."

So it wasn't just the newspaper that had let Lars know Wes was in town, but Wes let that pass for now.

"That's it?"

"Yeah. Pretty much."

Wes frowned. "Lars, I didn't see him from a distance. I got right up next to him. He talked to me."

"He talked to you? He was *alive*?"

Wes nodded. "When I got there, he was slumped down, unconscious. But I was able to bring him around."

Lars looked down at the table, then back at Wes. "Then what?"

"Then I tried to get him out, but he was stuck. I left to grab a knife, only before I could get back, the cockpit caught on fire. None of this was in the report you saw?"

Lars shook his head slightly. "No."

"Well, it should have been, because this guy here," Wes said, raising the article a few inches off the table, "isn't the guy I saw."

Neither of them said anything for several seconds.

Finally Lars leaned back. "I'm impressed and, well, shocked, really, that you were able to do as much as you did. But bear with me for a second. Is it possible you might not be remembering correctly? After all, stressful situations can mess with your head and make you think you saw something other than what you actually did."

"That had nothing to do with it," Wes insisted. Still, there was some truth in Lars's words. He closed his eyes for a moment, recalling the face of the man in the cockpit. But the one he saw still wasn't Adair's. "There must be someone unaccounted for. Some other pilot who's missing. That'll be the guy I saw."

"We don't have anyone unaccounted for."

Wes's phone beeped in his pocket. It was his alarm. He frowned. "I gotta get back."

"Yeah, me, too," Lars said.

"Can you do me a favor and check it out?"

"Check what out?"

"This picture. The pilot. Just make sure there wasn't a mistake. I saw the guy, Lars. It'll help put my mind at ease."

Lars rose from his seat and shrugged. "I don't know what you expect me to find, but okay. I'll check."

They walked around to the parking lot off the alley that ran behind the restaurant. Lars stopped next to a generic-looking sedan that Wes immediately pegged as base issue.

"Seriously? If terrorists ever knew the Navy made you drive around in that, they'd realize they'd already won."

Lars grimaced. "Yeah, well, we can't all be driving BMWs."

"You overestimate me. Back home I drive a Prius."

"Tree hugger, huh?"

"Only in my off hours."

Lars seemed to relax a little. Holding out his hand, he said, "It's good to see you again."

Wes shook it. "You'll let me know what you find out?"

"Of course. But can I be honest with you?"

"Sure."

Lars hesitated before he spoke. "I think chances are I'm not going to find anything wrong. So you might want to start assuming your mind's playing tricks on you."

"You're probably right." Wes smiled. "I'm glad we got together."

"Me, too." Lars opened the door of his sedan, then paused in the opening. "Welcome home."

CHAPTER
11

LARS ANDERSEN HAD JUST DRIVEN THROUGH the gate of the China Lake naval base when his cellphone rang. He grabbed his Bluetooth headset off the cigarette lighter and put it in his ear.

"Lieutenant Commander Andersen."

"Lars, it's Janice. Commander Knudsen just got here for our meeting. You're almost back, right?"

Lars checked his watch. The meeting with Knudsen was supposed to start in fifteen minutes. "Any way we can push it back an hour?"

"He's already in the conference room. Why? You can't make it?"

If Lars kept going on the road he was on, he'd be at his office in two minutes. Instead he turned left.

"You'll have to take it without me."

"He's not going to be happy," Janice said.

"Make something up. You can fill me in later."

"If that's what you want."

"No choice," he said, then disconnected the call. Immediately he punched in a new number.

"Commander Forman's office, Seaman Litoff speaking."

"This is Lieutenant Commander Andersen. I need to see the commander now."

"Sir, the commander isn't here at the moment."

"Where is he?"

"I'm afraid I'm not authorized to give you that information."

"Well, Seaman, I suggest you call your boss and tell him I'm on the way to his office and he's going to want to see me right away. Understood?"

"Yes, sir. Understood. Can you tell me what this is regarding?"

"No."

Lars disconnected the call.

CHAPTER

12

AS IT TURNED OUT, WES COULD HAVE STAYED longer at lunch.

"Our afternoon schedule just got canceled," Dione told the crew once everyone had regrouped at the motel.

"You've got to be kidding me," Monroe said.

"It's the crash," Dione explained.

Wes frowned, confused. "I thought we weren't going back out to the Pinnacles until Monday or Tuesday."

"I'm not talking about the Pinnacles. We had those Native American sites on the base this afternoon. But I just got a call from our Navy contact, who said because of the crash all unnecessary visitor passes have been revoked. That includes us."

"Well, that sucks," Alison said.

"Pool time," Danny said, smiling. Everyone turned and stared at him. "What? You guys brought suits, right?"

If they were going to have the afternoon off, Wes realized now might be the time to take care of that unfinished business, the errand his mother had asked him to do. He'd been dreading it, and had secretly hoped he'd be unable to make time to visit the storage facility. But he also knew it was something he *had* to do. Now was as good a time as—

"Just because the schedule got screwed up doesn't mean we can't get anything done," Dione said, looking directly at Danny. "We'll get some B-roll."

While Wes felt a sense of reprieve, Danny suddenly looked like a kid who'd been told the trip to Disneyland he was about to take was really heading for the city dump.

"All afternoon?" he asked.

"As long as it takes."

B-roll shots were usually taken on the go as a crew was shooting other things. The name was a holdover from the days when everything was shot on rolls of film. The A-roll, though few, if any, called it that, was the scripted shots, while B-roll was random shots taken as they came up.

"Danny, you and I will take the Highlander, and Wes, you can take the Escape," she said. "I'm looking for beautiful desert images. Anything you think will be interesting."

"Why do I need the chaperone?" Danny asked.

"Do you really have to ask?"

"What am I supposed to do? Just sit here?" Monroe asked.

"You've got the afternoon off," Dione said, looking at Monroe, but meaning Alison and Anna, too. "You're all free to do whatever you want. Tony, you can—"

"You're taking both cars," Monroe cut her off.

Dione pasted on her putting-up-with-the-talent smile. "You can rent a car for the day. We'll pay for it."

"So I have to rent my own car now?"

"I'll take care of it," Tony said, jumping in.

"Whatever," Monroe said. "I'll be in my room. Tell me when the car's here. And not one of those crappy subcompacts."

As Monroe walked away, Dione mouthed "Thank you" to Tony.

"She *does* know how to drive, right?" Alison asked, keeping her voice low.

They all silently stared at one another.

"I, um, assume so," Dione said.

"Has anyone actually seen her behind the wheel?" Alison asked.

Shaking heads all around.

Tony groaned. "Please tell me I don't have to drive her around."

"Absolutely not," Dione said. "She can drive herself if she wants to go anywhere, whether she knows how to or not. I want you to make a list of what we're going to need tomorrow. We'll be on the road most of the day, with no stores nearby that I know of, so you'll have to get supplies tonight when we get back. When you're done with the list, write up the production report for yesterday and today. I'll take a look at them later."

Dione glanced at Danny and Wes. "All right, guys. Shall we hit it?"

Danny retrieved his camera from the Escape and put it in the other SUV.

"So you're going to be all alone?" Anna asked Wes.

"Looks that way," Wes said.

She glanced at Dione. "Mind if I join him?"

An odd smile formed on Dione's face. "Fine by me." She opened the driver's door of the Highlander, then asked Wes, "Which way are you going to head?"

He shrugged. "Thought I could go north." He pointed

at the far end of the valley, where the hills met the Sierras. "Get some of the volcanic stuff."

"Great idea," she said as she climbed in. "We'll go east toward Death Valley."

"Death Valley?" Whatever else Danny added to his protest was rendered unintelligible as Dione pulled her door shut.

"You want me to drive so you can shoot?" Anna said to Wes.

"Maybe in a bit," Wes replied.

A few moments later they were on the road, air conditioner blasting.

"I think Dione might know," Wes threw out.

"Know what?"

"About us."

"Of course she does," Anna said. "I told her."

"You *told* her?"

"Dione's one of my best friends."

"I thought we'd decided to keep things quiet for a while."

"Do you see me shouting about it to everyone?" Anna asked. "Besides, you told Casey."

"Casey's my roommate. I didn't have a choice if you were going to stay over."

"Well, you had a choice. You could have just not had me come over."

"That was not an option, either."

Anna turned so that her back was to the door and she could take a good, long look at him. "Anyone else you tell?"

"You're changing the subject."

"Maybe I am, but I want to know. I know you haven't told Alison yet."

Wes shifted uncomfortably in his chair. He and Alison

had hooked up for a short time a year earlier. Anna knew all this, of course. It was the worst-kept secret on the crew. And while he was okay remaining friends, it was obvious Alison was still open to the possibility of more.

"She'll find out soon enough."

Anna watched him for a moment, the hint of a smile on her face. "So who else?"

He shook his head. "No one you've met."

"So there is someone else. Now I'm really intrigued."

Wes brought the Escape to a stop at the intersection of China Lake Boulevard and Inyokern Road. A turn to the right would take them to the front gate of the base, and a turn left would eventually take them to the highway. Wes turned left.

"Who?" Anna asked again.

Wes frowned. "Okay. My mom."

Silence.

"You told your mom about me?" Anna's tone was stunned.

"Yeah, I told my mom about you. It's not a big deal, okay?"

"You told your mom."

"Look, she always asks me if I'm seeing anyone, and I'm always telling her no. Last time when she asked, it just kind of . . . slipped."

"How does something like that kind of slip?"

"You don't know my mom."

Wes was afraid to glance over at her, scared of what her reaction would be. Would she think he was some sort of thirty-three-year-old mamma's boy, or maybe think it was too soon for him to say something to his mom, or, worst of all, realize that he was more serious about her than she was ever going to be about him?

Finally, he couldn't help himself and took a quick peek at her.

She was still staring at him, but not in the get-me-out-of-this-car kind of way he'd almost been expecting. She was smiling.

"What?" he asked.

She swiveled around so she was facing front again, then she put her arm on the back of his seat and began softly stroking his neck.

"I told my mom, too."

CHAPTER
13

THEY ALL ENDED UP AT DELTA SIERRA'S AGAIN that evening. This time, to the surprise of everyone, Monroe joined them.

"I'm still trying to figure out how the hell you ever lived here," Danny said, already working on his third beer. "I've never seen so much dirt in my life."

"I'm not quite sure how they did it in your family, Danny, but in mine, where I lived was, strangely, determined by my parents." Wes smirked.

"I thought you were from San Diego," Tony said.

"He moved to San Diego when he was a junior in high school," Alison informed everyone.

"Why?" Danny asked. "Your dad get transferred?"

"Divorce," Wes said before Alison could show off more of her knowledge of his life.

There were nods around the table, several in the knowing fashion of those who'd lived through the same thing.

"Any family still here?" Tony asked.

Wes shook his head but didn't elaborate. His dad had stayed in Ridgecrest, but had died a year and a half after

Wes had left town. The funeral had been held in Whittier, east of Los Angeles, where Wes's dad had grown up and his uncle still lived.

More pitchers of beer arrived, and the focus moved from Wes to Dione to Danny, and, inevitably, to Monroe.

"I know I'm not supposed to talk about it, *but*," Monroe said, the glaze of alcohol in her eyes, "my agent thinks I have the inside shot at a pilot for ABC."

"Really? That's great," Dione said. "What's it about?"

Monroe looked around the table. "You've got to keep this to yourself."

"Of course," Dione spoke for the group.

"It's an update of *Mork and Mindy*."

Danny nearly spit his beer across the table. "*Mork and Mindy*? Are you serious?"

"Why? What's wrong with that?"

"Who's going to play Mork?" Danny asked.

"See, that's the twist. In the remake . . . Mork's a woman!"

Everyone stared at her.

"So are you saying you're going to play Mork?" Anna asked slowly.

"Well, the character's name is different, of course. I'm not allowed to tell anyone that. But, yeah. That's the part I'm up for."

The silence that followed had almost reached the awkward point when Dione said, "Couldn't be happier for you, Monroe." Even halfway to drunk, she was able to fake it for the show's host.

Monroe beamed.

"We should celebrate," Dione suggested.

A devilish looked entered Monroe's eyes. "Tequila shots! A hundred bucks to whoever drinks the most."

There were groans and averted gazes around the table. All, that is, except for Dione. Her eyes narrowed as she announced, "You're on, Morkette. Tony, get the waitress."

Six shots arrived a few minutes later and the two women matched each other glass for glass.

As they were waiting for another round, Wes stood up and headed to the men's room. The bar had filled up a bit more, so he had to navigate around several groups before he entered the hallway that led to the restrooms.

"How do you think you get up there?"

Wes looked back. He hadn't realized Danny had followed him. "Up where?"

"On the wall. The pictures of the planes and the crews. Think you have to be regulars here?" Danny opened the bathroom door and let Wes pass through. "You know, like the shamrocks at Tom Bergin's back home on Fairfax. Or do you have to do something special?"

"I have no idea."

Danny finished first, washed his hands, then headed for the door. "You coming?"

"Go ahead," Wes said. "I'll be right there."

Wes stared into the mirror as he finished washing up. *The photos.* What if the pilot he'd seen at the crash was in one of them? If he was, Wes could show the picture to Lars as proof that he hadn't been seeing things.

He exited the bathroom with purpose, intent on closely examining the walls, but was immediately derailed when he found Anna standing in the hallway outside the women's bathroom. She started shaking her head the moment she saw him.

"Where's the paparazzi when you need them?" she asked.

"What's going on?"

She motioned toward the bathroom door. "Monroe is doing a little unintentional weight reduction."

"Oh, God."

There was a muffled retch from beyond the door, followed by, "Don't worry. You're not going to fall in."

"Dione?" Wes asked.

Anna nodded. "Best-friend duty. Though she's not that much better off herself. Help me take them back to the hotel?"

"Sure."

A few minutes later the door opened and Monroe and Dione staggered into the hallway, but not before bumping into the door frame and breaking out in laughter.

"Hey, Wes," Dione said.

"Wes!" Monroe echoed, none the worse for her time hovering above the toilet.

"Hey, I have an idea," Wes said. "We're going to head back to the motel. You want to come with us?"

Monroe shook her head. "Too early. I want to—" She stumbled against the wall, then closed her eyes and put her hand on her forehead. "Uh, yeah. Okay. Maybe that would be a good idea."

It turned out that everyone except Danny was ready to head back.

Wes took control of Monroe, while Anna and Alison acted as Dione's guides. By the time they reached Monroe's room, she was telling Wes what a great guy he was, how cute he was in that older, mid-thirties kind of way, and outright offering him a spot in her bed that night.

Wes politely declined, then waited outside as Anna and Alison dealt with getting *Close to Home*'s star under the covers. Dione had waited with him for a few minutes, trying not to sway, then wandered off to her own room before the other two women came back out.

"Well, that was fun, wasn't it?" Alison said, then yawned.

"Don't do that," Anna said. She tried unsuccessfully to keep from yawning herself. "Fine. I'm officially tired."

They started walking together in the direction of Anna's and Alison's rooms. First, though, they reached the corridor that led out to the parking lot and the side of the hotel where Wes's room was located. They paused there.

"You guys sleep well," Wes said. "I have a feeling some people are going to be cranky tomorrow."

"Think I'll be asleep before I even get in my room," Alison said.

"I know the feeling," Anna said.

But no one made the first move. Wes and Anna exchanged a glance while Alison leisurely hunted through her purse for her key.

Finally, Wes said, "All right. I'll see you both in the morning."

He headed off down the hallway without looking back. When he got to his room, his motel phone was ringing.

"Hello?"

"You're going to have to tell her." It was Anna.

"I know. I know," he said. "Did she say anything?"

"Come on, Wes. She didn't have to."

Wes frowned. Telling Alison about his relationship with Anna was not something he was looking forward to. "I'll try to find time tomorrow."

"I think that's an excellent idea." She paused. "So . . . you want me to come over?"

"Absolutely. You still have the extra key I gave you, right?"

"Why? Aren't you going to be there?"

"I thought maybe I should go back and check on Danny."

"Danny? He can take care of himself."

Wes laughed loudly.

"Fine," she said. "But he is *old* enough to take care of himself."

"I won't be long," he said. "I'll make sure he's fine, then come right back. Wait for me here?"

She was silent for a moment. "If I'm asleep when you come in, you're not getting any."

CHAPTER
14

WHAT WES REALLY WANTED TO DO WAS TAKE A look at the pictures in the bar and see if he could find one with the pilot in it. He knew he should have just told Anna that, but until he found his proof, he felt it was better if he kept it to himself. No one wants to come off as a conspiracy nut.

In the forty-five minutes it had taken to get Monroe settled and then walk back to the bar, the crowd at Delta Sierra's had doubled, and the sound level had gone up exponentially.

Wes spotted Danny right away. He had moved to the bar and seemed to have made a couple of new friends— two women who were in at least their mid-thirties, but dressed like they were still in high school. Thankfully, though, they were monopolizing all of Danny's attention, so Wes's return went unnoticed.

Wes started with the wall closest to the main door. Though some photos were in color, most were black-and-white. Where there was any terrain visible, he saw the unmistakable desert of the Mojave, plains of nothingness and in the distance barren hills and mountains.

Wes's eyes darted from frame to frame, searching for the face he'd seen. There were a couple of possibilities in some of the group shots, but these were so small, he couldn't be sure.

He'd gone about a third of the way through the room when he found an empty spot. Despite a thin layer of dust on the surrounding wall, the spot was clean. Whatever had been hanging there had been removed recently.

He finished the back wall and started making his way along the one that led toward the bar. Two more empty spots, one on top of the other. Recent.

"Wes! You came back!"

Wes winced. A part of him had been hoping he could avoid Danny, but no go. He put on a smile and walked over to the bar. "Came to see how you were doing."

"Me? I'm great. This place is awesome." Danny was standing between stools occupied by his new female friends, and definitely drunk. "Hey, let me introduce you."

The two women turned toward Wes, smiling.

"Ladies, this is my buddy Wes. He's the one I was telling you about. Wes, this is Regina." Danny tipped his beer toward the woman with a too-friendly look in her eyes.

She held out her hand and Wes shook it. But when he went to let go, she resisted for a moment, then stuck out her lower lip in an exaggerated pout when he finally pulled his hand free.

Danny put a familiar arm around the other woman. "And this is Dori."

She shook Wes's hand, mercifully with no lingering touch.

"Danny told us what you did," Regina said. "That was very brave."

"Let us buy you something to drink," Dori said.

"I'm fine," Wes told her. "Thanks, though."

"That wasn't a question," Dori said, then caught the bartender's attention and got Wes a beer.

"Thanks," he said.

Regina lifted her glass. "To the hero."

"I'm not a hero."

"To the hero," Dori repeated.

Wes clinked glasses with everyone, then raised the pint to his mouth. He let the liquid brush his lips, but he refrained from actually taking a drink.

"So, what were you doing?" Dori asked.

"Pardon?" Wes said.

She nodded toward the room beyond the bar. "You were checking out the walls."

"Who was checking out the walls?" Danny asked, a bit unsteady.

"Your friend. He was walking around the room, staring at them."

Wes shrugged. "I wasn't staring. I was just taking a look at the pictures."

"See anything interesting?" Regina asked.

"A bunch of pilots and planes," Wes said.

Regina reached out and put her arm around Wes's waist. "Want to share the stool, sweetie?"

He pulled himself back. "Actually, I need to use the restroom. I'll be back in a minute."

Her hand lingered on his hip. "I'll be waiting."

Wes angled himself through a break in the growing crowd and headed toward the restrooms. Just before the hallway, he turned to the left and finished examining the wall near the bar.

Nothing.

Whoever the pilot in the downed F-18 had been, his picture wasn't here.

Disappointed, Wes made a wide circle around the bar, avoiding Danny and his friends, and headed quickly for the exit. Just as he reached the far side, someone grabbed his arm.

"Thought you were coming back."

He turned to find Dori standing behind him.

"I'm tired," he said. "Gotta work early tomorrow."

"Danny doesn't seem worried about it."

"He'll pay for it in the morning."

"I think Regina likes you."

"I'm sure she's very nice," Wes said, "but I'm attached."

Dori frowned. "Kind of attached, or very attached?"

"Very."

"Really? Well, that's good news," she said, then added, "not for Regina, of course."

Wes faked a smile. "I'll see you later."

"Will you?"

"Good night, Dori. It was nice meeting you."

She regarded him for a moment. "Bye, Wes." She disappeared back into the crowd.

As Wes turned for the door, something on the wall behind the bar caught his eye. He stepped closer to get a better look. It was a framed photograph of Lieutenant Lawrence Adair, the same shot that had been in the paper. There was a black ribbon around the frame and several candles burning below it.

That's when it dawned on Wes. The missing photos on the walls, they must have also been of Adair. Taken down out of respect.

So *where* was Wes's pilot?

He frowned to himself, then straightened up. It had been worth a try.

After a quick glance back at the bar, he started to turn for the door, but paused. Someone had been looking in his direction. He turned back to see who it was, and was surprised to find Lieutenant Jenks, one of the pilots from the previous evening, staring back at him. The lieutenant smiled and raised his glass, tilting it in Wes's direction.

With a nod of acknowledgment, Wes turned back toward the door and left.

CHAPTER 15

ANNA WAS ASLEEP WHEN WES RETURNED, BUT stirred when the start-up tone rang out as he booted up his laptop.

"What are you doing?" she asked, barely able to keep her eyelids open.

"Go back to sleep. I just want to check something."

"You did understand what I said about no sex, right?"

"Right, if you're asleep. I promise to wake you first."

A pillow flew across the room, landing near his feet. "Not what I meant."

He put his computer on the small motel-room desk, then walked over to the bed.

"Get away from me." She giggled as she pulled the covers over her head.

He started to pull them down, but she held on tight, putting up a fight.

"I'll scream," she said.

"So will I," he said. "I'll claim you snuck in here and surprised me. I'll say that you've been stalking me, then we'll have to get a restraining order, and that'll just make this relationship thing all the more difficult."

She struggled with him some more, but he was able to inch the blanket down below her chin. He leaned in and kissed her. Her lips remained pressed tightly together for several moments, then they began to soften and part.

Finally she whispered, "You never told me what your mother said when you told her."

Wes kissed her again. "She said no woman is good enough for her son." Another kiss. "Of course, I told her that you were already aware of your inadequacies."

"Oh, really." She kissed him deeply. "Maybe you can detail them for me."

"Happy to." He smiled. "Just give me a few minutes to check something."

"Ugh," she said, pushing him off. "You really know how to kill the mood."

"Not kill it," he said, standing up. "Just put it on ice for a few minutes."

"And that's supposed to make me feel better?"

"It's all about anticipation."

As he sat back down at the desk, a second pillow sailed through the air and hit him in the back.

Wes accessed the footage from the camera auto-backup drive. He wanted to see what Danny had shot of the crash. The night before, there had been no real reason to look at it. But now, after the picture in the newspaper, and his fruitless search of the pictures at the bar, he wanted to make sure he *wasn't* crazy.

The first shots were just B-roll stuff of the Pinnacles. Then there was the wide shot of Monroe standing next to the unusual rock formations. This went on for nearly thirty seconds before the image swung quickly to the left, then down at the ground.

Suddenly the picture whipped up and focused on the

sky. Center frame was the plane. The image held for five seconds, then cut off.

The next shot started with a jolt. Shadows. Car mats. Shoes. Then the dash of the Highlander, and the desert outside. The picture bounced and jerked with the movement of the car.

Another shot. Still inside the SUV, this time with burning vegetation on all sides. In the distance was the back of the Escape Wes had been driving, and beyond that the cloud of dust and smoke that enveloped the plane.

The final shot started in the car, but the chaotic motion was gone. Suddenly the door opened and the picture moved outside. The frame moved up and down as the image quickly approached the downed jet, then steadied once it was in position.

It spun to the right and focused on Wes trying to get up to the cockpit, then caught his miscalculation as he nearly fell off. The image stayed on Wes while he pulled himself back up and leaned into the cockpit. Unfortunately, Danny had positioned himself so that Wes blocked the view of the pilot from the camera.

"Dammit," Wes whispered.

Danny sped forward, keeping the pace just slow enough so he could get an idea of what was going on. But the whole time there was no clear shot of the pilot.

Then Danny had followed him with the camera as he'd made his dash for the knife.

"For God's sakes, Danny," Wes said.

"What's wrong?" Anna asked.

"Nothing," he said. "Everything's fine."

Wes watched himself race past burning brush for the SUV. Anna ran out to meet him, handing him the knife. Then, as he turned to go, Dione stopped him.

As Wes pushed past her and headed back toward the

plane, the image panned quickly to the cockpit, then swung back to pick up Wes again.

Wes rewound to the cockpit shot, then hit Pause.

The image of the man's face was there for only a few frames before he turned his head to look back at Wes on the wing. Wes clicked through, frame by frame. Five total. NTSC, the video format used in the United States, ran at approximately thirty frames a second, which meant the man's face was on camera for only one-sixth of a second.

Wes studied each frame separately, but they were too blurry to distinguish anything. He then looped them so that they'd play over and over. In motion, unlike still images, there was just enough to get an idea of what the pilot looked like.

He did have to admit that it didn't definitively prove it wasn't Lieutenant Adair, but to his eyes, he was sure the man in the shot wasn't the same man whose picture had run in the paper.

"I thought you said you were only going to be a few minutes," Anna said.

"I am."

"It's already been twenty."

"No it hasn't."

"You're right. It's actually been twenty-three."

Wes glanced at the clock on his computer and was surprised to see she was right.

"Look, if you're going to work all night, I'm going back to my room."

There was the rustle of blankets and sheets.

"No, don't go," he said. "I'm just finishing up."

He saved the file to both the hard drive and his portable thumb drive. Behind him, he could hear Anna shuffle across the floor, then felt her lean over his shoulder and look at the screen.

"What are you doing?"

Wes closed the laptop and stood up. "If I tell you now, you'll fall asleep before I finish. How about we wait until morning?"

Before she could say anything, he picked her up and carried her to the bed.

"Don't think this is helping your cause," she said. "I'm going back to sleep."

"I doubt it."

"You do?"

"I do."

CHAPTER
16

WHEN WES RAN OUT OF HIS ROOM THE NEXT morning, he was already three minutes late for morning call time. But he slowed his pace as soon as he noticed no one else was at the SUVs yet. Behind him, he heard someone on the sidewalk, and wasn't surprised when Anna jogged up.

"We're first?" she asked.

"Looks like it."

Wes loaded the camera bag and the backup system into the rear of the Escape, then joined Anna in leaning against the front fender.

"Should we make sure they're alive?" she asked.

He checked the time on his phone. "Nah. Let's give them until seven forty-five."

It was 7:39 when Dione shuffled out of the courtyard corridor, face slack and a pair of Jackie O sunglasses covering her eyes. She was followed thirty seconds later by Alison, who merely looked tired, then by Tony, and finally by the host of *Close to Home*.

"I could have sworn we had to shovel Monroe into bed last night," Anna whispered to Wes.

Monroe was showing no ill effects from the tequila fest the night before.

"Maybe she's always hungover," Wes suggested.

Anna stifled a snort.

"Where's Danny?" Dione said, her voice at least an octave lower than usual.

Shrugs, and a few I-don't-knows.

"Has anyone called him?" she asked.

No one spoke up.

"Great," she said as she pulled out her cellphone.

Two seconds later Wes heard another phone ringing in the distance.

"I'm coming," Danny yelled.

They could all now see the second cameraman walking quickly toward them down the sidewalk that ran along the motel. And he wasn't alone.

Dori was draped under his arm, sporting the same age-inappropriate dress she'd been wearing the night before. They stopped in front of a Lincoln sedan, shared a few words, then kissed for several seconds.

Alison let out a groan. "I really didn't need to see that first thing in the morning."

"I really didn't need to see that ever," Tony said.

As Danny and Dori parted, Dori looked over and gave Wes a small wave.

This elicited a raised eyebrow from Anna.

"Don't ask," Wes said.

"Morning, gang," Danny said as he jogged over, surprisingly spry after a night of drinking. "Sorry I'm late. I got a little sidetracked."

"Can we just go?" Dione asked wearily.

Their first stop was Robber's Roost. It was basically a large, fractured boulder, with a couple of smaller piles of rock nearby, that bandits in the 1800s had used as a lookout for spotting stagecoaches bound for Los Angeles. It wasn't exactly the easiest place to shoot, but was a natural location for *Close to Home*.

Tony went up and down the rocks over a dozen times, wearing his hiking boots and a wide grin as he hauled equipment, then escorted Monroe into place.

"This is awesome," he said as he helped Dione up the side of the rock.

She groaned, then pushed her glasses up her nose. "'Awesome' isn't quite the word I'd use."

When they rolled into Red Rock Canyon just before 11 a.m., they were surprisingly still on schedule. The canyon was a fascinating mix of cliff faces, buttes, and tributary ravines lined by erosion-carved rocks. The colors, too, were striking—deep reds, whites, and, of course, nearly every shade of brown.

They spent the first hour and a half shooting B-roll, then broke for lunch at twelve-thirty.

Wes was just taking a bite of a roasted turkey sandwich when a dark sedan turned off the highway and drove slowly toward them, parking just behind the SUVs.

He took a step toward the sedan as the door opened and Lars got out.

"We can't be in trouble," Dione scoffed. "I got all the right permits."

"Relax," Wes said. "It's not the park service. It's a friend of mine."

"Hey, Wes," Lars said as he walked up.

"Didn't expect to see you out here."

"I was passing by and realized it was you and your friends, so thought I'd stop."

"You saw us from the road?" Wes asked, surprised.

"Yeah. When I noticed the cameras, I figured it had to be you."

"Everyone, this is my old friend, Lars Andersen," Wes said to the crew. "We grew up together. Lars, this is Danny, Alison, Tony, Dione, Anna, and Monroe."

There were a lot of hellos and nice-to-meet-yous.

"So this is what Hollywood's like, huh?" Lars said to Wes, once everyone else returned to lunch.

"Yeah, pretty glamorous. At least we're on schedule. We were supposed to shoot on the base yesterday, but that got canceled."

"I heard," Lars said. "Sorry about that, but standard procedure."

"Doesn't matter to me," Wes said, grinning. "I get paid whether we shoot or not."

Lars returned the smile. "I was wondering if you might have a minute to talk?"

Wes nodded. "Sure. We've got about ten until we start up again."

"Why don't we take a walk?" Lars suggested.

They followed the wall of the canyon away from the SUVs.

"So, what's up?" Wes asked once they were out of earshot of the others.

"I did some checking," Lars said. "Wes, the guy in the newspaper picture was the pilot of the plane."

"You're sure?"

Lars nodded, a sympathetic smile on his face. "I talked to some of the search-and-rescue team, reread through all the reports; there's no question. It was Adair." He paused. "Look. It's completely understandable. You were under a lot of stress. It's a wonder you remember seeing anyone at all."

"You're one hundred percent positive?"

"Absolutely. Multiple ID verification."

Wes sighed. "Guess I was wrong."

Lars put a hand on Wes's shoulder. "Don't worry about it. I'm glad you asked me to check. Better to know the truth than to just assume, right?" He paused. "Listen, when do you leave town?"

"Wednesday," Wes said.

"So you're here this weekend?"

Wes nodded.

"Will you be shooting or do you get some downtime?"

"No. A couple people have to go back to L.A. for the weekend, so we're off."

"Then come over tomorrow afternoon. We'll barbecue and talk about old times. What do you think?"

"Maybe," Wes said.

"I'll take that for a yes. Four-thirty, and bring beer."

Wes remained silent as they turned to head back.

"Don't beat yourself up. You went above and beyond yesterday for Adair. You should be proud of that."

"I was so sure."

"I told you, stress likes to mess with your mind."

"That photo . . . I could have sworn it was wrong."

"Hope this has made you feel a little better. Always good to get things settled."

"I guess."

"At least now you can stop wandering around bars looking at pictures."

Wes stopped walking. "What?"

Lars let out a resigned breath. "I heard about your visit to the bar last night. I didn't realize how seriously you were taking this."

Wes eyed his friend. "You didn't just come out here by chance, did you?"

Lars hesitated a moment, then shook his head. "No, I didn't."

"How did you find us?"

"I work for the Navy, Wes. If we can find a specific submarine in thousands of square miles of ocean, finding a film crew in Red Rock Canyon isn't difficult."

Wes paused a moment. "Then why the lie? And what about the pilot? Are you lying about him, too?"

"Whoa. I just came out here because I knew it was bothering you and thought it would be nice to clear your mind as soon as I had some info. I didn't come to get into an argument."

Wes took a breath and allowed himself to relax a little. He glanced toward the crew vehicles, then back at his friend. "What if I could prove I'm right?"

"Right about what?"

Wes hesitated, unsure if he should go on. But this was Lars, his old friend. They had trusted each other once. "We shot video of the accident, including a shot of the pilot's face. It's not Adair. I'll show you and you'll see."

Lars stared at him. "You have video? I thought the investigators had all your footage."

"How do you know that?"

"I already told you, I read the reports. So how can you possibly have video if they've got your original source?"

Wes silently cursed himself for saying more than he should have. "I just do."

Lars frowned. "Did you look at it?"

"Yes. Why? Are you afraid I might have seen something I shouldn't have?"

Lars stared off into the distance for a moment, then looked back, clearly annoyed. "Wes, this is an embarrassment for us. It's our plane. Our man died in it.

Whether it was a training issue or a mechanical one, this is a black eye for the Navy. Jesus, you have a bad day, you just reshoot. We have a bad day, someone dies. Your playing private investigator isn't helping anything, and it certainly isn't going to change reality. This is our tragedy. We're handling it in-house. I would think you'd get that."

Wes said nothing for a moment. "Of course I get that."

"Then for God's sake, just let us deal with it. *Please*."

A horn sounded behind them. Wes looked back and saw Dione waving at him.

"I'll drop it. All right? Sorry. I gotta get back to work."

"Wes, wait." Lars's tone softened. "I'm sorry. I'm not trying to make a big deal of this. We're all on edge because of the accident. I'm sure you can appreciate that. I really just wanted to let you know that I checked things out like I promised I would, but there's been no mistake."

"Yeah. Sure. Look, I gotta go."

"See you this weekend?"

"I'll think about it."

The horn honked again.

CHAPTER
17

"I'VE BEEN DYING TO ASK YOU ALL DAY," ANNA said as they entered Wes's room at the Desert Rose. "What was that all about?"

Wes set the camera bag in the closet. "What was what all about?"

"Your friend Lars. What did he want?"

"Nothing important."

He put the case containing the auto-backup system on the floor next to the desk, then went to grab a clean shirt, but stopped short. His suitcase wasn't there.

Anna plopped down on the bed. "Nothing? It didn't look like nothing."

Wes wheeled around, searching the room.

"What's wrong?" she asked.

"My suitcase. It's gone."

She pointed at the far side of the dresser. "What are you talking about? It's right there."

"Huh." He couldn't remember putting it there.

He pulled out a black polo shirt and exchanged it with the shirt he'd been wearing all day. "Do we need to stop by your room first?"

"Nope. You're going to have to take me as I am."

"I like the sound of that. Maybe we should just order in."

"No way. You're taking me out on the town," she said. "What there is of it."

He circled his arms around her and picked her up off the bed. "Are you sure?"

"Don't tempt me."

"That's exactly what I'm trying to do."

She slapped his arm and said, "Put me down. I'm hungry."

As they exited his room, Anna rummaged around in her purse.

"Damn," she said.

"What?"

"I don't have my lipstick."

"Sure you do," Wes said. "I saw you putting some on when we were out today."

"That's nice that you'd watch me primp, sweetie, but that was my daytime lipstick. I need my nighttime." She closed her purse. "Not here. I'll be right back."

"So we *are* going to your room."

"I'm going, you're getting the car started."

She tilted her head up and kissed him, then jogged off.

Wes had parked the Escape in the spot right outside his room. He fired up the engine, then turned on the satellite radio and tuned it to BBC One. Anna loved listening to the DJs' accents. He was fiddling with the A/C when the passenger door flew open.

"You were right. That was quick." He looked over.

Anna made no move to get in, a strange look on her face.

"What's wrong?" he asked, suddenly alert.

"I think there might be someone in my room."

They ran through a short passage to the other side and quickly reached her door. It was ajar.

"Did you leave it like that?" he asked.

Anna nodded.

Wes nudged it open and peered inside. It was quiet. He pushed it open more, then stepped across the threshold. The room was empty.

Confused, he glanced at Anna.

"Listen," she whispered.

He cocked his head and immediately registered a noise that shouldn't have been there.

"Is that the shower?" he asked.

She nodded.

"Don't tell me there's someone in it."

"I don't know for sure. I went in to check, but as soon as I saw the mirror, I ran out."

"The mirror?"

"You have to see."

Cautiously Wes stepped farther into the room, his gaze sweeping the space to make sure he didn't miss anything. Anna was right behind him.

"Go back outside," he told her, keeping his voice low.

"I'm not letting you do this alone. What if someone's in there?"

Frowning, Wes turned back to the bathroom. Though the door was half open, he knocked on the jamb. "Hello?"

No response.

Wes eased into the room, then put a hand on the plastic shower curtain. His other hand he balled into a fist, just in case.

"Hello?" he said again.

When there was still no answer, he yanked the curtain back and glanced inside.

He shrugged. "Empty."

Anna relaxed a little, but not completely. "The mirror."

Wes swiveled around so he could see the mirror that covered the wall behind the sinks. It was fogged up from the steam of the shower. Clearly visible across the surface, someone had written:

HE IS NOT WHO HE SAYS HE IS

Despite the warmth of the bathroom, a chill ran through Wes.

"This wasn't here before?" he asked.

"If I'd seen it earlier, don't you think I would have said something?"

"I mean did you ever steam up the mirror enough for this to appear?"

"I don't know. I don't remember it getting that foggy."

He reached out toward the final *S*.

"Don't," Anna said. "We should call the police."

"I just want to check something."

Wes could feel her tense behind him, but she said nothing more.

He touched the nail of his index finger to the bottom of the letter, then pulled it back. There was a small bit of whatever had been on the mirror now on his nail. He wiped it onto the pad of his thumb and rubbed it around.

"It feels like Vaseline," he said. "Did you use the bathroom this morning?"

She'd only had fifteen minutes from after she'd left Wes's room until they met up again at the SUVs.

"I took a quick shower."

"So you're sure this wasn't here then."

"Wes, it wasn't there," she snapped. She took a deep breath. "What do you think it means?"

"I don't know," Wes said.

"Maybe it's about the pilot," she said. "You know how you said the guy in the paper wasn't the same guy you saw? Maybe that's what this means."

"Maybe," he said. "Come on. I'll call the police."

CHAPTER
18

THE ON-DUTY MANAGER OF THE MOTEL WAS A
pudgy, balding man named Harold Barber. He had already come by and expressed his apologies. He offered
to move Anna to a new room—offer accepted, with the
request that it be near Wes's. He also said he would
comp her stay—offer also accepted on behalf of Dione,
who, in addition to Monroe, had gone back to L.A.
until Sunday night.

The police had sent more people than necessary for
what amounted to a little act of vandalism. But it was
still early on Friday night, so there probably wasn't
much else going on.

After a detective named Stevens asked Wes and Anna
several questions and then ascertained that nothing was
missing, he allowed them to take Anna's things to her
new room. They dropped most of the stuff off, then
grabbed what Anna needed for the next morning and
left.

"If I remember correctly, you said something earlier
about room service," she said.

"No night on the town?"

She shook her head.

"How about a movie instead? We can check pay-per-view."

"Perfect."

He opened the door to his room and let her pass inside.

"You pick the movie, and I'll order the food," he said.

"Chinese?"

"Will do."

Once they were both inside, he started to close the door, but stopped and looked out toward the parking lot.

"What's wrong?" Anna asked.

Wes scanned the lot, then shook his head. It must have just been his nerves.

"Nothing," he said, then shut the door.

CHAPTER 19

THE MAN SITTING IN THE BLUE SEDAN ACROSS
the parking lot lowered his binoculars and picked up the
phone lying beside him on the empty passenger seat.

Once the call was connected, he said, "Looks like
she's moved to the room next to his. . . . Just dropped
her suitcases off there, but they've gone to his place. . . .
If I had a guess, I'd say they're in for the night. . . . I
can't, police are still here." There was a long pause as he
listened. "Okay, so not tonight. What do you want me
to do, then? . . . Got it."

He disconnected the call, put the phone on the seat,
then settled back to wait and make sure the couple
didn't leave unexpectedly.

CHAPTER
20

WES'S EYES POPPED OPEN AT JUST AFTER 6 A.M. on Saturday morning. With no shoot that day, he tried to go back to sleep, but that wasn't happening. So he rolled onto his side and stared at Anna for several minutes, hoping she might sense his gaze and wake up. That, apparently, wasn't happening, either.

With a groan, he flipped over, crawled out of bed, and shuffled to his computer. He knew what he'd seen out at the Pinnacles, and it wasn't the guy the Navy was trying to force-feed everyone. If he could only find a little more proof, then maybe he could convince Lars of that.

The first thing he did was fire off an email to Casey back in L.A., then he opened Google Images in his browser and typed in the search parameters: "China Lake pilots." Over one million hits came back. He started flipping through the thumbnail pages quickly, scanning for the face he remembered from the crash.

A few minutes later, the icon for his email program began bouncing on his toolbar. It was a response from Casey.

The best site is called Drew's Military Action Site. You'll
need a user ID and password to get in. Try BAN4KOOL,
password onit47.
Why are you looking for military photos?

Wes typed in a quick reply.

Just some background stuff. Thanks for the help.

Drew's Military Action Site was basically a database
of military history. Wes went immediately to the Photos
section. Depending on what search parameters he put
in, Wes could access photos tagged "pilots," "Navy pilots," pilots assigned to China Lake, or pilots assigned
to any other post by branches, divisions, groups, and the
like.

He did China Lake first, but found nothing useful, so
he widened his search to all Navy pilots. He moved rapidly through page after page of shots—some solo, some
group. Then he stopped suddenly, his index finger a
mere fraction of an inch above the forward arrow key,
and stared at the screen.

It was a group shot. Twenty people, mostly men. And
in the middle row, third from the left, was the man from
the crash.

He was sure of it.

He looked for any information associated with the
picture, but there was none.

Scrolling back, he checked other group shots. Most
had information and names listed below them. *What the
hell?*

He tried to move the picture to his desktop, but the
image was locked and could not be dragged off. A prob-

lem, but not nearly as annoying as not finding any information with the picture. He took a computer snapshot of his screen, then opened the new image in Photoshop and cropped out everything but the group picture itself.

Once he'd saved that, he blew the picture up until the resolution deteriorated and the man's face became unrecognizable. He was only able to magnify the picture a couple of times before this happened. He backed it down until the man's face was clear again and saved it as a separate file, then stared at the image.

He wasn't crazy.

He hadn't been seeing things.

The man he knew he had tried to pull from the crash had been real.

He didn't have the guy's name, but he had his picture.

This he could show to Lars. The picture in conjunction with the video loop should be more than enough to prove he was right. At the very least, it would be enough to convince Lars he should look into it a little deeper. And once he did, he'd find out that Wes wasn't the one who was making things up.

There was one other thing he could do, too. A backup, just in case.

He opened a new email and attached the photo to it. In the message body, he wrote:

Casey,
Trying to identify third man from the left in the middle row. Any chance you can help? Best if you keep this on the sly, and not just from the company. Will explain later.
Wes

After he hit Send, the knot of frustration that had been gnawing at the back of his mind began to unravel. The situation had worked him up more than he'd expected.

But now he knew the truth. Now he'd be listened to.

CHAPTER 21

THE DAY HAD TURNED OUT TO BE THE HOTTEST one yet. Wes guessed it had to be just below one hundred degrees as he and Anna got out of the SUV at the self-storage facility. It was almost enough reason to climb back in and return to the hotel.

Almost.

They got directions from the woman in the office, then walked between the one-story buildings until they found the unit they were looking for.

There had been no shoot to put it off today, nothing that would make Wes too busy to carry out his mother's request. She had initially asked him to do it years ago, and when he'd told her he was coming up for the shoot, she reminded him again.

"Your father still had a lot of the old photos," she had told him over the phone before he'd left L.A. "I'd really like to get those. Everything else, well, whatever you don't want we'll donate to Goodwill."

He still wasn't sure he felt up to it, but he was here. And it was time.

"Wes?" Anna said.

He blinked and glanced over.

"Are you okay?"

"Yeah," he said. "Yeah, I'm fine."

"You're sure?"

He gave her a halfhearted smile, then slipped the key into the lock. It was stiff from the dry, dusty climate, but it didn't put up much of a fight and was soon off. Now the only thing separating him from what remained of his father's possessions was a metal roll-up door. He grabbed the handle and raised it out of the way.

The unit was about the size of a small, one-car garage, but much of it was hidden by a wall of cardboard boxes that filled the entrance. Someone had written short descriptors on the outside of each: *Kitchen, Clothes, Office, Books, Misc.*

Wes and Anna began moving them out of the unit and setting them on the asphalt to either side of the door, working slowly in deference to the temperature.

"How long has all this been here?" Anna asked after several minutes.

"About fifteen years, I guess."

"And you've never come to look through it before?"

He shook his head as he grabbed a box and carried it outside. "This is the first time I've been back."

Anna stopped and looked at him. "You mean since you moved away during high school?"

"Yeah."

They worked in silence for another minute.

"Didn't you see your dad after you left?"

"Of course I saw him," Wes said. "I just didn't see him here. He'd come down to San Diego."

Removing several more boxes revealed a second wall of them behind the first.

"Whoa," Anna said. "It's not all like this, is it?"

"If it is, we're stopping now."

Wes hopped up onto a couple of the boxes marked *Books,* and pulled out one of the top boxes of the second wall to look through the gap.

"I don't know if this is a good thing or not," he said, "but it looks like it's furniture after this."

Once he'd climbed back down, they finished off enough of the outer wall so they could get at the second one, then took a break to drink some of the water they'd brought along.

"Thanks," Anna said as he handed her a bottle. "I guess I don't understand why you never came back up here."

Wes uncapped his and took a long sip, then said, "He died a couple weeks after I graduated high school. Before that, it was always just easier for him to come to me."

"What about your friends? That guy Lars. Didn't you come back to visit them?"

He raised his bottle to his lips. "No," he replied, then tilted the bottle back.

He could feel her looking at him, waiting for more.

Finally she said, "Tell me about your father."

"Dad?" Wes paused. "Well, if you ever had a flat tire, he's the guy you'd want driving by. Seriously. Any time he saw someone pulled to the side of the road, he'd stop and see if he could help. Annoyed the hell out of my mom and me. Made us late to things more than once."

"Sounds like a good guy."

Wes smiled, then moved back into the unit and started in on the second wall. "Yeah, he was. He cared about things. A little too much, Mom said, but doing the right thing was important to him. He always stressed that to me. He'd say, 'It might not always be popular, but if it's what needs to be done, popular doesn't matter.'"

"You miss him, don't you?"

"Sure, wouldn't you if your dad was gone?"

"Every day," she said. She moved another box out of the way. "You've never actually told me how he died. If you don't want to, that's okay, but . . ."

"Car crash."

"Oh, Wes. I'm so sorry."

Wes shook his head like it didn't matter. "He was traveling up Nine Mile Canyon toward Kennedy Meadows in the Sierras. The road's narrow and really winding. No guardrails. It's also steep, hundreds of feet down. Apparently he misjudged and went off the side."

Anna took in a quick breath.

"They didn't even discover his car for almost a week. And only then because one of his friends got worried about him and alerted the police. By then it was just a burned-out hulk with a body inside. The only way they could ID him was from his dental records."

"That's awful."

"He must have been going camping. He did that a lot. Told me he liked the feel of waking up in the mountains. It was a nice change from all the brown down here."

They'd cleared enough away to get beyond the second wall of boxes, and stepped through into the main area of the unit. The area was lit by a 100-watt bulb that had automatically come on when they'd opened the door.

"My God, look at this stuff," Wes said.

There was furniture and filing cabinets and lamps and odds and ends stacked haphazardly throughout the central portion of the space.

"What are we looking for?" Anna asked.

"Photo albums, pictures. That kind of thing. My mom wants them."

He squeezed his way between two cabinets and started tilting things one way or the other to see what was behind them.

"Bingo," Anna called out a few minutes later. "This drawer is full of framed pictures. Most of them must be you." She paused for a moment, then laughed.

"What?"

"Nothing," she said, still giggling. After a moment she turned the photo she was looking at so he could see. "It's you at maybe two, I think. Your face is covered with chocolate, and the only other thing you're wearing is a diaper."

"Oh, God," he said. "Maybe you shouldn't actually be looking for the pictures."

"Too late." She looked at it again. "I think I'm going to have to keep this one myself."

"You might have a fight on your hands with my mom."

"Oh, don't worry. I'll take her."

Wes laughed, then went back into search mode. So far he had found nothing of interest. As far as he was concerned, they could donate it all. Then he noticed a chest-high wall of boxes near the back wall.

He pushed past a couple of kitchen chairs and an old end table, then leaned against the wall and peered into the space beyond.

"It *is* here," he said.

"What?" Anna asked.

He grinned broadly. "Better if I show you." He pulled a box marked *Den* off the pile. "We're going to have to move some of these."

They worked quickly, and soon the barrier was half gone.

Anna said, "Is that . . . a motorcycle?"

Wes grinned again. "Yeah. It's my dad's Triumph Bonneville. Got it when I was ten. Another officer who was transferring overseas couldn't take it with him."

Together they cleared a path through the furniture, then Wes wheeled the motorcycle out into the sunlight. The bike's gas tank and fenders were painted a rich green that even after all these years had faded little. And the black storage compartment behind the seat looked almost new.

"There's something else back here," Anna called from inside the unit. "Looks like a box of bike stuff."

She carried it out and set it on the ground near the motorcycle. Inside were a helmet, a file folder, and keys.

Wes pulled out the folder and opened it. Inside was his father's old maintenance log, the final entry of which had been made after his father's death:

Oil and gas drained. Battery removed.

There were some initials at the end of the entry, but they meant nothing to Wes. Whoever it was had cared enough to prep the cycle for storage. There was also an envelope that contained the pink slip.

"You think it'll start?" Anna asked.

"We'll have to make a stop at an auto store first to get some oil and a new battery . . . and then gas, of course. But I don't see why not. Dad always took good care of it. Let's finish up and we'll see if I'm right."

They spent the next hour hunting down photos, but came up with a lot less than Wes had been expecting.

After that they started returning all the boxes they'd removed to the unit.

As Wes came back from carrying another load inside, he found Anna hunched over a box on the asphalt, looking inside.

"We're not going through them," he said. "We're just carrying them back in."

With a smirk, she turned the box and pointed at the side where someone had scrawled in black ink *Photos*.

"Would this be what your mom wanted?" she asked innocently.

She pulled out a photo album, gave it a quick perusal, then dove deeper into the box. Next out came an old Tupperware container full of loose photographs. That was followed by a second container, then a group of four thinner albums.

"I think you may have just earned my mother's undying love," Wes said, smiling.

"I'm still going to fight her for the Chocolate Boy picture."

"I would have expected nothing less. Now quit browsing and put it all back in the box. I'll take it to the truck once we get everything else put away."

As he was picking up another box to return to the unit, Anna said, "This is interesting."

He stopped just long enough to see that she'd removed a couple more items from the box, then continued into the storage unit. "You suck at directions. I told you just leave the photos in the box. You can look at them back at the motel if you really want to."

"These aren't photo albums," she called out.

"Then just set them on top of one of the boxes we're leaving. We don't need them."

Her voice grew distant as he went back into the unit. "You might want to take a look first."

He laughed to himself, then set the box down and went back outside.

"All right. Show me what you found."

She held out one of the books and said, "Here."

He took it and opened it. She was right. It wasn't a photo album. It was a day planner covering the year Wes was in eighth grade. Wes immediately recognized his father's handwriting.

"I forgot about these," he said. "They're my dad's. His way of staying organized so that he didn't miss anything."

"Maybe you should keep them." She held out the other three.

He thought for a moment, then took them from her. "Maybe."

From the box she pulled out some more. They put them in order. There were planners that started from when Wes was seven, right up until—

"That's odd," Wes said.

"What?"

"There's not one for the year he died."

"Maybe after you left, he stopped," Anna suggested.

"No way. Not Dad. He would have definitely kept these up. He died in the summer, so there's a whole half a year that should be written down somewhere."

Anna looked through the books, just to double-check. "Maybe it's in another box."

If he hadn't seen the books, he never would have missed them. But now, especially since he knew they were filled with words written by his father, he felt he couldn't just forget about them. And it only made sense, then, to have the whole set.

He thought back, remembering those times he'd seen his father sitting at the table, writing in one of the planners.

"The kitchen," he said. "That's where he could have kept it."

They located all the boxes marked *Kitchen* and started looking through them. It was Wes who found it in a box full of old notepads and shoestrings and ads for restaurants and the other things he knew his father had simply stuffed into the kitchen junk drawer.

He opened the book and started thumbing through the pages, stopping when he reached the last weeks of his father's life.

There were notations about meetings at work and a reminder about someone named Charlie's birthday. With only a slight hesitation, Wes paused before turning the page to the week that contained the day his father died. Oddly, there was nothing about going on a trip. In fact, on the day after his father was killed in the crash, he had several meetings scheduled.

A one-day camping trip? Wes had never remembered his father going on one that short before.

Then something else caught his attention. It was a single word written in the 8:30 p.m. slot on the day before the crash:

Pudge

Wes stared at the name for a moment, unable to comprehend why it would be here.

Pudge?

It was a nickname Wes's dad had come up with.

The name his father had called Lars.

CHAPTER
22

LARS LIVED ON RANDALL STREET, ON THE RIGHT side, near where the road dead-ended. His house was a modified ranch, longer front-to-back than side-to-side, with a lawn, lush and green, like most of the others in the neighborhood—their owners attempting to ignore the fact they lived in the middle of the desert.

Wes and Anna pulled in to the driveway on his dad's Triumph and parked next to an old Ford F-150 pickup. He wasn't even off the bike when Lars ran outside, a bottle of beer in his hand.

"Is that what I think it is?" He was grinning ear to ear.

"You remember it?" Wes asked.

"Hell yes, I do. We all wanted one just like it." He circled the motorcycle. "Damn, it looks exactly like it did back then. You've kept it in great shape."

"Thanks." Wes didn't bother correcting him.

Anna walked up beside him and slipped her hand into his.

"You remember Anna," Wes said. "You met her yesterday at the shoot."

Lars shook Anna's hand. "You're one of the few I do remember."

Wes's eyebrow rose. "What exactly does that mean?"

"It means keep her close or she may be riding in my truck by the end of the evening."

"Is that the 4.6 liter or 5.4?" Anna asked, nodding back at the truck.

Both men looked surprised.

"Oh, I like her," Lars said. "You are definitely in trouble, my friend."

There was laughter all around as they headed across the lawn toward the front door.

"This wasn't your parents' house, was it?" Wes asked.

"You think I could afford this on a Navy salary, even in Ridgecrest?"

"But I thought they lived on the other side of town."

"Moved here after you took off."

Wes realized he hadn't asked his friend about his parents yet. "Are they . . ."

"Very much alive. Believe it or not, living on a golf course in Phoenix. Retired to the desert from the desert. Would have expected nothing less from them. What about your mom?"

"Still in San Diego."

"Glad to hear it," Lars said. "Come on. Let me show you around."

He led them inside and gave them the dime tour. Living room, three bedrooms, two baths, dining room, and a nice, large kitchen. All of it neatly furnished in that Spartan way men living alone liked.

"The only thing you need to remember is the bathroom," Lars said as he pulled open the sliding glass door that led to the backyard. "Because the party's out here."

And a party it was. Wes had thought it was just going to be the three of them, but there were half a dozen other people lounging around the pool, talking and laughing, and all with a bottle of beer or glass of wine close at hand.

Lars made the introductions. Bob and Mary Cooper, Trent Unger, William and Nancy Quincy, and Janice Meyers. All of the men and one of the women—Janice—were naval officers like Lars. Mary was Bob's wife, and Nancy was William's. Not that Wes expected to remember any of it.

"Something to drink?" Janice asked.

Wes deferred to Anna.

"I'll take a beer," she said.

Wes smiled. "Me, too. Thanks."

Everyone gathered around the newcomers as Janice pulled two bottles out of a cooler, popped the caps, and handed them over.

"Lars tells us you work in Hollywood," Trent said.

"Technically Los Angeles," Wes said. "But yeah, Hollywood, I guess."

"Do you work with any celebrities?" Nancy asked.

"Nobody anyone would have heard of." Wes glanced at Anna, the hint of mischief in his eyes. "But Anna's done makeup for Jennifer Garner."

"Are you serious? What's she like?" Nancy said, gaping at Anna.

"Uh . . . nice. Really nice."

"I *knew* she'd be nice."

Before Nancy could ask another question, Wes said, "Why is no one in the pool?"

"Yeah," Lars said. "I pay to keep that thing clean. I expect you all to use it."

Trent whipped off his T-shirt and threw it on a nearby chair. "I was just waiting for the go-ahead."

He took one step toward the water and jumped in cannonball-style.

Bob dropped his pants, revealing a pair of bright red swim trunks, then took off his shirt and jumped in next. William, Mary, and Janice followed. Only Nancy refrained, sipping wine and finding a lawn chair in the shade.

"You got my suit?" Wes asked Anna.

She pulled his trunks out of her purse.

"Jennifer Garner?" she whispered.

"Hey, I got you out of it."

"You got me into it, too."

He smiled, then headed back to the house to change. When he reemerged from the bathroom, he found Lars in the kitchen pulling a stack of hamburger patties out of the refrigerator.

"Let me help you," Wes said.

"Ah. Great timing." Lars nodded toward the open fridge. "If you could grab that plate of onions, and the cheese."

Wes retrieved the items, then shut the refrigerator door with his elbow.

He then watched his friend begin separating the patties and putting them on a plate. "Can I ask you something?"

"Sure. What's up?"

Wes hesitated a second, then said, "After I left, did you ever run into my dad?"

Lars paused what he was doing and looked over for a second. "Your dad? Yeah, I guess." He shrugged. "It's a small town."

"You two ever do anything together?"

"You mean like hang out?"

"Yeah."

"With your dad?"

"Yeah."

"No. Why would I have done that? He didn't even like me."

"What are you talking about?" Wes asked. "He liked you."

Lars smiled skeptically. "Yeah. Sure."

Wes gave it a moment, then asked, "You remember when he disappeared?"

Lars glanced at him, then turned his attention back to the patties. "Of course. It was in the paper. I was surprised that you didn't come back."

"No one told me until after they found his body and it was already on the way to Whittier."

Lars leaned back from the counter, his eyes full of sympathy. "Really? Damn, I'm sorry."

"It's okay," Wes said, shaking his head. "Do you remember the last time you saw him?"

Lars looked off to the side, quiet for a moment. When he spoke, there was almost a rehearsed cadence to his words. "Not specifically. Like I said earlier, probably ran into him in town somewhere. Maybe the grocery store. Who knows?"

"I was going through his things and I found his day planner. You want to hear something weird?"

"What?" Lars asked. The patties finished, he turned on the faucet and began washing his hands.

"The night before he died, there was a note about a meeting with someone at eight-thirty."

"Busy man."

Now Wes paused. "The person he was supposed to meet with was you."

"*Me?*" Lars said. "I don't think so."

"That's what it said. So you didn't meet with him?"

"Of course not."

"Maybe you just—"

The doorbell rang.

CHAPTER
23

LARS SET THE PLATE OF BURGERS DOWN ON THE counter, then walked out of the kitchen.

Wes frowned. He sensed that Lars was holding something back. Then again, maybe he was just making a big deal out of nothing. What he really should be talking to Lars about was the proof he'd found online about the pilot from the crash.

"Lieutenant Commander," a voice said from the front of the house. "Hope we're not late."

There was a pause, then Lars said, "No. Come in."

A moment later Lars came back into the kitchen with a couple of men in tow.

"Wes. Want you to meet a couple colleagues from the base," Lars said, his smile slightly strained. "Lieutenant Reid Wasserman and Lieutenant Ken Jenks."

"We've actually met already," Wasserman said, holding his hand out to Wes and grinning broadly. "You're the hero."

Wes cringed inside as he shook Wasserman's hand. Why was everyone calling him that? "Not a hero."

"You know each other?" Lars asked.

"Ran into him and his friends at Delta Sierra," Jenks explained, extending his hand and shaking with Wes. "Good to see you again."

Smiling uncomfortably, Wes said, "Thanks again for the drinks. But it really wasn't necessary."

"Wish we could have done more." Jenks took a step toward Wes. "I don't know about anyone else, but I know I'd really like to find out what went on out there after the plane went down."

Wes took a deep breath. "Uh . . . okay."

"Listen, guys," Lars cut in. "I promised Wes we wouldn't talk about the crash today. You understand, right?"

There was a moment of awkward silence, then Jenks said, "Sure, sure. Sorry. You've probably talked about it too much already."

"We weren't thinking," Wasserman added. "Just forget we asked anything."

Before anyone could say anything else, Lars held the plates with the hamburgers and the onions out toward the two men. "Can you guys do me a favor and carry these out to the grill?"

Jenks took the onions. "No problem."

"These look great," Wasserman said, hamburger plate in hand. "Enough for two each?"

"Should be," Lars said.

"Excellent."

A moment later the lieutenants were gone.

"Sorry about that," Lars said.

"Thanks for running interference. I appreciate it." Wes paused a moment, then, "Look, sorry about the thing with my dad. Seeing your name there just surprised me, I guess."

"I know that was a while ago," Lars said. "But I'm

pretty sure I'd remember something like that. I have no idea why I'm in his planner. I didn't see him that night."

"I shouldn't have brought it up."

"Not a big deal." Lars gave Wes a pat on the shoulder. "I'm hungry. Let's get those burgers going."

Wes hesitated. "Um . . . Lars . . . about the crash."

"Don't worry, I've already told the others it's a taboo subject."

"Thanks," Wes said. "But, well, I know you told me to drop it—"

Lars gave his friend a compassionate smile. "I told you to do that because there's nothing there. You're going to make yourself crazy otherwise."

"It's just . . . I found his picture."

"Whose picture?"

"The pilot's."

Lars's smile faltered a little. "Adair's picture was in the paper. I would say you didn't have to look very hard."

"I'm not talking about Adair. I'm talking about the pilot I saw in the cockpit."

Lars held up a hand. "For God's sakes. You need to drop this. Whatever you think you've found doesn't change the fact that Lieutenant Adair died in that plane crash. You've got it so screwed up in your head that your mind's creating images of someone who wasn't there."

"You think I'm making this up?"

"No. I think you believe it. But I told you before, it's the stress." He put a hand on Wes's back. "Come on. Let's just go out, grill up some burgers, and have a good time. Okay?"

Wes forced a smile, then nodded. "Sure."

CHAPTER
24

THE PARTY WENT ON ALL AFTERNOON. THERE was drinking and eating and splashing and laughing and a volleyball game that no one could agree on who won. By the time the sun had started to set, Wes and Anna had talked to just about everyone—about sports, about the TV industry, about living in the desert. But Lars had been true to his word. No one brought up the crash.

With the coming night, people started leaving until the only guests left were Wes, Anna, Jenks, and Wasserman. Wes had tried several times to get Lars alone again, but his friend was always in the middle of playing host. Wes wanted to finish the conversation they'd started in the kitchen, but it looked like that just wasn't going to happen, so he walked over to Anna. "Want to head back to the motel?"

"Sounds like a good idea to me."

Lars was sitting by the grill, a nearly empty bottle of beer by his feet. "You guys leaving?"

"I think so," Wes said.

Lars pushed himself out of the chair, then grabbed on

to Wes's arm as he found his balance. "I'm glad you could come."

"Wes." Jenks walked over from where he'd been poking at the remains in the potato chip bowl. "I was hoping to talk to you a little bit more about your job before you left." He leaned forward and added in a whisper they could all hear, "Not going to be in the Navy forever."

"Maybe some other time," Wes said.

"How do you get into something like that?" Jenks asked. "I mean, I assume you have to know someone, right?"

"It helps."

"I do some camera work on the base sometimes. Training stuff, that kind of thing. I was thinking there might be some online classes I could take to learn the more advanced techniques."

"I'm sure there are. I'm just not familiar with any."

Wes put a hand on Anna's back, but before he could start for the door, Jenks grabbed him gently by the arm.

"Do you know anyone who might know?" Jenks asked.

Wes forced a smile. "I'll tell you what. I'll do some checking, then email what I find out to Lars. That sound okay?"

Jenks glanced past Wes, then said, "Uh, yeah, sure. Thanks."

"No problem."

Jenks held out his hand. "It was great meeting both of you."

Wasserman had been on his phone near the sliding glass door, but when he saw Wes and Anna talking with Jenks, he put his hand over the receiver and approached them.

"Leaving already?" he said.

"Been a long day," Wes said.

"Come on," Wasserman said. "It's Saturday and it's still early. One more beer won't kill you." He stepped over to the tub and pulled out a wet bottle.

"They're tired," Lars insisted.

Wasserman dropped the bottle back in the container. "Only wanted to make sure they had a good time, Lieutenant Commander."

"We had a great time," Wes said.

Lars slid open the door. "I'll walk you out."

Streetlights lit up the cul-de-sac, giving it that comfortable, neighborhoody feel. As they neared his bike, Wes said, "I'd still like to talk."

"Sure, come by before you leave town and we can catch up. Just the two of us."

"I mean about what we were discussing earlier. The crash."

Lars closed his eyes and shook his head. "Wes, come on. We've already—"

"If what I have to show you doesn't sway you, I promise I'll let it go."

Lars thought for a moment. "You promise?"

"Yes. I promise," Wes said.

"Okay." He took a quick glance back at the house. "How about tomorrow? You're not working, right?"

"Not working."

"Good. We can go for a drive," Lars said. "I can pick you up at your motel around two."

"That sounds good," Wes said, then he and Anna climbed onto the bike. "Thanks."

He told Anna to hold on, then he swung the Triumph around and onto the street.

It was a beautiful night, the evening air warm but

pleasant, so Wes decided to take the long way back to the motel. For the first few blocks, it was bliss, then suddenly a dark coupe turned onto the road in front of them. Wes switched lanes and attempted to go around it, but had to quickly back off when the coupe mirrored his movement, in an unsettling reminder that other vehicles often didn't see motorcycles.

He eased the Triumph into the right lane and increased his speed.

The coupe pulled in front of him again.

"Come on," Wes said.

He could feel Anna glancing over his shoulder.

Instead of once more trying to get around the coupe, Wes decided to be rid of it completely. At the next block he turned right, then drove rapidly down to the stop sign and turned left, heading once more toward Inyokern Road.

He was nearly at the end of the block when the coupe raced into the next intersection, sliding sideways as it turned toward him.

"Wes, be careful!" Anna yelled.

As soon as the coupe had finished the turn, its engine roared and the vehicle all but leapt toward them.

Stopping wasn't an option. The only thing Wes could do to avoid being struck was to veer into the open field to his right.

"Grab on tight!" he shouted, then took the bike off the road.

The Triumph jumped and bounced on the uneven ground so much that Wes thought for a second he was going to lose it. But by some miracle he was able to maintain control and get them back onto the asphalt.

Behind them tires squealed loudly.

Wes glanced quickly over his shoulder and saw the

coupe spinning back around so it could make another run at them.

"Who *is* that?" Anna asked.

Wes had no idea, and he was too busy figuring out what to do next to answer her.

He took a hard right, and accelerated as fast as possible.

The coupe turned onto the road behind them. A glance back told Wes the car wasn't going fast enough to close the gap between them, but it wasn't letting up, either.

Wes had worked on enough true-crime shows to know exactly what he needed to do. *Don't stop until you get to the police station.* That meant getting down to China Lake Boulevard and heading back across town.

But at Norma Street he hit a Ridgecrest traffic jam— five cars all traveling in the lane he wanted to get into. He angled the bike sharply to the right and jumped it up onto the sidewalk. Anna squeezed him tightly, but remained silent.

The nearest car was pacing him, while the car behind it was in tailgate mode. The only space available was a small gap in front of the car beside him. Wes increased his speed, then flew off the short curb and shot into the opening. The trailing car honked several times, but before the horn cut out, the Triumph was already in the middle lane and speeding away.

Wes could see the coupe in his mirror. It had waited until all the cars had passed, and was in the process of pulling onto the street. Wes scanned the street signs, trying to remember which road went all the way through to China Lake Boulevard.

Perdew Avenue? Maybe . . . Yes. Yes, it does. But by

the time he remembered, he was already too far into the intersection to make the turn.

Graaf?

Possibly.

Reeves? Yes. Definitely Reeves.

"We're turning," he said, unsure if Anna could hear him.

He didn't slow the bike until the absolute last possible moment, and then only enough so that he wouldn't lose control. Leaning into the turn, he cut in front of an oncoming minivan, and poured on the speed again as the bike entered the new street.

The coupe had to stop to let the minivan pass, buying them a few extra seconds.

Even then, Anna's cry, "He's still behind us!" came sooner than he had hoped.

If they could only get to China Lake Boulevard, they should be okay. It was the main drag. It had more traffic. Wes could weave the Triumph in and around the other cars, easily losing the coupe.

They just needed to get there.

"Wes!"

The panic in Anna's voice was enough to make him look back. A vehicle had just come barreling out of the cross street they'd just passed. It was an SUV, dark like the coupe, with tinted windows. But it didn't turn after them. Instead it continued down the road it was on, and disappeared.

He kept the Triumph in the middle of the road, his eyes on the boulevard ahead.

They were only two blocks away when the SUV made a second appearance, this time racing out of the street ahead of them. But instead of continuing, it screeched to a stop in the middle of the road, directly in the bike's path.

Wes angled the Triumph so he could go around the back of the truck, but as soon as he made the adjustment, the SUV's reverse lights flashed on, and it moved once more into his way.

Wes released the accelerator and applied the breaks. "Hold on!"

At the last second, he shifted the handlebars and threw his weight so the back of the bike skidded around.

The smell of rubber burning on asphalt.

The whine of the engine.

Then—

Half thud, half crunch as the Triumph smacked sideways into the SUV.

Wes threw his right leg out to keep momentum from throwing them to the ground. One of the SUV's doors started to open, so he twisted the accelerator, hoping the bike had suffered no serious damage. The Triumph responded immediately, zipping forward past the SUV.

Wes raced to Ward, then took that to China Lake Boulevard.

As they were finally heading south on the boulevard, he shouted, "Are you all right?"

"Yeah," Anna called back.

"Can you tell if they're still behind us?"

He could feel her moving around for a moment, then, "I don't see them."

"Okay," Wes said.

But he didn't feel any relief until they pulled in to the police station parking lot.

CHAPTER 25

"SOMEONE *CHASED* YOU?"

Wes and Anna had been handed over to a plainclothes detective named Andrews. He looked to be about Wes's age, and was obviously having a hard time believing their story.

"Yes," Wes said. "From Downs all the way to China Lake Boulevard."

Andrews glanced at his notes. "Two cars."

"At first it was only the coupe," Anna chimed in. "The SUV didn't show up until the end."

"That's the car you ran into?"

"Yes," Wes said. "If nothing else, the rear half on the driver's side should be pretty scratched up."

"You didn't get a look at the driver?"

"The windows were tinted."

"What about the make?" the detective asked. "Or a license number? For either car?"

"I was a little busy trying to get away," Wes said. He rubbed his left shoulder. It had taken the brunt of the collision. Though the rear fender of the bike had also been bent a little. *Sorry, Dad.* Anna had continued to say that she was okay, but he was pretty sure she was just trying to keep him from worrying.

"There's got to be someone who saw everything," Wes added. "We passed several cars."

Andrews picked up Wes's driver's license from the table. "Mr. Stewart, you do realize that you're not licensed to drive a motorcycle, don't you?"

Wes looked at the detective, his eyes narrowing. "Yes. I realize that. I plan on taking care of that next week. But that has nothing to do with what happened to us tonight."

"We'll have someone check it out," Andrews said finally, continuing to study the license a moment longer before finally handing it back. "I'm going to let you off this time, considering what you say you've been through. I'll even let you drive the bike back to your motel. But I'd advise you not to ride it again until you get your license sorted out. If you're stopped, you *will* be cited, and your bike will be impounded."

"Thanks," Wes said, trying not to let his annoyance show.

"I'll have one of our officers follow you back. Just in case your friends show up again."

Wes was about to tell him it wasn't necessary, but he could see that Anna liked the idea. "That would be nice. Thanks, again."

"We'll call you if we need any more information." Andrews stood up.

"Or if you find out who did this to us?" Wes asked.

"Of course."

CHAPTER
26

BY THE TIME WES AND ANNA PULLED IN TO THE parking lot of the Desert Rose Motel, it was almost 10 p.m.

"Not exactly the night I had planned," he said.

Anna got off the bike. "Well, it wasn't dull, that's for sure."

As he joined her on the sidewalk, he noticed she was favoring her left side. "Are you all right?"

"Fine."

"Is it your arm?"

She frowned, then shook her head. "My ribs. Jammed my elbow into them when we hit."

"You think you cracked one?"

"I said I'm fine. It's just bruised."

"Maybe we should take you to the emergency room."

"Whoa. Who needs to go to the emergency room?" Danny had just exited the corridor to the courtyard, his new friend Dori stuck to his side.

"Nobody," Anna said quickly, her voice strong. "I just tripped and banged into something, and Wes is overreacting."

"Protective of your girlfriend, are you?" Dori said.

Danny let out a laugh. "Anna is Wes's girlfriend? He wishes."

Dori merely smiled, but the look in her eye let Wes know she suspected she was right.

"Hey, we're going to grab something to eat, then head over to the bar," Danny said. "Wanna come?"

"I don't think so," Wes said.

"Come on, Danny," Dori said. "They want to be alone."

"Ha. Alone. Right. Well, if you get bored or thirsty or want to look at more of those pictures, you know where to find us."

"Sure."

Danny tipped a hat he wasn't wearing, then continued down the walkway.

Wes and Anna had only taken a few steps toward his room when Wes stopped. "Our suits. Here." He handed her his room key and returned to the bike. They'd stashed their chlorine-soaked swimsuits in the compartment behind the Triumph's seat.

But he'd barely got it open when Anna rushed back out of his room. "Call nine-one-one."

He scrambled for the phone in his pocket. "Is your pain worse?"

"It's not me."

CHAPTER
27

IN THE MOVIES, WHEN SOMEONE CAME HOME to find their place had been searched, it usually looked like a government-declared disaster area. That wasn't quite what Wes found when he entered his hotel room, but close enough.

Everything that had been in his suitcase—shirts, underwear, socks, pants, a few books—had been tossed into a pile on the floor. The bed was skewed, the mattress twisted at a forty-five-degree angle from the box spring, the sheets and blankets ripped off and thrown in a separate pile against the far wall. Though Wes hadn't used the dresser, all the drawers had been pulled out and were either on the floor or hanging in their openings. And in the bathroom, the contents of his shaving kit had been dumped into the sink.

Panicked, he ran over to the closet and jerked the door open. Surprisingly, the camera was still there. But the relief was only short-lived when he realized the backpack with his laptop and the case with the backup system for the cameras were both gone.

"No!" he yelled.

Anna came up behind him. "What is it?"

"They took the computers."

While they waited for the police, Wes and Anna searched her room to see if anyone had been there, but it was untouched.

The same investigator from the previous evening, Detective Stevens, showed up accompanied by Detective Andrews. After a quick examination of Wes's room, the night manager loaned them the motel office so they could talk to Wes in private.

"Not a good couple days for you," Stevens said. "Detective Andrews told me about earlier tonight."

"I've had better weekends," Wes said.

"It's only half over," Andrews quipped.

"Thanks for that," Wes said. "But what happened earlier tonight has to be connected to this."

Stevens took out a notebook. "What makes you say that?"

"Don't you see? The people chasing us were just buying time while their friends went through my room."

Stevens held his gaze for a moment, but only said, "Perhaps."

"Well, if they were," Andrews said, "you've got a lot of people wanting to cause you trouble. At least one each in those cars, and someone here. So who is it you pissed off?"

Wes did have one idea, but he shook his head. "No one."

"No enemies in town? Someone who might want to do you harm?"

"This is the first time I've been here in seventeen years. So no."

"You're from L.A., right? Any problems down there that might have followed you up?"

"No. Of course not. Look, whoever did this was obviously interested in our equipment, and was just waiting for an opportunity to take it."

"Perhaps," Stevens said again.

"But your camera's still here," Andrews pointed out. "Odd to leave that but take everything else, don't you think?"

"I don't know. Maybe they're more interested in computer equipment," Wes said.

"Do you think this is related to what happened in Miss Mendes's room last night?" Stevens asked.

Wes hesitated. This was getting close to his own theory. "It *is* kind of coincidental, don't you think?"

There were several more questions, all variations on ones already asked. When Wes was done, he found Anna in the lobby with Alison, so he slumped into the chair across from them.

"The manager said he'd put you in the room on the other side of mine," Anna said. "He also said he's comping you, too. Think he's afraid we're going to say something bad about the place on the show."

"We *should* say something," Alison said. "Anna's room last night. Yours tonight. Who's next? Me?"

"I doubt it," Wes said.

Alison didn't look convinced. "I'll tell you one thing, I'm sleeping with a chair jammed under the doorknob until we leave."

They fell silent for several moments.

"Should we tell the others?" Anna asked.

"Danny's busy with his new lady friend," Wes reminded her.

Alison rolled her eyes, disgusted. "The way you said that just sounds wrong."

"Tell me a way to say it that sounds right."

Alison paused for a moment. "Wow. I can't think of one."

"What about Tony?" Anna said.

"His room's next to mine," Alison said. "I could tell him."

Wes nodded. "Sure. Go ahead."

The door to the outside opened, and the night manager walked in, all energy and nerves. "Mr. Stewart, I've got you all set. I even sent someone out to get you some toiletries."

"That wasn't necessary," Wes told him.

The manager waved him off. "I also wanted to let you all know that we are adding extra security every night for the remainder of your stay."

"Thank you," Anna said.

"Let me get you your keys."

The man all but jogged to the reception desk. A moment later he was back with two keycards, one a spare in case Wes needed it.

As Wes took them he said, "I don't remember seeing any damage to my room door. Could whoever broke in have had their own key?"

"I don't see how," the manager said, immediately defensive.

"Then how do you think they got in?"

"I guess that's what the police will have to figure out." He gave them a quick smile. "Please let us know if there is anything else you need."

He made a hasty retreat to the reception desk.

"Don't think he liked the question," Alison said.

Wes rubbed the bridge of his nose. "I don't know about you guys, but I'm beat." He stood up and led them outside.

Detective Andrews was standing near the doorway to Wes's old room, talking to one of his colleagues.

"Any chance I could get my clothes?" Wes asked.

The two cops stopped talking and looked at Wes. After a moment Andrews said, "Hold on."

He disappeared inside the trashed room, then returned a few seconds later.

"Yeah. It's fine," Andrews said. "But we're going to have to keep the suitcase for evidence."

"Why?" Wes asked.

"We got a partial fingerprint on the lock. Need to send it to the lab in Bakersfield."

"I guess that's something," Wes said. "Can I go in now?"

"Yeah, just don't touch anything else."

"We'll help you," Anna said.

Before they entered the room, another thought came to Wes. "What about the camera and its case? Can we take those, too?"

Andrews pinched his mouth in annoyance. "Stevens, they want to know if they can take the camera bag, too."

Wes crossed the threshold, hoping his presence would press the point. The other detective was near the bed, looking through a notebook. There were two uniformed officers present, one with a still camera and one putting Wes's suitcase in a large plastic bag.

"Stevens?" Andrews said.

Stevens glanced up. "Huh? Yeah. That's fine. It's clean."

Wes was about to ask Alison to get the camera bag, but she made a beeline for his clothes before he could. "She might need some help," he said to Anna, then grabbed the camera bag himself.

Once they were loaded up, they headed over to his new room. As he was fumbling with the keycard, he heard a car pull in to one of the spots behind him and its door open.

"What's going on?"

Wes looked over his shoulder in time to see Danny get out of the passenger side of an old Lincoln Continental.

"Switching rooms," Wes said.

The driver's door opened, and Dori stepped out. "What's with all the police?"

"Weren't you guys going out to dinner and then the bar?" Anna asked Danny.

"Just ate," he said. "Gonna walk to the bar from here. So, what *is* with all the police?"

"Someone broke into his room," Alison said.

"You're kidding," Danny said.

Wes went into the new room and put the camera bag in the closet. "You can dump the clothes on the dresser."

Danny and Dori followed everyone inside.

"Do they know who?" Dori asked.

Anna shook her head.

"Did they take anything?" Danny asked.

"My laptop," Wes said. "And the auto-backup drive."

"Oh, crap. The footage," Danny said. "Who the hell would do that?"

Wes shook his head, more in defeat than as an answer. "Can we talk about this later?"

"Great idea," Anna said. She started for the door. "Let's give him a little space, huh?"

"Sure, sure," Danny said, but didn't move. "Man, that sucks."

"Danny," Anna said.

"Come on, babe." Dori wrapped her arm through

Danny's and pulled him toward the door. "Wes, I'm so sorry. Danny's right. That does suck."

Wes nodded, but said nothing.

Anna glanced at Wes, then left, but Alison lingered inside a moment longer.

"If you need someone to talk to, I'm just around the corner."

"Thanks," he said.

She smiled, and looked for a moment like she was going to say something else. But whatever it was, she decided to keep it to herself, and left.

Once Wes was alone, Danny's final question ran through his mind again.

Who the hell would *do that?*

The idea Wes had had earlier hadn't gone away. But there was no way he could be right.

No way.

CHAPTER
28

BOOM.

Wes popped open his eyes.

He was in bed, the room still dark, a sheen of sweat covering his arms and chest.

"Are you all right?" Anna whispered.

Boom. Boom.

Wes turned toward the sound. "What the hell is—"

"Wes, are you awake?" It was Alison, her muffled voice coming from the other side of the door.

He and Anna shared a confused look.

"Hold on," he said loud enough for Alison to hear. To Anna he whispered, "Stay here. I'll see what she wants."

He glanced at the digital clock on the nightstand. 2:53 a.m.

Two hours of sleep. Great.

He grabbed his T-shirt and his jeans off the floor and pulled them on as he headed across the room. When he got to the door, he cracked it open just wide enough to look out. Alison, dressed in a pair of lime green sweats and an L.A. Dodger's baseball cap, stood alone just on the other side.

"What's going on?" Wes asked.

"Sorry," she said. Her arms were crossed and she rocked slightly left and right. "I know this hasn't been a great night for you, but I tried knocking on Anna's door and she didn't answer. And there was no way I was going to try Danny's."

"What's going on?"

"Can I come in?"

Wes hesitated. "Hold on." He closed the door and glanced back at Anna. "She wants to come in."

"Why?"

Wes shrugged. "She looks upset."

Anna sighed, then scrambled out of the bed, grabbed her clothes, and headed into the bathroom. Wes waited until she was out of sight before he opened the door and let Alison in.

"Thanks," she said.

Wes shut the door behind her. "You want to sit down?"

She shook her head.

"Okay," he said, then waited.

She fidgeted for a moment, biting the inside of her cheek.

"You want to tell me what's going on?" he asked.

More fidgeting. She was starting to open her mouth when the bathroom door swung open, and Anna, now dressed, sheepishly emerged.

"Hi," she said.

Alison stared at her as if she wasn't sure Anna was really there. Then her shoulders sagged a little. "Sorry. I . . . um . . . I didn't mean to disturb . . . I'll just . . . I'll—"

"No, it's all right." Wes hesitated, then added, "I'm sorry. I should have told you before."

"You don't have to tell me anything."

He could tell she wanted to leave, but she didn't move.

"Anna and I have been going out for several months."

She bit the inside of her lip again, then said, "Great," without any enthusiasm. "Good for you guys."

Wes reached out to touch her arm, but she pulled away.

"Don't," she said. "I . . . I . . ."

"Alison, why don't you tell us what's going on?" Anna said.

Alison shot her a dirty look, but then quickly closed her eyes, took a deep breath, and seemed to relax a little. "Sorry, I'm just worried."

"About what?"

"Tony. He's not back yet."

"How do you know?" Wes asked.

"I knocked on his door to tell him about the break-in, but he didn't answer. That was hours ago and he's still not back."

"You've been awake this whole time?" Wes asked.

She gaped at him as if the answer should be obvious. "I'm freaked out, and when I get freaked out, I can't sleep. You know that."

"Could he have decided to go back to L.A.?" Wes asked.

Alison shook her head. "How would he get there? He didn't have a car. Besides, he would have told one of us."

"Maybe he hooked up with someone like Danny did," Anna suggested, "and went home with them."

Alison was quiet for a moment. "I hadn't thought of that."

"God, let's hope he didn't hook up with someone like

Danny did," Wes said. "She'd be old enough to be his mother."

A smile from Anna, but Alison's expression didn't change.

"He'll probably show up sometime tomorrow hungover and smiling," Anna said.

Alison took another deep breath. "You're probably right. That's got to be what happened. Nothing like a little overreacting, huh?"

"Totally understandable," Wes reassured her.

She took a step toward the door. "I'll get out of your hair."

"You want me to walk you back to your room?" Wes asked, realizing a second after it was out of his mouth that it was the wrong thing to say.

But before Alison could jump on him, Anna said, "I'll do it."

Alison pulled open the door, then turned back. "Just tell me, am I the last one to know about you two?"

Wes shook his head. "Not even close. Dione's the only one on the crew who knows."

A wan smile and a nod, then Alison stepped outside, Anna following behind her.

Several minutes later Anna let herself back in.

"Well done," she said. "I see your people skills are in top form."

"I know. I could have handled that a little better."

"Yeah. I can think of about two dozen ways right off the top of my head."

"Sorry."

The smirk that had been on her face held for a moment longer, then melted. She walked over and put her arms around him. "At least she knows now."

"Yeah," he said, trying to smile. "So what did you two talk about?"

"She's my friend. I just wanted to make sure she's going to be okay."

"And is she?"

He could feel her shoulders go up and down. "Hope so."

As they climbed back into bed she asked, "So what were you dreaming about?"

"Huh?"

"You sounded like you were having a bad dream when Alison knocked on the door."

"Was I?" he said. *The dirt. The plane. Anna in danger.* "I don't remember."

CHAPTER 29

"THEY TOOK *WHAT*?"

Wes had waited until after breakfast Sunday morning to call Dione with the news.

"We got lucky," he said.

"Tell me how we possibly got lucky."

"We don't have to reshoot."

Dione said nothing for a moment. "Don't jerk me around, Wes. Are you serious?"

"Serious," he said. "We lost the backup. But I hadn't removed the original footage from the cards in the cameras yet. We *will* need a new backup drive, but we won't have to shoot anything again. The only thing we're missing is the footage on the card the Navy took. And we should be getting that back sometime this week." Well, he did have one thing from that card, the loop of the pilot that he'd saved to the thumb drive in his pocket. But he wasn't going to tell her that. "Of course, without the laptop I can't start editing."

"I can live with that," she said, brightening.

"Tell me that again when I give you the bill for a new computer."

"Sorry," she said. "I'm being a jackass. Are you all right?"

"I'm fine. Just pissed."

"Understandable. Did the motel give you a new room?"

"Yeah," he said. "They're comping my stay. Anna's room, too."

"Why Anna's?"

He winced. He'd forgotten Dione had already been gone when that happened. "Someone broke into her room Friday night. Didn't take anything, but it was enough for the motel to move her into the room next to mine."

"Jesus, Wes. What the hell's going on up there?"

Wes didn't know what to say.

"Was it the same people who broke into yours?" she asked.

"The police don't know yet."

"Anything else you want to tell me?"

Well, there was the chase. But he decided to save that bit of news until she got back. "No. That's it for now."

"I would hope so," she said, then paused. "Okay, here's what we're going to do. Check if there's anyplace there where you can get a new drive. If you can't find one, text me and I'll get one before I head back up."

"Okay."

"And, Wes, no more excitement, all right?"

"I'll do what I can."

Once he hung up, he went over to Anna's room.

"How'd she take it?" Anna asked.

"Not well at first, but better after I told her we hadn't really lost anything. She wants me to try and find a new drive. Want to come along?"

"I think I might just stay here and take a nap."

Neither of them had slept well. "Sure. We can grab lunch before Lars comes by."

"Sounds good," she said.

"Have you heard from Alison?"

"I called her while you were talking to Dione. She says Tony must have really hit the jackpot, because he's not back yet."

"He's not?"

"Said she tried calling his cell, but it went straight to voicemail."

"I'm sure he's okay."

"Yeah. Me, too."

But the silence that followed belied their confidence.

"If he comes back while I'm gone, call me," Wes said.

"I will."

He pulled the Escape keys out of his pocket and set them on the dresser. "In case you need to go somewhere."

"What are you going to take?"

"The Triumph," he said.

"Uh, excuse me. But do I need to remind you what the nice detective said last night?"

Detective Andrews. Driving without a proper license. *Damn.* He'd forgotten about that.

"You take the SUV," Anna said, picking up the keys and handing them back. "I won't need to go anywhere." The corner of her mouth began to turn upward. "But if I do, I can just ask Danny's friend for a lift."

Wes laughed and opened the door. He then turned to Anna and gave her a kiss right there in the doorway where anyone in the parking lot could have seen.

She arched an eyebrow.

"What?" he asked, a portrait of innocence.

This time she initiated the kiss.

CHAPTER
30

THE ESCAPE WAS PARKED RIGHT BESIDE THE Triumph.

Wes climbed into the driver's seat of the SUV and started to close the door. That's when he spotted something tucked between the motorcycle's gas tank and handlebars.

He got back out and stepped over to the bike. The object was a yellowed piece of paper that looked like it came from an old newspaper. There were enough random gusts of wind in the desert that finding a piece of trash lodged in his bike wasn't particularly surprising.

But he realized as he pulled it out that if it had been trash, it would have been battered and torn by the wind and the terrain. There were no tears in this piece of paper, no places where it was punctured by branches or rocks or God knew what.

There was something more telling, too. The paper wasn't a crinkled ball or even a scrap. It was a neatly folded, three-by-three-inch square.

Wes flipped it around, looking at both sides, then, worried that it might fall apart along the creases, carefully teased it open. He was pleased with himself that he was able to keep it from falling apart. But this sense of satisfaction lasted only until he focused on the article inside.

At the top was a school photo of a thick-necked kid of probably sixteen or seventeen. Though it was black-and-white, it was easy to tell the kid had blond hair. It was also easy to tell, despite the smile on his lips, that he was a jerk.

Or perhaps that was only Wes's interpretation, since he had known the boy.

Jack Rice.

The kids at Murray Junior High used to have a nickname for him. The Tormentor.

In the teenage years, brawn still ruled over brains, and since Jack had a lot of the former and very little of the latter, he was one of the kings. A Class A asshole, through and through.

Wes had stopped riding the bus to school in seventh grade because Jack used to get into the seat behind him and slam his fists into Wes's back. Wes much preferred taking the extra time to walk the three miles instead of suffering from the pain of one of Jack's blows for the rest of the day.

There was a headline below the photo:

LOCAL BOY NAMED TO
ALL-DISTRICT JV TEAM

Wes didn't read the article. He knew it wasn't important.

But he also knew there was no chance this was trash, either.

This article had been left for him.

CHAPTER
31

"HE JUST LEFT." THE MAN WAS BACK IN HIS sedan, parked near where he'd been the night before.

He reached for his binoculars, then trained them on the woman's room.

"No, she stayed behind."

He focused on the room's window, but the curtains were pulled, so he could see nothing.

"Not the motorcycle. The SUV." He listened, then rolled his eyes. "Relax. He still found it."

He set the binoculars back down.

"No, he didn't seem happy at all."

CHAPTER
32

IT TOOK WES SEVEN MINUTES TO GET FROM THE motel parking lot to the driveway of Lars's house, his mission to find a hard drive all but forgotten. The truck that had been there the day before was gone, so Wes pulled in to its space and jammed the Escape into park.

The article he'd found on the motorcycle was clutched tightly in his hand as he marched up to the front entrance. Skipping the bell, he pounded on the door with his empty fist.

Nothing.

He pounded again, then strained to hear anything from inside. Silence.

He leaned over and rapped on the glass of the living room window.

Still no answer. Wes walked around the side of the house, unlatched the gate, and entered the backyard. The pool area was deserted, and a look through the back windows confirmed that the house was as devoid of people on this side as it had been out front.

"Can I help you?"

Wes nearly jumped at the sound of the voice. He

turned and found a middle-aged man standing near the corner of the house, a rake held at his side.

"I . . . was just looking for Lars. He didn't answer his door, and he's supposed to be here."

"You a friend of his?"

"Yeah," Wes said, then added, "an old friend."

The man looked at him for a moment, then nodded toward the front of the house. "His truck's gone, so he's not home."

"Thought maybe he'd parked it in the garage," Wes said.

"Never does."

"Thanks." Wes started for the gate. "Guess I'll come back later."

"Good idea."

Once Wes was in the Escape, he pulled out his phone and tried calling Lars, but was sent straight to voice-mail. Lars was either out of range or his phone was off—both real possibilities in this area of spotty signal strength.

He *could* be working. Of course, if that were the case, would he have suggested they get together early that afternoon? Unlikely.

Shopping, then? Maybe, but doubtful. Church? Not the old Lars.

What the hell else was there to do on a Sunday morning?

When the answer hit him, it was so obvious he wondered why he hadn't thought of it right away.

Football.

Wes pulled out his phone and found an NFL schedule on the Web. Sure enough, the Pittsburgh Steelers were playing the early game. On the West Coast that meant game time was at 10 a.m.

Though Lars had grown up in the desert, he'd been born in Pennsylvania. And since his dad was a huge Steelers fan, the same mania had naturally passed on to his son.

If Lars wasn't at home watching the game, he had to be watching it somewhere. A friend's house? If so, Wes was going to be out of luck. There was another possibility, though.

He started the engine and threw the SUV into reverse.

He'd seen a few bars along China Lake Boulevard. If those didn't pan out, there had to be others.

The plot of land Checkers Bar and Grill was located on had been empty in Wes's day, and might as well have been empty now. There were only three cars parked in the lot, and none were Lars's truck. A few blocks away was The Pile On. It had a dozen vehicles parked out front. Even better, two were trucks that were similar to Lars's.

Wes parked and went inside.

A mixture of cheers and groans greeted him as he passed through the door. But they weren't for him. Instead, they were aimed at several televisions mounted above the bar, each showing a different game. Wes scanned the crowd.

No Lars.

The next few places—including a stop at Delta Sierra—produced the same results.

It was in the fifth place, a sports bar off Ridgecrest Boulevard called Tommy T's, built on the site of the old bowling alley, that he found his friend.

Lars was sitting at a table with Janice and Bob from the pool party, his eyes so focused on the Steelers game he didn't even see Wes walk up. Pittsburgh had the ball and was barely ahead of Cincinnati, 14–12.

"Close game," Wes said.

"Hey, Wes," Janice said.

Lars broke eye contact with the television and looked genuinely surprised to see his friend. "Wes? Hey, great. Pull up a chair, and we'll make room for you."

Bob smiled and nodded. "How you doing?"

Wes returned the nod. "I'm okay." To Lars, he said, "Think we could talk for a minute?"

"Sure," his friend replied, his gaze already back on the TV. "Don't worry. I'm listening."

"Privately." Wes glanced at the other two. "No offense."

Both Janice and Bob waved it off like they understood.

Lars, though, waited until the end of a play, grimaced, then glanced at Wes. "Halftime's in about five minutes. Can it wait?"

"No."

Lars looked back at the screen for a moment, then sighed and stood up. "Fine. But I swear, if something happens while I'm away, you'll never hear the end of it."

Wes led them out of the bar and over to a spot near the back of the building where he thought they wouldn't be disturbed.

"So what couldn't wait?" Lars asked.

"This." Wes handed him the article.

Lars looked confused as he unfolded the paper. Then, as soon as he saw the picture, his eyes widened in surprise.

"Not very subtle," Wes said.

"Subtle? What do you mean?"

"You almost blew it. I took the car and not the bike, so almost didn't see it."

"Are you trying to tell me someone left this for you?"

"You should have just slipped it under the door to my room. That way there wouldn't have been a chance I could have missed it."

"You think this is from *me*?"

Wes could contain his anger no longer. "Of course it's from you! Who the hell else could have left it?"

"I have no idea. But I do know it wasn't me."

Wes grabbed the article out of his friend's hand. "Wasn't having your people chasing Anna and me all around town while you had others breaking in to my room and taking all our footage enough for you? Or did you think that maybe you needed to do something a little extra to convince me to back off?"

"Slow down," Lars said. "Broke in to your room?"

"Like you don't already know. Your people took my computer and our backup drive. Not the camera, though, and it was probably the most expensive thing in the room. They knew exactly what they wanted, because you told them, didn't you?"

"Jesus, Wes. *I* had *nothing* to do with any of this."

"The shot of the pilot from the crash? You were the only one who knew I had that. So yeah, I think you might have had something to do with it."

"I don't care what you think. It wasn't me," Lars shot back.

"And this?" Wes glared, raising the article a few inches. "Not you, either?"

"I would *never* have left you that. Never. So back off!"

"Correct me if I'm wrong," Wes said, trying to keep his anger from overwhelming him, "but there are only three people on this entire planet who could have known what this article would mean to me. I didn't leave it for myself. So if it wasn't you, then it would have had to have been Mandy. And I can't imagine her ever doing this."

Lars glared at Wes. "That's not even funny."

"Of course it's not. Mandy would never do something like that. And if she didn't do it, then it must have been you."

"Shut up."

Wes pulled out his phone. "Maybe we should call her. Just to clear her name from the list of suspects. Bet you don't want me to do that, do you? Do you know if she's still in town, or did she move away somewhere?"

Lars said nothing for several seconds, then the confused look on his face started to fade. "You . . . you don't know, do you?"

"Know what?"

"I couldn't believe it when you didn't show up. Just run away, forget about all your old friends, and don't even come back when . . . God, I thought you were an asshole. Then I thought *I* was an asshole for considering you a friend. But you never knew, did you? That's why you didn't come back."

"What are you talking about, Lars?"

"Mandy's dead, Wes. She died a year after you left."

Wes stared at his friend, stunned into silence.

"I was sure your dad must have told you," Lars said.

Wes shook his head. "He didn't say a word." He knew instantly his father would have said nothing, fearing Wes would have tried to come back. "How . . . did it happen?"

Lars looked off toward the hills. "Suicide. Senior year."

How was that possible? Wes thought. Mandy dead? *Sixteen years* dead? That couldn't be right. And by *suicide*?

"She wasn't that kind of person."

"It happened exactly one year after that night," Lars told him.

He didn't have to say which night.

As Wes leaned against the wall, his body began shaking slightly. Lars reached down and picked something up off the ground. It was the article. Wes hadn't even realized he'd dropped it.

"I didn't leave this for you," Lars said. "I would never have done that."

"But no one else knew," Wes whispered. It was true to a point. His father had known. But he, like Mandy, was gone. "How . . . how did she do it?"

"She took sleeping pills, then climbed into a bathtub full of water and never got out."

"That . . . doesn't sound like something she'd do."

"Well, I guess you didn't know her as well as you thought you did."

"Why? Did you think that was something she'd do?" Wes snapped.

Lars leaned against the wall next to Wes. "No. I didn't."

An image of Mandy Johansson flashed in Wes's mind. It was Halloween, junior year. She'd come to school dressed as Dorothy from *The Wizard of Oz,* and had spent most of the day teasing Wes about his attempt to look like Harvey Keitel in *Pulp Fiction.*

"I'm sorry. I really thought you knew," Lars said.

Wes shook his head, his mind still in the past. He should have kept in touch. Maybe that would have helped. Maybe he could have pulled her through the darkness that must have overtaken her.

"Tell me about the break-in," Lars said.

"Like you don't know," Wes said, but most of the fight had left him.

"No. I don't. Tell me what happened."

Wes told Lars about the chase, and then getting back to the motel only to find that he'd been robbed. By the end, Lars was staring at him, stunned. If he was acting, his performance was Oscar worthy.

"Jesus. And the article?"

"I found it tucked below the handlebars of the Triumph thirty minutes ago."

"So it happened sometime between after you got home last night and then."

"Obviously."

"I just mean, it couldn't have happened during the break-in, because you were on the motorcycle when that happened."

"They could have come back," Wes said, but Lars had a point.

"You think they were just after your footage?"

"What else?" Wes said. "The only things they took were the things that held our shots."

"But why? What's the value in that?"

Wes stared at his old friend for a moment, trying to get a read on him. Finally he said, "Okay, for the moment, let's say you had nothing to do with it. But come on. Even you should be able to see they wanted to take any proof I had that the dead pilot isn't who everyone said he is."

"The crash again," Lars said, shaking his head.

"Hell yes, the crash again. And I *did* have proof." Still had it, in fact, on his thumb drive. But he'd keep that to himself for the time being.

Lars took a couple steps away, processing. "I don't know what else to tell you about the crash. Whatever

you had would not have proved anything but the truth."
He looked at Wes. "Why does this matter to you so
much?"

"The pilot who was trapped in the cockpit when I got
there was *not* the same man the Navy is saying died. I
was just trying to get you to actually listen to me, but
everyone's just been trying to shut me up. Why? You're
in the service, Lars. This is one of *your* colleagues. The
question is, why *doesn't* it matter to you?"

Lars opened his mouth to speak, stopped himself,
then said, "Of course it matters to me. Do you think I
ignored what you were saying? We're handling this in-
ternally, and your prodding isn't helping." He paused
for a moment. "Look, what if I could prove to you Adair
was the pilot? Would you accept that?"

"Prove how?"

"Hold on." Lars pulled out a cellphone, then walked
out of earshot and made a call.

Wes looked at the article again. Mandy. Dead. He figured she'd grown up, moved away, gone on to better
things. Not this. Never this.

As Lars walked back up, Wes slipped the clipping into
his pocket.

"Come on," Lars said.

"Where are we going?"

"To show you that you're wrong."

CHAPTER
33

"ARE YOU SURE WE'RE GOING THE RIGHT WAY?"
Mandy asked from the front passenger seat.

She was excited, and probably a little anxious. It *was* her first party at the Rocks, after all. Wes and Lars were pros compared to her.

"I'm sure," Wes said from the driver's seat.

The dirt road was really not much of a road at all— two ruts on either side, beaten down by the tires of those who'd passed this way before, and a narrow, deeper gouge running roughly between them, cut there by the infrequent desert rains.

Wes turned the wheel suddenly, barely missing a rock sticking out of the ground on the right side. In the backseat, he heard Lars tumble sideways and the sound of several bottles clinking together.

"Careful!" Lars said. "You don't want me to break any of these in here, do you? Try explaining that to your folks."

Wes eased off the accelerator. "You should be holding on to them."

"I *am* holding on to them."

"Dip!" Wes yelled out.

The van lurched downward, then jerked up just as quickly.

"Woohoo!" Mandy cried out.

"Holy crap," Lars said.

When the road evened out, Wes said, "We need some kind of code phrase to let each other know we're ready to leave."

"Leave?" Mandy said. "We haven't even got there yet."

"Yeah, but if any of us gets to the point where they want to go, then we all go. That was the deal."

"Right," Mandy said, sounding less than happy. "I remember."

"So the code word?" Lars said.

"Dip!" Wes yelled out.

The car bounced again.

"I'm not sure 'dip' would be a good word to use," Lars said. "Hard to work into a sentence."

"Very funny, jackass," Wes said.

"Why don't we just say we want to go?" Mandy suggested.

"Because that would be completely uncool," Lars told her. "We want to sneak away so people think we're still there. We don't want them knowing we left early. They'd think we were a bunch of losers."

"Even if they do, at least we won't be the only losers there," Wes said. "Tommy from the debate team said he's coming with some of his friends from band."

They all laughed.

"Some of the guys from the football team are going to be there, too," Mandy said.

"Really?" Lars said. "That sucks."

"How do you know that?" Wes asked her.

"Jack told me."

"Jack?" Wes asked.

"Jack Rice."

"Why were you talking to that jerk?" Lars asked.

"He's not so bad once you get to know him."

Wes rolled his eyes. "You've got to be kidding me."

"Question number two," Lars said. "Why would anyone want to get to know him?"

"Exactly what I was thinking," Wes said.

"You guys are idiots," she said.

"*We're* the idiots? Who's the one getting all kissy-kissy with Jack Rice?" Lars said.

"I *never* said anything about . . ." Instead of finishing the sentence, Mandy punched Lars in the arm.

The VW swerved a few inches off the road, brushing the front fender against a creosote bush. "Hey! Careful. You want to kill us?"

"A little sensitive on the whole Jack thing, aren't you?" Lars said, rubbing his arm.

Mandy groaned. "Just stop talking. Both of you."

They drove in silence for nearly a minute before Lars said, "We, uh, never came up with our exit phrase."

A wry smile grew on Wes's lips. "How about 'There's Jack'?"

He was already ducking when Mandy's fist slammed into his shoulder.

CHAPTER 34

THEY RODE IN LARS'S TRUCK TO THE MAIN ENtrance of the China Lake Naval Air Weapons Station, neither of them saying a word. Just before the gate, Lars pulled in to the visitor center parking area.

Wes started to get out with him, but Lars shook his head. "No. You stay here."

Lars disappeared into the building for a few minutes. When he climbed back into the cab, he handed Wes a piece of plastic.

"I'm sure you know what to do with this."

It was a visitor's badge, complete with a clip. Wes attached it to his shirt as Lars pulled back onto the road and drove over to the gate. Once the guard there checked both their badges, he waved the truck through, and just like that, they were on the base.

If driving through Ridgecrest after all this time had been strange, being back on the base was absolutely surreal. There was so much that hadn't changed since Wes had been a ten-year-old riding in his parents' VW van, and so much that was completely different.

Whole swaths of base housing had disappeared, leaving empty desert. From what Wes could tell, both of the houses his family had lived in on the base were gone. It was as if a specialized bomb had gone off and had left only roads and sidewalks and desert, but no debris at all.

Wes tried to guess where they were going, but once they'd passed Michelson Lab, his geographical knowledge from his youth ran out. All he could tell was that they were heading north into the open desert portion of the base, which probably meant Armitage Field.

Lars wasn't saying anything, but it was apparent he was growing more and more tense with each mile. Twice he looked over at Wes, scrutinizing him, but he remained silent. Whatever he was thinking, he wasn't sharing.

They came to a second checkpoint. One of the guards took Wes's badge and reentered the guard hut, where she made a phone call.

When she returned, she passed the badge through the window, saluted Lars, and said, "Have a good day, sir."

As they neared the airfield, two jets rose into the air, one right after the other, and streaked toward the sky above the Sierra Nevadas, the wail of their engines momentarily drowning everything else out.

Lars turned down a road that ran just east of the hangars, then pulled up in front of a building surrounded by an eight-foot-high barbed-wire-topped fence. The gate across the entrance was closed, but as soon as they stopped, an armed guard exited the building and pushed the gate open wide enough to accommodate Lars's truck. Lars then pulled into a parking spot and turned the engine off.

"So what's here?" Wes asked, looking at the building.

Lars opened his door and climbed out. "Your proof," he said without looking back.

Wes hesitated a few seconds, then got out, too.

The door to the building opened just before they reached it. Lars didn't miss a step as he passed inside. The Big Brother feel of it bothered Wes, but he continued to follow his friend.

Just inside was another armed guard. Like his buddy at the gate, he was unsmiling. Beyond him two other men waited. One wore a khaki naval uniform, and the other a white lab coat over shirt, tie, and slacks.

The uniformed man saluted Lars. "Lieutenant Commander. Good to see you, sir."

Lars returned the salute.

"Lieutenant Commander Andersen," the civilian said, shaking hands with Lars.

"Thank you for doing this," Lars said. He gestured toward Wes. "This is Wes Stewart. Wes, this is Dr. Handler and Lieutenant Truax."

"Mr. Stewart," Lieutenant Truax said, shaking Wes's hand.

"Are either of you carrying cellphones?" Dr. Handler asked. "There is some very sensitive equipment in the building, so please turn them off for the duration of your visit." Once they'd complied, the doctor said, "If you'd be so kind as to follow me."

Dr. Handler led them down a central hallway to a door marked RESTRICTED ACCESS, then paused. "We'd appreciate it if you didn't talk about what you will see here. It's not necessarily classified, but it could be . . . well, disturbing to certain people. We're only showing you this at the request of the lieutenant commander."

"I understand," Wes said.

There was an access pad on the wall beside the door. As the doctor waved his badge in front of it, the lock clicked. He pushed the door open and a wave of cool air spilled out.

"There are coats just inside," Lieutenant Truax said.

One by one they stepped through. The room they entered wasn't much larger than the mudroom of Wes's aunt's house in Wisconsin and appeared to serve a similar purpose. Hanging from pegs on the wall were several black jackets. They were separated by size. Lieutenant Truax took one down and handed it to Wes.

"It's not that cold," Wes said.

"It will be," Lieutenant Truax told him as he donned his own jacket.

"We're only using this facility because of the sensitive nature of this case," Dr. Handler added. "I hope you can overlook the inconvenience."

With a shrug, Wes pulled his on.

Once they were all properly attired, the doctor opened the door at the opposite side of the room. The air that came out this time was not cool, but cold.

The new room was about forty feet deep and fifty across. White cabinets lined three of the walls, while a long counter with several sinks lined the other. In the center were three large, evenly spaced tables, the two closest of which were empty. The third, however, was not.

The doctor led them to it. "This isn't going to be pleasant."

On top, a white sheet covered the obvious form of a body.

"Are you ready?" Lars asked Wes.

"Yeah, sure."

The doctor pulled the sheet back just enough to reveal the body's head and shoulders. The corpse was so se-

verely damaged by fire it was almost impossible to imagine the person it had once been.

Bile began rising from Wes's stomach.

"Are you okay?" Dr. Handler asked.

"I'm fine," Wes said, attempting to sound convincing.

"This is Lieutenant Adair," the doctor explained. "I
understand you think there might be a problem with
identification? I can assure you this is the lieutenant.
Both DNA test and dental records have proved that."

Wes gave his nausea a few seconds to settle, then took
another look at the face, trying to spot any familiar features. But it was impossible. Anything recognizable had
been obliterated by flames.

"If you knew who he was already, why did you run a
DNA test?" he asked.

"Dr. Handler did the test because *you* questioned the
man's identity," Lars said, annoyed.

"Okay. If you say it's Lieutenant Adair, then I'm sure
it is."

Lars stared at his friend for a moment, then frowned.
"Lieutenant Truax, could you please tell Wes why you're
here?"

"Yes, sir," Truax said. "I was with the search-and-
rescue team deployed to the crash site."

Wes gave Truax a second look, but couldn't remember him from the accident site. Still, there had been
dozens of people running around, so the fact that the
lieutenant was unfamiliar didn't mean much.

"Lieutenant Truax was one of the men who removed
the pilot's body from the plane," Lars said. "Isn't that
correct, Lieutenant?"

"Yes, sir. That's correct."

Lars nodded at the corpse. "And is this the body of
the man you pulled out?"

"Yes, sir."

"Did you know Lieutenant Adair?" Lars asked.

The lieutenant paused. "Yes, sir. I've met him."

"Did you realize it was Lieutenant Adair when you recovered the body?"

"Yes, sir."

"Because someone told you who it was?"

"No, sir. I recognized him."

"But you didn't get there until after he'd already been burned in the fire," Wes said. "How the hell could you have recognized him?"

"I didn't recognize him from his face, sir. It was his scar."

"Scar?"

Lieutenant Truax nodded. "On his arm."

"Here," Dr. Handler said.

He lifted the sheet and pulled an arm out from underneath. He twisted it ninety degrees, and there, in a diagonal slash across the side of the corpse's arm, was a three-inch scar.

"Told me he got that cutting wood when he was a teenager," the lieutenant explained. "Said a bow saw slipped."

Dr. Handler placed the arm back under the sheet.

"Thank you, Lieutenant." Lars looked at Wes. "If there's anything else you want to ask, now is the time."

Wes shook his head. "No. You've been very thorough. Thank you."

The doctor led everyone back through the building and outside. There he first shook Wes's hand and then Lars's.

"I hope this helped," the doctor said.

Lars and Wes got into the truck. Once they were back

on the road, Wes said, "I don't know. Maybe you were right. Maybe it *was* him who I saw."

Lars let out a low, exasperated laugh and shook his head. "Maybe?"

"I'm saying I could have been wrong . . . I just . . . Look, if you say that was the guy who was in the cockpit, then I guess I believe you." He didn't know what else to say. Seeing the dead man had kind of knocked him sideways.

Lars said nothing for nearly a minute. "I want to make one more stop."

CHAPTER
35

THE HOUSE WAS IN THE SECTION OF THE BASE
reserved for high-ranking officers. If Lars hadn't been
living in town, this was probably the area he would have
called home.

"So who lives here?" Wes asked once they were both
out of the car.

"Follow me," Lars said.

The home was on a small hill that rose above the
street. A set of seven steps led up to a walkway that split
the green front lawn into two on its way to the front
door.

Lars pushed the doorbell, and it was only a few seconds before a man in his mid-forties answered. He was
dressed in slacks and a button-down shirt, and looked
very familiar to Wes.

"Lieutenant Commander Andersen," the man said.

"Commander Forman," Lars replied.

Forman? This was the guy who had questioned Wes
at the crash site. Without the uniform, Wes hadn't made
the connection.

"Hello, Commander," Wes said.

"How are you doing, Wes?" Forman said with a smile.

"Fine, sir."

"It's good to see you again, despite what I assume are the circumstances of your visit." He glanced at Lars. "I take it there are still questions."

"I don't think he's completely convinced, sir." Lars's tone sounded almost like an apology.

Wes looked at his friend, surprised. "I said that I believe—"

"Why don't you come in?" Forman said, cutting him off. "Can I get either of you gentlemen something to drink?"

"No, thank you, sir," Wes and Lars replied in unison.

"Please, follow me." He led them to an office near the kitchen. Door shut, they all sat down—the commander behind the desk, and Wes and Lars on the sofa in front of it.

"Wes, I trust that you recall my task is to find out exactly what caused one of our F-18s to belly flop in the desert and kill its pilot."

"Yes, sir."

"I've been doing nothing but working at finding those answers since immediately after the incident. I take my job very seriously. Kind of like your old man did when he was stationed here."

Wes sat up a little, caught off guard by the mention of his father. "I'm sorry, sir?"

"When we first met, you mentioned that your father worked on the base when you were younger, so I looked him up. Dennis Stewart was a good man. Hell of an officer. Died much too young."

Wes frowned. "I'm not sure what this has to do with why we're here."

Forman leaned forward. "Lieutenant Commander Andersen tells me that you claim the man flying the plane was not Lieutenant Adair. I can't for the life of me figure out why you would say that."

Wes shot a look at his friend. "I was only raising a question, sir. He's already—"

Again, Forman stopped him mid-sentence. "Now don't go getting all upset. Lars came to me asking if there might have been a mistake when we ID'd the pilot. He was very concerned."

Wes relaxed a bit. Of course Lars would have gone to Commander Forman. Wes himself had asked his friend to check things out.

"As you can imagine, I was also concerned," Forman continued. "Even more so once Lars explained the information was coming from you, the last man to see the pilot alive. So trust me when I say I've made it my personal mission to make sure there's been no mistake. I ordered my team to go above and beyond in IDing the body. Interviews with the ground crew, DNA testing, triple-checking identifying marks, talking to the search-and-rescue teams." The commander switched his attention to Lars. "Were you able to connect with Lieutenant Truax?"

"Yes, sir," Lars said.

"Good." His gaze returned to Wes. "Then you know that Lieutenant Truax was one of the responders who removed the body, and that he also positively ID'd Lieutenant Adair."

"Yes, sir," Wes said.

"Then you must believe me when I say there were no mistakes here."

Wes said, "I understand a lot of care was taken."

After a few more seconds, Forman said, "Yet you still have doubts." It wasn't a question.

Wes lowered his head for a moment, uncomfortable. He was unsure what to say, because, quite honestly, he was unsure what he thought. He'd seen what he'd seen at the crash site, but he'd also seen the body Lieutenant Truax had identified as Adair. He chose to remain silent.

The commander leaned back in his chair, a contemplative look on his face. From somewhere outside came the distant squeal of a child playing.

As the silence in the office lengthened, there was a second squeal, this one followed by laughter.

The commander suddenly pushed his chair back and stood up. "Wes, if you have a moment, I'd like to introduce you to my wife."

"Uh, sure," Wes said, surprised by the change of topic.

Forman came around his desk. "She's out back. Lars, please join us."

"Yes, sir."

Forman led them to a sliding glass door off a family room at the back of the house. Outside, Wes saw a woman, maybe a few years younger than the commander, sitting on a patio chair, shielded from the sun by a large umbrella stuck through the center of a patio table. She was looking toward a part of the yard Wes couldn't see.

As the commander pulled the door open, a child's voice yelled out, "My turn!"

The commander motioned for Wes and Lars to go first, then he followed.

A rectangle of cement served as a patio, but the rest of the yard, like the front, was lush and green. In the area Wes hadn't been able to see from inside was a wooden play set complete with slide, swings, and monkey bars. There were two girls standing at the bottom of the ladder to the slide, pushing each other.

"Darla, let your little sister go first this time," the woman in the chair said.

"But she went first last time!" the taller of the two girls complained.

"And you went first the two times before that," the woman reminded her.

Reluctantly the taller girl stood to the side and let her sister go up the ladder.

"Sweetheart," Commander Forman said, "I want you to meet someone."

With a smile, Mrs. Forman stood up, but was careful to remain in the shade.

"You know Lieutenant Commander Andersen, I believe," Forman said.

"Of course. It's good to see you again." She held out her hand. "We met at the Everts' party, if I'm not mistaken."

Lars took the offered hand and gave it a gentle shake. "Yes, ma'am. That's correct."

"And this is Wesley Stewart," the commander said. "Mr. Stewart, this is my wife."

"Glad to meet you, Mrs. Forman," Wes said.

She laughed as they shook. "Please, call me Shelly."

"Wes grew up here," the commander said. "He and Lars went to high school together."

"You grew up here, too?" she said, looking at Lars.

"Yes, ma'am."

"And now you're stationed here. You must be a glutton for punishment."

"Shelly's not the biggest fan of the desert," the commander explained.

"When you think Navy, you think oceans and beaches, not tumbleweeds and rattlesnakes," she said.

One of the children screamed, and all the adults turned to see what had happened. The older girl was sitting on the ground at the base of the slide, tears in her eyes.

"Excuse me." Shelly headed toward the play set. "What happened, sweetie?"

"Two daughters," Wes said. "That's going to be fun when they're old enough to date."

"They're not ours," the commander said. "We also have two kids, a boy and a girl. But they're both in college."

Shelly returned, the older girl in her arms and the younger one tagging along behind them.

"Came down too hard on her backside," Shelly explained, rubbing the girl's hip. "Lieutenant Commander, Wes, this is Darla and her sister, Rachel."

Wes bent down so he was at Rachel's height. "Nice to meet you."

"Nice to meet you, too," Rachel said.

Darla tucked her head into Shelly's shoulder and said nothing.

"Who wants a juice box?" Shelly asked.

"Oh, me!" Rachel said.

"Darla?" Shelly asked.

The older girl nodded.

"Come on, then. Into the kitchen."

Rachel ran ahead and made a valiant yet unsuccessful attempt to open the door. As soon as Shelly got there, she applied the extra help needed, and then they all went inside.

"Cute girls," Wes said. "But if there's nothing else, Commander, maybe we should go."

"They're Lieutenant Adair's."

Wes blinked. "I'm sorry?"

"Darla and Rachel. They're Lieutenant Adair's children."

Wes looked toward the sliding door the girls had just disappeared behind.

"No matter what you think you saw," the commander said, "those girls lost their father. It's bad enough he made an error that caused the crash. Don't you see? If you start raising these questions, giving them false hope, the ones you'll hurt most in the end will be them. Their father was on that plane, Wes. Whatever you think you saw, you were wrong."

CHAPTER
36

"DO YOU BELIEVE ME NOW?" LARS ASKED.

They were parked in his truck next to Wes's rented Escape outside Tommy T's Sports Bar. Wes was staring out the window at nothing.

"It was a mistake," Lars said. "Understandable, given the circumstances, but still a mistake."

Wes reached for the door handle, but he stopped and turned to look at his high school friend. "You know, for a little bit there I was starting to think that maybe I *had* been wrong. Maybe the face I remembered wasn't the one I really saw."

"But you don't believe it now? You just met his children, for God's sakes."

Wes let out a snort and shook his head. Perhaps if Lars had taken him home after seeing the body, he would have been convinced enough to drop it. But then Forman and the kids coupled with everything else? Lars had tried a little *too* hard to convince him. And that just pissed him off.

"Goodbye, Lars," he said, then opened the door and climbed out.

"Wes, goddammit!"

Wes crossed over to the SUV and got in without answering.

Lars watched him for a moment, then pulled his truck out of its parking spot and sped off.

Wes started the Escape and pulled out of the lot. He ended up two cars behind Lars's truck at the corner of Ridgecrest and China Lake Boulevard. Lars should have continued straight and not turned right until he got to Norma or Downs, but instead he turned onto China Lake, so he was still a few cars ahead as Wes drove toward the motel.

As they neared the Desert Rose, Wes considered turning into the parking lot, but instead he decided to stay on the road, suspicious about where his childhood friend might be headed. Soon they passed the hospital and most of the handful of businesses strung between there and Inyokern Road.

When Wes got in sight of the intersection, he made a quick left at the triangle cutoff in front of the movie theater and immediately pulled to the curb. Lars's truck approached the stop. Then, as Wes already knew would happen, Lars turned right, toward the base.

Wes waited until he was sure Lars had gone through the gate, then he made a U-turn and headed back to the motel, certain now he was being conned.

CHAPTER
37

"SO?" COMMANDER FORMAN ASKED.

Lars frowned for a moment, then shook his head.

"Dammit! Your job is to make this problem go away."

Lars frowned. "I'm aware of that, sir. But—"

"Being aware of it and doing what you've been ordered to do are not the same thing. I expect you to deal with this problem." He stared at Lars, then said, "I want to show you something."

Forman picked up a remote control off his desk and popped on the TV that sat on a cabinet in the corner of the office. The screen was blank for a few moments, then video began to play. It was of the downed F-18, only minutes after it had crashed. The footage Danny DeLeon had shot. Lars watched Wes struggle to get to the cockpit, then lean over the pilot. Forman paused the image.

"A goddamn action hero," he said. "This is the kind of stuff the media would love. Since he already works in that business, it would be easy for him to get someone interested. You need to stop this now. We're all in the line of fire on this, but you, Lieutenant Commander, are dead center and the first to go down."

Lars sat back. "Why me, sir?"

"Need I remind you that you are the one who wrote the protocols that were to be followed on the flight? Those protocols were a very tight map. If someone were to examine them closely, they would see that certain tests that would have been logical next steps were not included."

"But you're the one who instructed me to—"

"And you're the one who signed off on them. If anything comes down, your neck will be more exposed than most. So it's in your best interest to get this done. Am I clear?"

Lars's mouth suddenly felt dry.

"Well?"

Lars nodded. "Yes, sir. I'll do what I can."

"Do more."

It was an obvious dismissal. Lars got up, but then hesitated at the door.

"Yes?" Forman asked, impatient.

"Sir, I understand that you felt it was necessary to get Wes's computer and hard drive."

"Is there a question?"

Lars hesitated. "Was it also necessary to break in and take them?"

The commander stared blankly at Lars. "What do you think?"

"He would have given me that material if I had asked him."

"He gave us the material once before, but he failed to tell us about the copy. What makes you think he wouldn't have done that again?"

"But breaking into his room?"

"Are you trying to sound like a fool? We do what we must. Now, if you will excuse me."

This time the dismissal was final.

CHAPTER
38

WES WAS SURPRISED TO FIND ANNA AND ALISON waiting in his room when he came back.

"Did you find one?" Anna asked.

"One what?" he asked.

"Backup drive."

"Had a change of plans."

"Then you'd better call Dione," she told him. "She's called here twice looking for you. Said she tried your cell, but it went straight to voicemail."

He'd forgotten Dr. Handler had had him turn it off. He pulled it out and pushed the power switch.

"So where did you go?" she asked.

"I was with Lars," he said, giving her a look he hoped would convey his desire not to get into it with Alison in the room. "Were you guys waiting for me?"

Anna glanced at Alison. "It's Tony."

"He's still not back," Alison said.

"You're sure?"

"I tried his cell and he wasn't answering, either," she snapped.

"Well, maybe he had it off like me," he shot back. He

took a breath. "Look. It's our day off. He probably just wanted to get away from all of us. God knows I've felt that way on shoots before."

Alison bit her lip, her face tense.

"What?" he asked.

When she didn't answer right away, Anna said, "We ran into Danny. He told us he saw Tony at Delta Sierra last night. Said Tony was heading back to the motel around one a.m."

"Alone," Alison added.

Wes sat on the bed next to her. He put a hand on her back, expecting her to flinch, but she didn't. "Think about it. Would you have told Danny you were going home with someone?"

Her gaze flicked away, then at him again, a bit of doubt in her eyes.

"Yeah, neither would I," he said. "Tony strikes me as pretty smart, so I'm sure he wouldn't have, either."

"But that doesn't mean he *did* go with someone."

Wes nodded. "You're right. It doesn't."

"It's just, you know, with what's been happening around here . . . it makes me nervous. Like maybe something happened to him."

Wes thought for a moment. "Have you checked inside his room?"

Alison shook her head. "Just knocked."

He scooted over, picked up the motel phone, and dialed zero.

"Front desk," the woman on the other end said.

"Can I speak to the manager, please?"

"That would be me, sir," she said.

"I need to check on a friend. He's not answering his phone or his door, and we're worried he might be sick or something. Could we get you to open his door for us? Just to check."

"Of course," she said. "What's the room number?"

Wes moved the handset away from his mouth. "What's Tony's room number?"

"One seventy-eight," Alison told him.

"One seventy-eight," Wes repeated into the phone. "I'll meet you there."

CHAPTER
39

THE MANAGER ARRIVED AT TONY'S ROOM ONLY a few moments after they did, and pulled an electronic keycard out of her pocket. But before she slipped it into the lock, she knocked.

"Motel management."

No response.

She put the key into the slot, then turned the knob and pushed the door open. "Hello, motel management."

Wes craned his neck so he could see around her, but the room was dark.

"Hello?" the woman said again.

She flipped on the light switch and took a step into the room, Alison, Anna, and Wes crowding in behind her.

"Tony?" Alison said.

"Doesn't look like anyone's here," the manager said.

The bed was made and the room was neat.

"Has housekeeping come in yet?" Wes asked.

"I checked that before I came over," the woman said. "They haven't done this room yet."

Wes could feel a chill in his spine.

"Tony?" Anna called out.

She stepped around the manager and headed toward the bathroom.

"I'm not sure you should be in here," the woman told her.

"Tony?" Anna said. She disappeared into the bathroom, but stepped back out a moment later. "Not there."

"Does it look like anything's missing?" Wes asked.

Anna pointed at the bag sitting by the desk. "His suitcase is still here."

"His hiking boots, too," Alison added.

"Wes." Anna was standing next to the bed, looking down at the nightstand.

Wes moved out from behind the manager. "What is it?"

She reached down and picked something up.

"You shouldn't touch anything," the manager chimed. "That's not your property."

Anna looked at the object for a moment, then held it out so they could all see.

It was a cellphone.

"Tony's?" Wes asked.

"Looks like it," she said. "Hold on." She fiddled with it for a few seconds, then glanced at Alison. "Try calling him again."

Alison pulled out her mobile and made the call. There was a delay of three seconds, then the phone in Anna's hand started ringing.

"Oh, God," Alison said.

"Doesn't mean anything," Wes said. "Just that he went to the bar without it."

"But he wouldn't have left it here all day, too. He's supposed to be on call. Even on the days off."

She was right. Being a PA for *Close to Home* meant being available 24/7.

"Your friend isn't here," the manager said, moving toward the door. "I think we should all leave."

Wes nodded. "Thanks for letting us check."

Anna joined them, still holding the phone.

"I think you should leave that here," the woman said.

"We'll give it to our friend as soon as we see him," Wes promised.

The manager didn't look happy, but she made no further protest as she ushered them out, then closed the door and left.

"This is not good," Alison said, her eyes darting every few seconds back to Tony's door. "He wouldn't have left his phone."

Anna was looking down at the cell and pushing a series of buttons. "He only made two calls yesterday, and received one. All Dione, so work related."

Alison let out an exasperated breath. "I'm telling you, something is seriously wrong."

"Maybe we should call the police," Anna suggested.

Wes thought for a moment, then nodded. "Yeah. That's probably a good idea."

The officer who answered the call put Wes through to a familiar voice.

"Detective Stevens."

"Hello, Detective. It's Wes Stewart. The man whose motel room was—"

"I know who you are, Mr. Stewart. Did you find something else missing?"

"I'm not calling about the break-in."

A pause. "Okay. What can I do for you?"

"A colleague of ours, Tony Hall, he's missing."

"How long?"

"The last time anyone saw him was around one a.m."

"So just about twelve hours ago."

Anna and Alison were both watching Wes, concerned.

"Yes. He hasn't been back to his room, and he left his—"

"Are there any signs of trouble?" Stevens asked.

"Not exactly, but he left his cellphone behind and he's supposed to be on call all day."

Both women nodded in agreement.

"How old is he?"

"I don't know." Wes glanced at Alison. "He's probably about twenty-four."

"Twenty-three," Alison said, correcting him.

"Twenty-three," Wes told the detective.

"Where was he last seen?"

"Delta Sierra."

"The bar?"

"Yes."

A pause. "I'll note that you called," the detective said. "If he's still missing tomorrow, call me back, but for now I wouldn't worry about it. He's probably just sleeping it off somewhere."

"But what if something bad *has* happened?"

The line was quiet for a moment. "Have you considered the fact that this friend of yours might be responsible for breaking in to your room?"

"What?"

"It's a possibility, isn't it?"

"You can't be serious."

"You can call me in the morning if he's still missing," Stevens said, then hung up.

Wes held the phone to his ear for a moment longer, surprised at how the conversation had gone. When he lowered it, Alison immediately asked, "What happened?"

"You're not going to believe this. He suggested that Tony might be responsible for breaking into my room."

"Are you kidding me?" Alison said.

"That's ridiculous," Anna said. "No way it was Tony."

"Of course it wasn't," Wes agreed.

"Are they at least going to look for him?" Anna asked.

Wes shook his head. "The detective said he wouldn't do anything until the morning."

"But what if Tony's in trouble?" Alison blurted out. "Tomorrow might be too late!"

"Unless we have evidence that something's wrong, I don't think they'll do anything yet."

"What about his cellphone?" she asked incredulously. "That's evidence!"

"It is," Anna said, her tone calmer than Alison's. "But it's really only evidence that he doesn't have it with him."

"So we're just supposed to sit around and do nothing?" Alison threw her arm out in frustration, but she misjudged her position, and her fingers rapped loudly against Tony's window.

The noise reverberated through the empty courtyard, silencing all three of them.

Alison's shoulders dropped. "Sorry."

"We're all upset," Anna said.

Wes hesitated, then said, "It probably won't do any good, but we could look around for him ourselves."

Alison's face brightened. "That's a great idea."

As they were exiting the courtyard and heading to the parking lot, Wes's cell rang.

Alison looked at him as he pulled it out. He knew she was hoping it was Tony, but the name on the display was DIONE. He shook his head, and tapped ACCEPT.

"Finally," Dione said. "I've been trying to reach you for hours. Your phone was off."

"Yeah, I know. Sorry."

"Did you get the hard drive?"

"No."

"I was afraid of that." She paused. "Okay, I'll get one on my way out of town. Probably means I won't—"

"We've got another problem," he interrupted her. "Tony's missing." He gave her a quick update.

"Jesus, Wes. Maybe I should head up there right now."

"That's up to you," he said. "But I doubt there's much more you could be doing."

She let out a frustrated groan. "Call me the second he turns up."

"Will do."

He hung up and looked at the other two.

"Let's go."

CHAPTER
40

THE MAN CALLED TO REPORT IN, BUT AFTER FOUR rings he was sent to voicemail. He hung up before the beep.

No messages. Nothing recorded. If the call was not picked up, he was to try again later.

Great, he thought. The one time he needed to have an immediate conversation, and there was no answer.

Minutes earlier the target and two women—one identified as the target's girlfriend, the other a coworker—had come out of the motel and walked over to their SUV.

It looked for a moment as if they were all going to get in, then the target had said something, and mounted the motorcycle while the women got into the Escape. When the vehicles left, the SUV headed north and the motorcycle south.

The question was, should the man follow the motorcycle, the SUV, or just stay where he was?

"Dammit," he said.

He contemplated his choices for half a second, then started the car.

If it was the wrong decision, he'd hear about it later. But he knew he had to do something.

When in doubt, he thought, keep the target in sight.

CHAPTER
41

WES HOPPED ON THE TRIUMPH, NOT WORRYING about any potential ticket. With two vehicles they could cover a lot more ground. He'd braced himself for an objection from Anna, but she hadn't said a word.

They agreed to check in with each other every fifteen minutes, then took off in opposite directions.

Where the hell are you, Tony?

He stopped at bars and restaurants, and cruised around fast-food places, looking through the windows for the show's missing crew member. But so far, nothing. The periodic check-ins with Anna revealed that she and Alison were faring no better.

Wanting to make sure they covered everything, Wes headed over to Burroughs High. The school was within the Ridgecrest city limits, but was tucked up against the base, with a chain-link fence separating it from Navy property.

The last house Wes and his family had lived in before relocating into town had been in a housing tract known as the B K-parts on the other side of the base fence. Now where there had once been lawns and homes, there was only desert and asphalt streets leading nowhere.

He tried to remember exactly where his house had stood, but even the trees that had been planted throughout the neighborhood were gone. He visualized the walk he used to take home every day, watching his imaginary self make the journey again. *There,* he thought after a few moments. *Right there.*

Maybe.

The truth was, without any definitive markers he was only able to approximate its location. He felt hollow, like a part of his life had never existed.

He turned his attention to the still-standing school.

There were only two cars in the faculty parking lot, a Honda Accord and an old Dodge pickup. Both had faculty stickers in their windows, the pickup also sporting a Burroughs Burros booster bumper sticker on the tailgate.

Burroughs was basically an outdoor campus—long, rectangular buildings separated by wide areas of dirt and the occasional bit of grass. Wes drove the bike up a handicap ramp and onto the sidewalk, then slowly moved in and around the different halls. When he'd covered everything, he stopped near the administration building and called Anna.

"Anything?" he asked.

"Not a sign. How about you?"

"Same. Where are you now?"

"Just checked out a place called Lucky Liquor. Showed them a picture Alison had on her camera of Tony, but no one recognized him."

He frowned. "Let's give it another hour, then meet back at the motel. We should be able to cover most of the likely spots by then."

"All right."

Wes looked around at the school. Tony wasn't here, had never been here. It had been a long shot at best. Anna and Alison were more likely to find a lead at Lucky Liquor than he had been riding around Burroughs.

He sped away from the high school and turned back onto China Lake Boulevard, passing the McDonald's he'd worked at the summer before his junior year, then turned left on Ridgecrest Boulevard.

He checked the bar where he'd found Lars that morning, then two more before he ended up on the road to the fairgrounds at the eastern edge of town. These were the grounds used by traveling carnivals that, when Wes lived there, had come to town twice a year. He drove slowly along the west side, but saw no one.

Just as he was about to head back toward town, a sign at the far end of the facility caught his eye.

RIDGECREST MEMORIAL CEMETERY

At the bottom was a large black arrow pointing left down an intersecting road.

Wes checked the time, hesitated, then took the turn.

There were a few scattered houses off to either side, but the desert between them grew wider and wider the farther he went, until only the space between remained.

It was another few minutes before he reached a wrought-iron gate built into the middle of a five-foot-high cinder-block wall. He pulled to a stop in the small, empty parking area and cut the engine.

Beyond the gate, the graveyard stretched outward for several acres, surrounded on all sides by more wall. It was mostly covered with green, but there were more than a few spots of brown where the grass had lost the battle against the relentless heat and sun.

All the markers were embedded in the ground, the majority white marble. Because of the fierce winds in the spring and the fall, old-fashioned vertical markers would never have lasted for long.

Wes spotted a small enclosure against the wall near the gate. Above the doorless entry a sign read DIREC-TORY. Wes flipped through the pages, finding the name he was looking for about a third of the way through. The grid number was E68. He consulted the map at the front of the book, then set off across the cemetery.

When he got to the correct area, it took him a few moments to find the marker he was looking for.

> *Amanda "Mandy" Johansson*
> *Beloved Daughter*
> *Cherished Sister*

Below that were the dates of her birth and death.

If Lars hadn't gotten the job first, Mandy would have been Wes's best friend. As it was, they had been close since meeting in Mr. Raef's English class at Murray Junior High.

"It wasn't your fault, Mandy," Wes said. He removed a couple of stray blades of grass from her marker. "I should have come back . . . I'm . . . I'm sorry."

CHAPTER
42

THE ONLY PERSON WHO SAW THEM LEAVE WAS Michael Dillman.

"Don't tell me you're going home already?" Dillman had asked.

"Beer run," Lars announced.

Dillman grinned. "Cool. Bring me back a couple, huh? Something good."

"You got it," Lars shouted over his shoulder.

Dillman wandered back toward the path to the party while Wes, Lars, and Mandy climbed into the VW van.

They rode down the hill in silence, both Wes and Lars stealing glances at Mandy and at each other. Mandy, though, had withdrawn into herself and was staring blankly at the dashboard.

"It's going to be all right," Wes said, just before they reached the highway.

She mumbled something, then shook her head.

"It'll be fine," Lars said, trying to sound upbeat.

"It's all my fault. I shouldn't have been . . . I shouldn't have . . ."

"Mandy, there's no way it's your fault." Wes looked over at her. "You can't think that way."

"It *is* my fault! Who else's could it be? Oh, God, I can't believe it."

Wes veered the van to the side of the road and stopped. He turned to her and grabbed her hands. She jerked back slightly, but he didn't let go. "You did absolutely *nothing* wrong. Not a damn thing. You are *not* to blame for what happened."

She looked up. In her eyes Wes could see fear and helplessness and despair.

Her hands began trembling in his. "Someone's going to find out," she whispered. "And when they do . . ." Her gaze started to dart around, panicked. "I need to get out." She pulled her hands away, and grabbed at the door handle, but missed. "I need to get out!"

Wes reached for her shoulder. "Hold on."

She screamed, "No!" Then she shoved the handle downward. The door opened and she all but fell outside.

"Mandy!" Wes yelled.

She stumbled away from the van, into the darkness.

Without a word, both Wes and Lars jumped out and ran across the desert after her. When they finally reached her, she was on the ground, retching and crying. For the next thirty minutes, they could do little but watch that she didn't hurt herself as she sobbed. Finally they tried to coax her back to the van.

It was the pact that finally did it.

"How can you be sure?" Mandy said, her tears finally subsiding.

"We're sure."

"Say it again."

"We'll never tell a soul," Lars said.

"We'll never tell a soul," Wes repeated. "I promise, no one will ever find out."

She stared at the two boys for several seconds as if she was waiting for one of them to take it back.

When they didn't, she nodded. "Okay. I promise, too."

CHAPTER
43

WES'S PHONE RANG, BRINGING HIM BACK TO
the here and now. He pushed himself up off the ground
next to Mandy's grave and pulled his cell out. It was
Anna.

"We can call off the dogs," she said.

"You found him?"

"Not exactly. But Dori saw him this morning. Said he
was heading up to Mount Whitney for the day with
some friends he'd met."

"Thank God," Wes said, relief washing over him.
"Where are you?"

"We're back at the hotel."

"I'll be there in fifteen minutes."

As he drove away from the cemetery, he passed a
sedan pulled to the side of the road. Thinking someone
might have broken down, he slowed, but it appeared to
be empty, and he didn't see anyone around. He also
didn't remember it being there before, but of course his
focus had been on other things. Tony. Mandy.

The past.

Half a minute later, he'd forgotten all about it.

CHAPTER
44

LARS SPENT THE REST OF SUNDAY AFTERNOON in his office on the base. No one else was in, so he was completely undisturbed.

He was a party to the events that had taken the life of an F-18 pilot. He'd written the protocols per the commander's instructions. These were the procedures the pilot was to follow as he used the system that had been specially installed on the aircraft. They'd been organized in a way that, if followed, everything would go fine. But two sequences had been left out, ones that would have made sense given the nature of the test flight. Lars had known it was a problem at the time, but with the commander's assurances, he'd convinced himself that everything would be fine.

But everything had not been fine. Most pilots would have stuck to the protocols and followed orders. But not this pilot. For some reason, Adair had decided on his own to test the missing sequences. And, predictably, the plane had gone down, and a naval officer was dead.

Those damn protocols. If only he had listened to his instincts and refused to issue them. If he had, he wouldn't be caught in a cover-up, ordered to do whatever it took to keep a friend quiet, just to keep his naval career from imploding and avoid spending the rest of his life in prison.

He could hear the distant echo of a voice in his head. Wes's.

No, not quite Wes's. It was a combo of Wes and Wes's dad.

Sometimes the hardest thing to do—

He shut it off. He didn't want to hear it.

Pulling his computer keyboard forward, he hit the space bar and woke up the screen. He brought up the website for the *High Desert Tribune* and searched for all articles pertaining to the crash. There were two more, both follow-ups to the original article. Nothing he didn't already know. A wider Web search revealed that several national outlets had picked up on the initial crash story, but there had been nothing new since. If Wes had plans on leaking what he had to the media, he hadn't done so yet.

Lars took a moment to think about what to do next, then logged on to the China Lake operations system, and used his clearance to access personnel records. In the search section, he typed in "Adair, Lawrence" then hit Find.

The name came up, but when Lars tried clicking on the link that should have taken him to the pilot's personnel file, nothing happened.

He reloaded the page in case there'd been an error, but the result was the same.

He was just about to switch over to the Pentagon site when his desk phone rang.

"Lieutenant Commander Andersen," he said.

"Sir, this is Lieutenant Tyler," a woman on the other

end said. "We've just received a notification that someone has tried to access restricted information from your
computer."

"Who is *we*, Lieutenant?" he asked.

"Cyber Command, sir," she said. "Are you attempting to access information concerning a Lieutenant
Adair?"

Cyber Command? "Yes, I am. What's the problem?"

"May I ask, sir, why?"

"I'm working with Commander Forman," Lars told
her. "The investigation into last week's crash."

He heard computer keys clacking, followed by a short
pause.

"Sir, I'm sorry, but you're not on the list of those with
approved access."

"Lieutenant, I'm on special assignment for Commander Forman. I'm sure he has access. Call him. He'll
confirm I should be allowed to view the file."

"Please hold the line."

Click.

Lars rubbed his fingers across his chin. Okay, yes, re-
stricting Lieutenant Adair's file made sense. It was standard during an investigation. But what was with the
heavy-handed response?

The line clicked again.

"Thank you for your time, Lieutenant Commander."

Before Lars could respond, the woman hung up.

He set the handset back in its cradle. *What the hell
was that all about? Did he have access or not?*

Before he'd even removed his hand, the phone rang
again. He jerked in surprise, then picked it up.

"Lieutenant Commander Andersen."

"Lars, I just got a call from Cyber Command." It was

Commander Forman. "I understand you've been trying to look at Lieutenant Adair's personnel file."

"Yes, sir. I'm sorry. I didn't realize that it was restricted."

"Why do you need to look at it?"

Lars's mind kicked into overdrive. "I was looking for the reference to Adair's distinguishing marks."

The commander remained silent for several seconds. "Why would you need to do that?"

"Thought if I could print that out and show it to Wes, it would confirm what he'd seen this morning with Dr. Handler and Lieutenant Truax. Lieutenant Adair had a scar on his—"

"I'd rather not show classified documents to civilians, if you don't mind," the commander said, cutting him off. "Find some other way of convincing him."

"Okay, sir," Lars said. "If that's what you'd like."

"That's what I'd like. I'll inform Cyber Command that it was a misunderstanding."

"I appreciate that, sir."

Lars hung up and stared at the phone for a moment. There was definitely something weird going on.

He looked down at the piece of paper on the desk.

Lieutenant Lawrence Adair.

He ripped it from the pad and stuck it in his pocket. He knew he couldn't find what he was looking for in his office, so he headed out to his car.

His first stop was the temporary offices that had been set up as investigation central for the crash. He feared that Forman might have dropped in, but the commander wasn't there. Only a skeleton crew of two lieutenants and a few enlisted men were present.

"Lieutenant Commander," one of the lieutenants said. "Is there something I can do for you?"

"I'd like to see the most up-to-date reports, please."

"Of course. One moment, sir."

The lieutenant retrieved a file from a locked cabinet and gave it to Lars.

"Thank you." Lars took it into an empty office and shut the door.

The file should have contained any ancillary reports, whether preliminary or final, plus a draft of the overall status. But several of the items he knew should be there weren't. Including a copy of Adair's personnel record.

He tapped his index finger against the table absently as he worked through what he should do next. After a few moments he started a final pass of the report, then stopped when he noticed the signature at the bottom of the report on the DNA results. It was an approval signature. *His* signature.

Only he had never signed that report. He carefully scanned the others to see if his name appeared elsewhere, but this was the only place.

Why was his signature on the DNA report? And what about the reports that weren't here? Was his signature on them, too?

A chill ran through him. He was already in neck deep because of the protocols, but it seemed that wasn't enough. Commander Forman was making sure a big, fat arrow was pointing right at Lars.

He stared at a blank spot on the desk, paralyzed. He had to do something, but what?

He sat there for nearly ten minutes, his mind churning. Finally, he knew what he had to do.

With a deep breath, he closed the folder, and exited the office.

CHAPTER
45

"I'LL GRAB SOME CLOTHES FOR TOMORROW and be over in a few minutes," Anna said.

They'd just returned to the motel from dinner.

"Don't be too long," Wes said.

"Or what?"

"Or I might be the one who's asleep."

Smirking, she shook her head. "Should have taken that nap with me."

While Anna went for her things, Wes let himself into his room.

The red light on the phone was lit. He made a quick stop in the bathroom, then retrieved the message.

"Wes, it's Lars. I'll . . . uh . . . I'll call back."

Wes stabbed a finger at the number three button, erasing the message. He then turned on the TV and climbed onto the bed. As he pulled out one of the pillows to put behind his back, he realized there was something stuck to the cloth case.

It was a neatly folded piece of newsprint, safetypinned to the pillow's cover.

Reluctantly he undid the pin and opened the paper.

Most of the page was the remnants of an article about school board elections. But whoever had left it had conveniently circled a smaller, one-column article in black ink.

BHS STUDENT DIES AT HOME

Ridgecrest emergency services were called to the home of the Johansson family on Rancho Street yesterday afternoon. Inside, they found a young woman in cardiac arrest. According to Fire Department liaison Lisbeth Klausen, EMTs immediately began lifesaving procedures, but their efforts proved unsuccessful.

A family spokesman indentified the woman as Amanda Johansson, 17-year-old daughter of Dean and Lauraine Johansson, and a senior at Burroughs High School. It is believed Miss Johansson was home alone at the time.

Wes could feel tears welling in his eyes. Two short paragraphs announcing her death were all that Mandy got.

It was so stark. So impersonal.

He wiped his eyes, then threw back the bedspread to make sure there was nothing else underneath. All he found were sheets.

A knock on the door startled him. He pulled the spread back onto the bed, then went to see who it was.

Anna was there, but she wasn't alone. Behind her were Detectives Stevens and Andrews.

"What's . . . up?" Wes said.

"Sorry to bother you so late on a Sunday evening, Mr. Stewart," Stevens said.

"Did you find my stuff?"

"I wish that's why we were here."

When Stevens didn't elaborate, Wes said, "Then what is it?"

"We'd like you to come down to the station with us." Stevens smiled without warmth. "We have something we want to show you."

"You can't tell me what it is here?"

"Easier if you come with us."

Andrews pointed at a sedan in the lot. "Our car's right over there."

CHAPTER
46

DETECTIVE STEVENS LED WES INTO A SMALL,
windowless office and motioned for him to take a seat in
front of the desk. Andrews grabbed the other guest
chair.

"We apologize for having to bring you all the way
down here," Stevens said.

"So what did you want to show me?"

"It's actually more to listen to than show. I'm sure
you're familiar with anonymous tip lines?"

"Uh . . . sure."

"We may be a small force but we have one, too. Most
of the tips turn out to be nothing. You know, angry
neighbor stuff, or someone just trying to mess around
with us. I'll be honest with you, we probably write off
ninety percent of them the moment we hear them."

"Okay, but what does this have to do with me?" Wes
asked.

"We received another call a little over an hour ago.
Probably would have dismissed it, too, but, well . . . Can
I play it for you?"

"That's why we're here, right?"

Stevens answered with a nod, then turned to his computer. "All right. Here we go."

An initial hiss was followed by an electronic time stamp, then a moment of dead air. *"There is a man staying at the Desert Rose Motel named Wesley Stewart. He has information about a crime that happened when he used to live here. You should talk to him."* A couple of clicks, then the speaker went silent.

The voice had been muffled. Monotone. No telling if it was male or female.

Stevens looked at Wes. "So what do you think?"

Wes tried to look confused but unfazed. "What do *I* think?"

Andrews chuckled. "Pretty crazy, huh?"

"More bizarre than anything else."

"Any idea what it could mean?" Stevens asked.

Wes shook his head. "I haven't the slightest. Do you?"

"What about the voice? Do you recognize it?"

"No. It could be anyone."

"It mentioned you left town a long time ago," Andrews said. "Is that true?"

"Yeah . . . I grew up here."

"Right." Andrews pulled out a notebook. "Grew up on base, right? Navy brat?"

"Yeah."

"When did you leave?"

Wes narrowed his eyes. "A long time ago. When I was a teenager."

"How long?"

Wes hesitated a second. "Seventeen years."

"Wanted to get out of here as quick as you could, huh? Go start your career in Hollywood?"

"Something like that."

Stevens asked, "So if you've been gone so long, why

do you think someone would have called and said all that?"

"I haven't the slightest idea," Wes replied. "Whoever left that must be pulling a prank on you."

Andrews smiled. "I had the same thought, didn't I, Stevens?"

"You did," Stevens said.

"I mean, really, it's kind of random. Maybe we should ask you about all our cold cases and see what you might have had to do with them." Andrews looked at Wes again. "Of course, you *have* had a lot of things happening around you this weekend."

Wes cocked his head. "Excuse me?"

"Come on. This isn't the first time we've spoken since you came back to town. In fact it's not even the second. So I guess we're wondering why, if you lived here all those years ago, and are just in town to shoot an episode of . . . ," he flipped through his notebook, "*Close to Home,* an anonymous caller would use your name?"

"And *I'm* supposed to know the answer?" Wes said.

"We were hoping," Stevens said.

Wes shrugged. "I don't know. Maybe they saw my name in the paper the other day, and thought it would be fun to screw around with an out-of-towner."

"Your name was in the paper?" Stevens asked.

Wes looked at Stevens, then at Andrews. Both detectives stared blankly back.

"The F-18 crash?" he said. "I was the first one on scene?"

"That's right," Stevens said. "I do remember reading that now."

"Some jerk probably just went, 'Eenie, meenie, miney, moe,' and picked my name out of the article."

"Perhaps," Stevens said.

The two detectives shared another look, then Andrews said, "Two break-ins, an apparent car chase, a missing person, and now this? I don't have a good feeling about you."

Wes leaned forward. "Are you implying I might be responsible for any of those things?"

"We're not *implying* anything," Andrews said.

"My involvement in the break-ins and the chase were either as the victim or the friend of the victim, nothing more. And this message you received? It's garbage." Wes stood up. "So if there's nothing else, I'm going back to my motel."

Stevens appeared to be lost in thought for a moment, then he nodded and said, "I'm sorry we troubled you."

Wes got the distinct feeling neither of the detectives was particularly sorry, but he refrained from saying as much, and turned to leave. "Excuse me," he said to the still-sitting Andrews.

"You'll need a ride back, Mr. Stewart," Andrews said.

"I think I'll walk."

"Don't be ridiculous," Andrews insisted, rising to his feet. "I'll drive you."

Wes started to protest, but stopped. Walking back would take him at least twenty minutes, while the ride would only last three. "Fine."

They rode in silence. The only time the detective said anything was when Wes got out of the car at the Desert Rose. "Stay out of trouble, Mr. Stewart."

Wes shut the door without replying. As the police car disappeared, so did the anger that had been masking the feeling of nausea he'd had since he'd heard the message in Stevens's office.

The anonymous tip had definitely not been a prank.

CHAPTER
47

ANNA THREW HER ARMS AROUND HIM AS HE
walked through the door. "What did they want?"

"It was a joke," Wes said.

Her face scrunched together. "Joke?"

"Well . . . not so much a joke." He told her about the
anonymous tip.

"That's just weird," she said.

"No kidding."

"Couldn't the police have asked you about it here?"

"They wanted me to hear it. They were hoping I could
identify the caller."

"Could you?"

He shook his head. "No. Whoever it was disguised
their voice."

"What did the police say?"

Wes hesitated, then decided to tell her about Andrews's insinuation that he might be involved with the
other crimes.

She stared at him dumbfounded. "You're leaving out
the punch line, right?"

"I wish I was."

"That's stupid. You didn't have any—"

He held up a hand, stopping her. "I know. But it doesn't matter. Right now I just want to take a shower and crawl into bed."

He went into the bathroom and began to take his shirt off.

"Lars called," Anna said. She was standing in the doorway.

Wes immediately tensed.

"He wants to talk to you."

"I'll bet he does." He tossed his shirt on the floor.

"He was acting funny, too," Anna said.

"Not surprising." He put some paste on his toothbrush and started to brush his teeth.

"Well, he's calling back in fifteen minutes."

He pulled the toothbrush out. "Then he'll have to leave a message, because I'm not talking to him."

"I kind of promised you would," she said sheepishly.

"You what?"

"Sorry. Didn't think it would be a problem." She paused. "But it was a promise."

Wes groaned. "Fine!"

He took a quick shower, and had just pulled on some clean clothes when the phone rang.

"Hello?" he said.

"Wes . . . it's Lars. Look, first off, I'm sorry about this morning."

"Fine. Forgiven. Thanks for calling." Wes started to pull the receiver away from his ear.

"Wait. That's not why I called. Are you still there?"

As Wes raised the phone back to his ear, his cell vibrated in his pocket, indicating he'd gotten a text. He ignored it and said, "For the moment."

"Anger aside, what I took you to see today—"

"I don't want to talk about what we saw."

"Sure. I get that. All I'm asking is that you give me a moment."

Wes's phone vibrated again. Annoyed, he pulled it out. There were two texts, but what caught Wes off guard was that they were both from Lars.

As he accessed them Lars said, "I know you've meant well, that your questions about Adair are only because you were concerned . . ."

Wes read the first message.

Phones bugged. We need to talk.

". . . can appreciate that. And as I said before, your mistake was understandable . . ."

The second message read:

Will be behind hospital. 5 mins.

"I hope I'm making sense," Lars said. "You under-stand what I'm getting at?"

Wes hesitated. "I think so." Once more his phone buzzed.

Careful u r not followed.

Wes paused, thinking.

"Are you still there?" Lars asked.

A further moment of silence, then Wes made a decision and said, "Yeah, sorry. The shoot, the crash. You're right, it's been very stressful. And seeing Adair's body today? I don't know, I think it kind of freaked me out. . . . I guess what I'm saying is I think I probably misremember the crash. I apologize for any trouble I caused you, and I promise I won't bring it up again."

"It's not easy seeing a man die," Lars said. "It didn't help that you weren't able to get him out of there in time. But, in truth, you did all you could. Thank you for that."

"I don't know. I guess you're right."

"I've gotta run, but I'm glad we were able to talk."

"Yeah. Me too. Take care," Wes said, then hung up.

"Is everything okay?" Anna asked.

He was breathing deeply in and out, trying to calm down. "Everything's fine."

She was about to ask another question, but he held his finger to his lips. She looked at him, confused. He motioned for her to follow him, then led her into the bathroom. There he carefully closed the door, and handed her the phone so she could read the texts from Lars.

When she finished, she looked stunned. "Bugged?" she whispered. "Is he serious?"

"I don't know," he whispered back.

"Are you going to meet him?"

Wes nodded. "Yeah. If he's lying, I'll know soon enough."

"I'm coming with you."

"Not a good idea."

"Why not?"

"He's only expecting me. I don't know how he'll react if you come along."

The look on her face made it clear that wasn't the answer she wanted to hear.

"I promise I'll tell you everything when I get back."

She continued frowning, but nodded in resignation. "I'll wait here. But call me if something changes."

"I will."

When she kissed him, he could feel her concern.

"Be careful," she whispered in his ear.

CHAPTER

48

"HE JUST LEFT HIS ROOM," THE MAN IN THE sedan said. "No, alone. The woman's still inside. . . . Hold on."

The man watched Wes Stewart move down the walkway that ran along the motel. Stewart had already passed his motorcycle, so the man assumed he was heading for the Escape. But instead of getting into the SUV, Stewart turned down the passageway that led toward the swimming pool and interior courtyard of the motel.

"I think he might be going to visit one of the other people he's here with. . . . No, can't see him anymore. But he's done this before. He's usually back within thirty minutes. . . . All right. I'll stay where I am."

The man returned his attention to the door of Wes's room.

CHAPTER
49

AFTER WORKING HIS WAY THROUGH THE DES-
ert Rose, Wes jogged across the back edge of the large,
empty field that separated the motel from the hospital,
and into the hospital parking lot. Two minutes later he
found Lars sitting in his pickup near the entrance to the
emergency room.

Wes opened the passenger door and climbed inside.

Lars was gripping the steering wheel, looking left and
right, tense and agitated.

"What the hell's going on?" Wes asked.

Lars snapped his head around. "Did anyone follow
you?"

"No. Tell me what's going on."

"You're sure no one saw you leave?"

Wes shrugged, surprised by Lars's seeming paranoia.
"I don't think so. I snuck out through the back."

Lars seemed to relax just a fraction. "Okay. Good.
We might be all right."

"Lars, what's going on?"

Lars put a hand over his face and sighed. "We need to
go now."

"Go where?"

Lars looked at the seat behind them. "It'll be tight, but you'll fit behind the seat."

Wes glanced at the gap between the top of the bench seat and the back wall of the cab. It couldn't have been more than five inches. "You want me to get back there? Why?"

"Because I can't get to where we need to go if anyone knows you're with me."

"And where's that?"

Lars looked at Wes. "You'll know soon enough."

"I'm not going anywhere until you tell me what this is about."

There was uncertainty in Lars's eyes. "Things . . ." He looked away for a moment, then back. "Just get behind the seat, okay? You'll understand everything soon enough."

Wes put a hand on the door handle, thinking this might have been a mistake.

"Please," Lars said. "We trusted each other once; I'm asking you to trust me again."

Wes hesitated. They *had* trusted each other once. But in the past few days, his old friend hadn't given him much reason to do it again. Still, there was something in Lars's eyes, in his voice, something that hinted at the Lars Wes used to know. "The minute I think you're trying to pull something, I'm out of here."

"Deal."

They got out of the truck and flipped the back of the bench seat forward. Though the space at the bottom was wider than at the top, it was still going to be a tight squeeze.

"I can move it up a few inches, but that's about it," Lars said.

"I'll take whatever you can give me."

Once Wes was lying down, Lars disappeared for a moment, then returned with an old, dark blue blanket from the bed of the truck.

"Just in case," he said as he spread it over Wes. "You okay?"

Wes pushed the blanket off his face so he could breathe. "Never been better."

Lars swung the seat back up. For half a second Wes thought it was going to smash him in the nose, but it stopped a half inch short.

There was absolutely no padding in the space behind the seat. Just metal sticking out at odd angles, digging deep into his back. And dirt, there was plenty of that, too.

"I'm going to move the bench up," Lars said once he'd climbed behind the wheel.

A clunk, then a metallic groan as the bench slid forward, giving Wes about two more inches.

"That's as far as I can go."

It wasn't much, but it felt luxurious compared to what it had been like moments before. That was until they started driving, and Wes wished Lars had left it where it was. The extra space allowed Wes to bang against the objects sticking out of the wall instead of being snug up against them.

At first he tracked their location by the turns they were taking, but he quickly got lost. So he closed his eyes and tried to think of something other than bruised kidneys. A few minutes later the truck rolled to a stop.

"Keep still and don't say a word," Lars whispered.

Wes heard the window crank down, then felt the hint of fresh air.

"Lieutenant Commander," a voice said from outside. "I have a message for you. Hold on just a moment."

They were on the base, Wes realized.

A moment later the voice of the guard was back. "Here you are, sir."

The crinkle of paper was followed by a "Thank you" from Lars.

As the truck started moving, Wes could hear the paper crinkle again, then Lars swore. "He knows something's up."

"Who does?"

"Just stay quiet. And . . . and if we get pulled over, make sure you're covered and keep still. I'm already in enough trouble as it is. If they find you, it'll be a lot worse. For both of us."

Wes knew that was true. He'd been snuck onto a military base. God knew how many federal laws that violated. Just getting caught would probably get them both at least a couple of years in prison.

Lars turned the truck every minute or so. It got to the point where it seemed to Wes like at times they were actually going in circles. Then suddenly they sped up, made two quick turns, and jammed to a stop. Lars switched the engine off and doused the headlights.

There was a thump as Lars lay across the bench seat. Wes wanted to ask what was going on, but was smart enough to remain silent.

They stayed like that for nearly five minutes before Lars finally sat back up. Nothing for a moment, then the engine came back to life and the truck started moving again.

More minutes passed, then Lars said, "You were right before. I was supposed to meet him that night."

Wes wasn't following. *Meet who? What night? The night of the crash?*

Then it hit him. Not the night of the crash. Another night, years ago.

His father's day planner. *Pudge at 8:30.*

"I chickened out. He wanted my help, but I chickened out."

"Help with what?" Wes asked.

Lars grunted, but said nothing more.

Wes asked him again, but didn't even get a grunt this time.

Several minutes later the truck pulled to a stop and Lars cut the engine.

"Stay here," he whispered.

The door opened, he got out, then it closed again.

Silence, both inside and outside the cab. A quiet Sunday night.

Questions about his father, and Lars, and why they would have met, swam through Wes's mind.

Lars came back after ten minutes. Without a word, he unlatched the seat and tilted it forward, then he pulled the blanket off.

"Here," he said, extending his free hand to Wes.

With Lars's help, Wes struggled up, then out, every muscle screaming in pain.

They were parked next to a rectangular, two-story, flat-top building. It was white, and had outside breezeways on both the first and second levels. Wes turned and saw two more identical buildings to the side. All unmistakably military.

He did a full three-sixty. There were three more buildings on the other side of a narrow road, but otherwise, there was only desert in all directions.

"Come on," Lars said.

"Wait. What were you supposed to help my father with?"

"Not now. We don't have time."

"Lars, we're talking about my dad!"

"Later."

"Do you know why he went up Nine Mile Canyon?"

But Lars was already jogging along the side of the building, toward a door at the top of a short set of concrete steps. Wes hesitated a moment, then followed. As soon as he reached the steps, Lars opened the metal door, revealing a stairwell inside. Without a word, they went up.

The stairs ended at the second-floor landing. From there, Lars led Wes onto the breezeway. Along the wall were five metal doors. Lars hurried down to the one at the far end, his footsteps echoing softly through the empty night, and pulled the door open. He motioned for Wes to enter.

The room was about fifteen feet wide by twenty long. There were three desks, each covered with books and papers. The wall on the left was a heavily used, floor-to-ceiling dry-erase board, while the wall on the right and the one directly across from the door sported waist-high, wood-framed windows.

Lars moved quickly to the corner where the two windowed walls met. He looked out one, then the other for several seconds before turning back to Wes. "You can see both routes from here."

He pointed through the window to the left, indicating where the road that ran between the buildings met with another that curved out into the darkness of the desert. Through the window to the right, he pointed at a narrower road that passed between two of the buildings on the other side of the main road and then led out into a different part of the wilderness.

"If you see anything, *anything*, you tell me right away."

"Hold on," Wes said. "What, exactly, are we doing here?"

Lars took a moment, then said, "You were right about Adair."

"Hold on. You're telling me for sure the pilot wasn't Adair?"

Lars nodded. "That's what I'm telling you."

"You've known this all along?"

"No," Lars said quickly. "That part of things I didn't know until this evening."

"What things?"

"Look, the reason we came out here is because there's information that will prove you were right, but I can't just access it anywhere. I called in a favor and got the password to a secure computer terminal downstairs that does have access to the info. It's not a perfect solution. But they won't realize it right away, and our location out here will hopefully buy us a little extra time for me to find everything. What I need you to do is watch the roads and warn me if anyone's coming." He turned the phone on the closest desk to face them. "There's an internal intercom in this building. When I get downstairs, I'll call you on this line." He pointed at an unlit indicator on the phone. "Just press that and we'll be connected. All right?"

Wes looked at his friend for a moment, then nodded. "Yeah. All right."

CHAPTER
50

AFTER FORTY MINUTES PASSED WITHOUT STEW-
art returning to his room, the man in the car began to
get annoyed. When it hit an hour, his annoyance became
concern. Not for Stewart, but for the possibility that
Stewart had given him the slip.

He waited an additional ten, then made the call he
was dreading, and was told to look around the motel
and see if he could find the missing cameraman.

He checked the rooms the rest of the crew were staying in, listening at doors and windows to see if he could
hear Stewart inside. Most were quiet. The only exception was the sound of a TV in one.

He thought for a second that maybe Stewart had
snuck off to have a little fun with the other woman in
the crew who'd stayed for the weekend, the tall one. But
when he checked her room, there was only silence.

Before getting back in the car, he checked Stewart's
room, just in case the guy had returned as stealthily as
he left. Didn't sound like it, though.

The son of a bitch was messing up the plan. Tonight
was supposed to be *the* night.

"I have no idea where he went," he said, checking back in. "As far as I can tell, he's not anywhere on the grounds. . . . No, she's still there." He listened, then cocked his head, surprised. "Are you sure? . . . Okay, okay, if that's what you want. . . . Yes, I'll call as soon as it's done."

The man hung up, not completely sure how he felt. Changes were never something he was comfortable with. But what could he do?

He looked at his watch, marking the time, then leaned back, saving his energy for later.

CHAPTER
51

"HOW'S IT LOOKING?" LARS ASKED OVER THE speakerphone.

"Quiet," Wes said.

Night in the desert meant miles and miles of nothing but dark. Wes would be able to see the headlights of any approaching vehicle in plenty of time for him and Lars to get away. So far the roads to the isolated set of buildings had remained empty.

"Good."

"How's it going there?"

"I'm in," Lars said. "Just searching for the files on the flight."

Wes continued to scan the desert, hearing only the clacking of a keyboard through the phone's speaker. He became so lost in the darkness that it was several seconds before he registered that the typing had stopped.

"Lars?"

"Give me a minute." Lars's voice sounded hushed and anxious.

Wes checked each road again. There was a faint light

off in the distance through the window on the right, but as far as he could tell, it wasn't in-line with the road.

"Did you find something or not?" he asked.

"I can work faster if you don't ask questions," Lars told him.

More typing.

Wes looked out the windows again. The light he'd seen before was gone.

"The roads are still empty," he reported.

A grunted acknowledgment, then nothing but key-strokes for nearly ten minutes.

Suddenly Lars said, "Got it!"

"What did you find?"

"Proof. I'm printing it out. Get back into the truck now!"

Wes reached forward to cut the intercom connection, but held up as he noticed movement out the window to his left. There was something on the road in the distance. It was almost as dark as the landscape, but it was moving fast.

"Lars, we have company!"

"I thought you said the roads were empty."

"They're coming in with their lights off. There are at least two of them. West road. I'd give us three minutes, tops."

"Get your ass down here! Now!"

CHAPTER
52

WES FLEW ALONG THE SECOND-FLOOR BREEZE-
way and dove through the door into the stairwell. Taking the steps three at a time, he hit the first-floor door
twenty seconds after he'd hung up the phone.

"Lars?" he called out.

The five office doors of the first floor were all closed.
He moved quickly from one to another, trying each. The
fourth knob he turned was unlocked.

"Lars," he said, sticking his head inside. "They'll be
here any second. We need to go!"

His friend was across the room, standing next to a
printer.

"Two more sheets," he said. "Go wait in the truck."

"Just leave them."

"I can't. This is the only thing that will keep us alive."

"What the hell's going on?"

Lars didn't answer, so Wes pushed out of the doorway and raced to the end of the building. He peeked
around the edge. From this angle he could see where the
road that ran between the buildings intersected with
the road the cars were on. As of yet, it was clear.

Hearing a door close behind him, he looked back. Lars was heading toward the truck, several sheets of paper in his hand.

Wes checked the intersection again. It was no longer empty.

"We're not going to make it," he yelled, running to join his friend. "They'll be here in just a couple of seconds."

"Here." Lars shoved the papers into Wes's hand. "Hide somewhere. I'll distract them."

"What?"

"You said yourself we're not going to make it. If they find you here, we both go to jail. If it's just me, I'll get a hand slap. When we're all gone, walk back, and find a way off the base without being seen. Can you do that?"

Wes was scared to death, but he nodded.

They could now hear engines approaching.

Wes started to turn away, but Lars grabbed him. "Wait." He snatched back one of the papers, pulled out a pen, and scribbled on the back of the sheet. "That's the key," he said, shoving it at Wes. "Now go! Hide!"

Wes turned and ran straight into the desert.

About one hundred feet out, he found a shallow ravine cut by an ancient flash flood. It was just deep enough for him to lie flat below the prevailing ground level. Once prone, he tilted his head up and looked back at the buildings.

Lars was in the truck and had started it up. But he only went a dozen feet before a dark sedan darted out from around the corner of the building and skidded to a stop half a car length in front of him.

Brake lights flashed, and the truck slammed to a stop. Just then a second car swung around the back of the building and cut off any potential retreat. Two more cars soon joined the first near the front, then, almost as one, doors flew open, and over a dozen armed men rushed out, their weapons pointed directly at the truck.

This is not going to be just a slap on the hand.

Wes heard sharp, raised voices, but couldn't make out the words. Then the driver's door of the truck opened, and Lars stepped out, his arms above his head.

"On your knees!" a single voice barked, just loud enough for Wes to hear.

Lars immediately complied.

The men surrounding him began closing in, their weapons still drawn. When they were within ten feet, two of the men behind Lars rushed forward. They grabbed Lars's arms and shoved them down. One of the men pulled something out of a pocket and secured Lars's hands, then they yanked him to his feet.

More voices as most of the guns were lowered. One man walked up until he was standing just a few feet in front of Lars. Even at this distance, Wes recognized Lieutenant Jenks.

After about a minute, Jenks looked back at the other men. As one, the remaining guns that had not been stowed were lowered. More talk, and then Lars was led to one of the sedans. Jenks opened the rear door and guided Lars's head as he climbed in, then Jenks got in after him. Two others got into the front. The doors were barely shut when the sedan made a quick U-turn and sped off the way it had come.

Wes watched the twelve remaining men, willing them to get into their cars and leave, too. But instead, they gathered together. When they finally split, two went over to Lars's truck and began searching through the cab. Six others headed to the first-floor breezeway of the building, disappearing from view. And while the final four men got into a sedan, instead of leaving, they began driving between the buildings, stopping every once in a while to shine a handheld searchlight at one of the structures.

After several minutes the car disappeared behind the buildings on the far side of the road. Just when Wes was beginning to think maybe it had driven off, headlights swept out from around the end of the building to Wes's left.

The sedan now drove slowly along the edge of the raw desert, the spotlight beam pointing into the wilderness as the vehicle drew closer and closer to Wes's position.

Run! The word reverberated in his head. But he held his position, knowing that if he *did* take off, there was no question he'd be spotted.

The sound of an engine roaring to life caused Wes to look back toward the buildings. It was Lars's truck. The headlights were on, and the two men who had been searching it were sitting inside. Someone trotted out of the building and over to the truck, the headlight temporarily lighting him up.

Wasserman.

He leaned in the open window for several seconds, then turned back to the building as the truck drove away.

Wes cursed silently. There had been a small part of him hoping they would leave the truck behind. He'd been toying with the idea of using it to get out of there.

He looked back at the sedan with the spotlight. It was almost parallel to his position now.

Again the urge to flee nearly overwhelmed him. But he resisted. He wasn't simply trespassing on private property. This was a military base. If he ran, there wouldn't be a shout ordering him to stop. The only shout would be from the gun firing the bullet aimed at his back.

When the spotlight touched the bushes only a few feet to his left, Wes tucked his head down as far as he could, burying his face in the dirt.

Five seconds passed. Then ten.

With each breath, he felt like he was inhaling more dust than air. But he didn't move, not even a fraction of an inch. He waited for the sound of car doors opening, then shouting and weapons being drawn, but the only thing he heard was his own heartbeat.

Finally, when he was sure he should have already been spotted, he twisted his head to the right and opened an eye. His view of the world was limited to sky and the edge of the shallow ravine. But it was all dark.

He listened intently, trying to pick out the sound of the sedan. After a moment, he heard the tires passing over dirt, faint and getting fainter.

The relief that coursed through him was tempered by the knowledge he wasn't out of trouble yet. He held his position, and counted off the minutes in his head, telling himself he'd take another look when he reached ten. Then when he did, he made himself take another five just to be safe.

Once that had passed, he carefully raised himself up so that he could see above the crest of the depression.

Unbroken night on all sides.

He focused on the buildings. Both the sedan that had been circling with the spotlight and the ones that had still been parked were gone.

He did a full scan, examining every inch in case this was some kind of trick.

No one.

He was alone.

CHAPTER
53

IN MANY WAYS, THE JOURNEY TO GET OFF THE base was more nerve-racking than lying in the ditch waiting to be caught. Keeping at least twenty feet off the road, Wes paralleled the route the sedans had arrived on, hoping that if he suddenly needed to hide, he could do so without being seen.

He had determined his location first by spotting the distant shadowy line of the Sierra Nevada Mountains to the west, then by the much closer form of B Mountain—so called because of the white *B* painted on the front each year by the Burroughs High School senior class—just to the north.

The quickest way to the fence would have been to take a hard left to the south, toward the highway to Trona, where he could probably hitch a ride. But going in that direction would have meant crossing a couple of miles of untouched desert. Not necessarily an attractive option.

If he went west, though, he would not only be heading in the direction of the motel, but also toward a portion of the fence where he felt confident he could find an easy place to get over.

So onward he hiked, ever mindful of any light he saw or sound he heard.

An hour later, he reached the road that led up to where his house used to stand. It was on this very strip of asphalt that he'd first gotten behind the wheel of a car. It had been his mom's 1975 VW van. Red bottom, white top, with a stick shift longer than his arm. He'd stalled twice, but eventually got it to the top of the incline.

Now he ascended it on foot, then crossed into the area that had once been the neighborhood he'd grown up in. Just that afternoon he'd looked at it from the other side of the fence, but now he was actually standing on the same streets where he'd played.

Angling southwest, he headed toward the fence that separated the area from the high school. Teens had been hopping that particular section since before Wes was born. That meant there'd be at least one spot along the expanse that could easily be scaled.

It wasn't until he'd already passed it that he realized he'd walked right through the space where his family's home had been. But as he turned back to look, what caught his attention wasn't the structural ghost from his childhood, but two sets of headlights moving quickly up the hill, one right after the other.

"Dammit." He started running.

He had to assume he'd been seen. The problem was there was absolutely nowhere to hide in his old neighborhood. His only hope lay with the high school on the other side of the fence.

There was no time to hunt for the easiest section, so Wes headed straight for the expanse closest to him. When he was three feet away, he leapt, his hands reaching for the support rail that ran across the top. As soon as he clamped on, he pulled himself up and over. But while he might now be on the town side of the fence, he was still in plain sight.

Wes ran, his eyes desperately searching for a place to hide. The closest structure was the school administration building, but he wouldn't be able to reach it without being seen first. He glanced left and right, trying to locate an alternative.

There! he thought, angling slightly to the left.

His target was a six-foot-high red cinder-block wall with the words SHERMAN E. BURROUGHS HIGH SCHOOL on the front.

He sprinted flat out, skidding around the wall just as the first set of headlights crested the hill.

He peered around the edge of his hiding place and watched the cars race into his old housing tract. Almost immediately spotlight beams shot out from the windows and began panning across the empty land. One of the cars came near the section of the fence Wes had gone over, but its light never turned toward the high school.

The cars then headed toward Hubbard Circle on the other side of Knox Road. Once they'd moved off, Wes made a dash for the admin building, then moved deeper into the school. By the time he reached the student parking lot near the lecture center, the cars on the base were gone.

He allowed himself a moment to lean against the building and catch his breath. As he did he felt a stinging sensation along his ribs on his right side. He reached down and found an inch-long, upside-down L-shaped tear in his T-shirt. Underneath, his skin was sticky with blood. It must have happened when he'd hopped the fence.

He winced as he probed the wound. He didn't think it

needed stitches, but it did need to be cleaned as soon as possible. Scratched arm, singed wrist, cut on his rib cage, and no doubt bruises everywhere else from the ride in the back of Lars's truck—there was nothing like coming home.

CHAPTER
54

WES FINALLY REACHED THE DESERT ROSE MOTEL at nearly 2 a.m., a sorry mix of pain and exhaustion. He carefully opened the door to his room so as to not wake Anna, but he needn't have been so cautious. She wasn't there. She'd apparently gotten tired of waiting for him and gone back to her own room. He thought about letting her know he was back, but he was just too exhausted. She'd be mad at him in the morning, but he convinced himself it was better to just let her sleep.

He took four Advils, then forced himself into the shower and washed out his wound. The gash was as unattractive as it was painful, but his initial instincts had been correct—he wasn't going to need any stitches.

Once he was finished with the shower, he found a couple of Band-Aids in his shaving kit and slapped them over the wound—inadequate at best, but better than nothing—then stretched out on the bed with the papers Lars had shoved in his hand. The last thing he remembered was looking at the top sheet and trying to make sense of the words. Sleep had other ideas.

CHAPTER
55

AT 7 A.M. WES WOKE IN THE SAME POSITION HE'D fallen asleep in. The papers were in a pile on the bed next to his outstretched hand. He picked them up and shoved them partly under the pile of clothes that were still on the dresser, then trudged into the bathroom.

He skipped a shower and just splashed some water on his face to wake up. He then dressed, threw a Padres baseball cap over his head, and headed out. By the time he got to the SUVs, Dione, Danny, and Monroe were already there.

"What happened?" Dione asked. "You guys have a party last night?"

"Not that I know of," Wes said.

"Then where the hell is everyone?"

"So glad you're back, Dione."

"Please tell me that PA guy is bringing coffee," Monroe rasped.

If anyone looked like they'd been at a party the night before, it was Monroe. She was wearing dark shades, and had the energy of a piece of petrified wood. Wes, remembering how well she'd bounced back after the night of tequila shots, wondered what she could have done over the weekend to cause her current condition.

Dione took a few steps away from the cars and motioned for Wes to follow her. "Did you read Tony the riot act?"

"I haven't seen him yet," Wes said. "I was out last night."

"Great. So I have to do it." She frowned, then looked down at the clipboard with her schedule and other information.

Wes winced, remembering the papers Lars had given him.

"What?" she asked.

"Left something in my room." He looked around. "I'll be right back."

"Check on the others while you're over there," Dione said. "Tell them to move it."

"Sure."

Wes headed across the parking lot, but he'd barely reached the walkway when Alison came racing out of the courtyard passageway.

She immediately spotted him and ran over. "He's not back," she said.

"Tony?" Wes said. "I thought—"

"He still hasn't come back."

She put a hand on Wes's arm and started pulling him toward the passageway.

"I was awake until one, and then up again at six," she told him, her voice panicked. "I've already knocked on his door a dozen times."

Wes stopped her. "Get the manager. I'll try the door."

Alison nodded, then headed toward the motel office as Wes ran in the other direction. The first thing he did when he reached Tony's door was try the knob. As expected, it was locked.

"Tony!" he yelled, pounding on the door. "Tony!"

As he started to yell a third time, Dione came jogging around the corner.

"I saw Alison and she just pointed in this direction," she said. "What's going on?"

"Tony's not back," Wes said. He pounded again. "Tony!"

Just then Alison and Harold Barber, the manager who had given Anna her new room, showed up. Unlike the manager from the day before, Barber immediately stuck the master keycard in the slot and pushed the door open.

Everything in the room was exactly as it had been when they'd checked on Sunday.

"Oh, God," Alison said.

Wes ran to the phone on the nightstand and called 911.

CHAPTER
56

TWO SQUAD CARS SPED INTO THE PARKING LOT,
lights blazing but sirens off. As soon as he saw them, Wes
stepped out from between the cars and waved them down.

"What the hell are the police doing here?" Monroe
asked.

"Tony's *missing*," Dione said. "All his stuff is here
and he's not. Something happened to him."

"Oh," seemed to be all Monroe could muster.

The two police cars pulled to a stop, and the officers
got out—one from the lead car and two from the trailing. Wes walked quickly over.

"Are you the one who placed the call?" the lead officer asked. His nametag read "Rockwell."

"Yes," Wes said.

"I understand someone's missing?"

"Our PA."

The officer's brow furrowed. "PA?"

"Production assistant," Wes explained. "We're working on a TV show."

Rockwell nodded. "What's the missing person's name?"

Wes spent two minutes giving him details.

Once he was finished, Rockwell said, "Can you show us where his room is?"

"Of course."

Wes and Alison led the officers to the room. Barber was still there, standing guard at the door. At Rockwell's direction, he opened it again. The officer and his two colleagues stepped over the threshold and looked in.

"Have any of you been inside?" Rockwell asked.

"A couple of us," Wes said. "Seeing if he was here."

"Anyone touch anything?"

"Only me. I used the phone to call you."

"Okay. We need to secure the scene until the detectives and the techs get here. Stay around, though. They're going to want to talk to you."

"We shouldn't have stopped looking for him yesterday," Alison said as she and Wes headed back to where the rest of the crew was waiting.

"We wouldn't have found him," Wes said. "He was hiking, remember? Maybe he's lost. Once they find out exactly where he went, they'll send people to look for him." As soon as they reached the walkway next to the parking lot, Wes looked around. "Where's Anna?"

"Shouldn't you be the one who knows the answer to that?" Alison couldn't quite keep the sarcasm out of her voice.

"Tell Dione what's happening," he told her. "I'll be right back."

He went over to Anna's room, but didn't have her spare keycard on him, so he knocked.

He could hear something inside, but no one answered. The noise was faint.

"Anna?" he said, knocking again. The door remained closed.

He walked quickly back to his room, retrieved the spare keycard, and returned to her door. He knocked one more time, then slipped the card into the lock.

After he pushed the door open, he froze.

The room reminded him in nearly every detail of Tony's.

Clean.

Bed not slept in.

The only difference was the clock radio on the night-stand playing low in the background.

There was no one there.

Anna was gone.

CHAPTER
57

"ANNA!"

Wes rushed into the bathroom, but it was empty.

He realized with dread that he'd fallen asleep next door thinking she was just on the other side of the wall, but she hadn't been.

That meant the last place she'd been . . .

. . . was his room.

He ran out the door and nearly crashed into Danny on the sidewalk.

"Whoa. Slow down," Danny said.

Wes threw open the door to his room and raced inside. He scanned the space with new eyes, looking for any clue as to what might have happened to Anna.

"Hey, you all right?" Danny was standing in the entryway.

Wes dropped to his hands and knees and looked under the bed. About six inches in, there was a wood-sided pedestal that prevented anything from being pushed all the way under.

He checked the bathroom. Only his toiletries and Anna's toothbrush sticking out of a glass.

"Wes, what's going on?" Danny asked.

"Get the police," Wes said. "They're over at Tony's room."

"What? Why?"

"Just do it! Please."

Danny nodded and headed quickly out of the room.

Wes stepped back into the bedroom and took another look around.

First Tony and now Anna? What in God's name was happening?

His gaze stopped at the closet. It had double doors that opened to either side. The door on the left was sticking open a half inch. He knew he hadn't left it that way. He approached it, fearful of what he might find, but knowing he had to look. He placed a couple of fingers against the edge near the top and pulled.

For a second he forgot to breathe.

Someone had taken one of the suit hangers and turned it ninety degrees. Taped on the wooden crossbar was a newspaper clipping. It was folded in half, so he couldn't see what the article was.

He removed it from the hanger and opened it up.

LOCAL STUDENT MISSING

Under the headline was a picture of Jack Rice.

Danny reentered the room, Officer Rockwell right behind him.

"Mr. Stewart," Rockwell said. "You wanted to see me?"

Without even thinking, Wes folded the article and slipped it into his pocket, then said, "Someone else is—"

"What the hell is that?" Danny asked.

At first Wes thought Danny had seen him hide the

paper, but he was pointing at something behind Wes's shoulder.

Wes turned. Mounted on the inside of the open closet door was a full-length mirror. On it was a viscous substance that Wes recognized immediately.

Vaseline. Just like in Anna's original room.

There were words on Wes's mirror, also, only they were harder to distinguish because there was no steam to help make them stand out. Still, Wes could discern the message.

YOUR FAULT

CHAPTER
58

WES AND THE OTHERS WERE GATHERED IN A meeting room just off the motel lobby. Monroe was the only one sitting. Everyone else was either leaning against a wall or standing.

All, that is, except for Wes. He couldn't stop pacing.

"That's really annoying," Monroe said as he walked past her chair for the third time.

"Shut up, Monroe," Alison said.

Monroe sat up. "What did you say?"

"I said shut up."

"You shut up!" Monroe yelled.

"Really? That's the best you can come up with?"

"I don't know who the hell you think you are, but—"

"For God's sakes, Monroe, listen to yourself," Dione said. "You're acting like a jackass. There are two people missing, friends of ours. This isn't about you."

That quieted everyone.

Wes continued, undeterred, his mind going a million miles a second. The only thing he was sure of was that Commander Forman was behind Anna's disappearance.

He must have thought he could use her as leverage to keep Wes quiet.

But what about Tony?

That was a piece that didn't fit.

Unfortunately, Wes was sure telling the police about Forman's involvement would hamper the search more than help. They were already leaning toward the possibility that Wes had something to do with the other events. So it was doubtful any theory he put forward would be believed, especially a theory that centered on a Navy commander kidnapping citizens in order to cover up the identity of the person who had died in a fighter crash. No, if he wanted the police to believe him, he would have to bring them stronger evidence than he currently had. Irrefutable evidence. Evidence that started with the papers Lars had given him the night before. Unfortunately, those were still in his room. He needed to retrieve them, examine them, then work out what to do from there.

The door opened, and a uniformed officer ushered Dori inside.

"Got here as soon as I could," she said.

Danny walked over to her. "It's okay. They haven't talked to any of us yet."

Dione was looking at them, one brow raised.

"She was the last one to see Tony," Danny said. "I thought the police would want to talk to her. So I gave her a call."

Dione nodded. "Good thinking."

"I'm not sure how much help I'm going to be," Dori said.

"Did you see the people he was with?" Alison asked, hopeful.

"No . . . I don't know, maybe. It's possible they were

there, too. But he didn't introduce me to anyone. And I was at the counter when he left, so I didn't see who he walked out with."

"Maybe there was a security camera," Alison suggested. "Maybe they have footage of Tony and the others."

Dori's face brightened. "I hadn't thought of that."

As Wes walked by Danny and Dori, Dori reached out and touched his arm. "I can tell how important Anna is to you. I'm sure she's okay."

"Thanks," he mumbled.

The door opened again. This time Detectives Stevens and Andrews came in. One by one they began taking people into another room for questioning. They saved Wes for last, but just before they walked him out, Stevens said to the rest of the group, "You can all return to your rooms. But for at least the next couple of days, you're to remain in town."

"Hey," Monroe said, "I wasn't even here this weekend. There's no reason I need to stay."

"I'm sorry, Miss Banks. There are no exceptions."

"That's ridiculous!"

"Can it, Monroe," Dione said.

"Mr. Stewart," Stevens said, "if you'll come with us."

Dione caught Wes's eye. "We'll be in my room when you're done."

The cops led Wes through the motel lobby and into a staff break room. Inside, there were two small tables with three chairs each. They took the table nearest the door.

"So here we are again," Andrews said, sitting across from Wes.

Stevens flipped through some pages on the legal pad. "According to Officer Rockwell, you didn't realize that

Miss Mendes was gone until the police were already here to investigate Mr. Hall's disappearance."

"Yes."

"He also says that you and Miss Mendes are an item."

An item. The term sounded ridiculous to Wes. "Yes."

"And though you had separate rooms, you've stated you often shared the same room."

Wes nodded. "Everything I told the officer earlier is accurate."

"I'm sure it is," Stevens said. "We're just trying to be thorough. You understand."

Wes looked around the room, and tried to relax.

"It says here that you went out for a little bit last night while Miss Mendes remained in your room. But when you got back, she was no longer there."

"Again, correct."

"Is there a reason you didn't check her room at that time?"

"It was late. We had an early start this morning, so I thought I'd let her sleep."

"So the first time you realized something was wrong was when she didn't show up this morning?"

"Not exactly," Wes said. "At first I just thought that maybe she'd overslept. I didn't realize something was wrong until I went into her room."

"With the spare key she'd given you."

"Yes."

Stevens nodded. "And where did you go last night?"

"I'm sorry?"

"When you left Miss Mendes here at the motel. Where did you go?"

"I wasn't tired," Wes said. He'd prepped for this question. "So I decided to go for a walk."

"Do you do that often?"

"Sometimes."

"Once a week? Twice a week? Every other night?"

"Just when I feel like it."

Stevens eyed him for a moment. "All right. So you just went for a walk. How long?"

"Ended up being a few hours," he said. Alison's mention of security cameras earlier made him want to keep things close to reality time-wise in case the motel had them, too.

"That's some walk. Where did you go?"

Wes shrugged. "Just around. Looking for places I used to know when I lived here." He paused. "Ended up at a friend's house, but he wasn't there. Waited around for a while, but he didn't show up."

"So no one saw you?"

"Could have," Wes said. "But if you're asking me if I spoke to anyone, then no."

"Who was the friend?" Detective Andrews asked.

"Lars Andersen. We grew up together."

"And his address?"

"It's west of here. On Randall. I don't remember the street number."

"It *is* kind of curious, isn't it?" Stevens said.

"What is?"

Stevens leaned back. "Just one more thing where you're the common denominator."

Wes looked from one detective to the other. "I told you before, the only thing I have to do with any of this is that I'm one of the victims. It's asinine to be wasting time on this. Anna and Tony are in trouble. They need our help."

"We don't know for sure if they're in trouble or not," Andrews said. "If you had nothing to do with it, maybe they ran off together?"

Wes was momentarily speechless. "Are you kidding me?"

"It's another possibility, isn't it?"

"No. It's not."

"Mr. Stewart," Stevens said, "there's no reason to get upset."

Wes almost said something more, but cut himself off. It was clear the police weren't going to be any help. He needed to get this over with so he could find Anna and Tony himself.

"I'm sorry," Wes said, then took a deep breath. "As far as I know, there was absolutely nothing between Anna and Tony. She and I have a very good relationship. She's not the kind of person who would have been messing around with someone else behind my back. She's the kind of person who would have just told me."

"If that's the case, then you're a lucky man," Stevens said.

"Yes. I am," Wes said, not feeling lucky at all.

CHAPTER
59

EVERYONE BUT MONROE WAS GATHERED IN Dione's room. According to Danny, the host of *Close to Home* was in her room on the phone with her agent.

Dione was just finishing up a call of her own as she let Wes in.

"Well, that's official," she said as soon as she'd hung up. "Production on our 'High Desert' episode is suspended."

"It wasn't like we could shoot anything right now anyway," Danny said.

There were murmurs of ascent.

"Did the police tell you anything?" Dione asked Wes.

Wes shook his head. "Just asked me questions."

"So now what?" Alison asked. "We just stay here and wait?"

"I think as long as we stay within city limits, we're fine," Dione said.

Alison folded her arms across her chest. "Well, that makes a huge difference."

"I'm getting hungry," Danny said. "Anyone interested in getting something to eat? Wes?"

"I think I'm going to pass," Wes said. "I'll check back with you all later."

He started for the door, anxious to take a look at Lars's papers.

"Where are you going?" Alison asked.

"I don't know. Out. I just need some air."

Alison started to get up. "I'll go with you."

"No. I kind of want to be alone. Okay?" His words came out sharper than he'd expected, so it wasn't surprising Alison looked like she'd been slapped. He knew he should tell her he was sorry, but he just needed to get out of there.

He headed for his room, but when he got there he found it still full of police.

"I'm sorry, sir," the cop at the door said. "I can't let you in."

"It's my room."

"The crime techs are still looking around. You'll have to come back later."

Dammit. Wes thought for a moment. "Can I at least grab a clean shirt? I hadn't expected to spend all day in this one."

The cop looked back into the room, then said, "Where is it?"

Wes pointed at the pile of clothes on the dresser. "It'd be easier if I just grabbed it."

The cop frowned, then jerked his head toward the pile. "Make it quick."

"Thank you."

At the dresser, Wes made a show of going through the clothes. As he did, he moved a black T-shirt out so that it completely covered Lars's papers. Then he bundled it all up and walked back across the room.

Though his instinct was to race out and find someplace where he could look at the pages undisturbed, he didn't want to raise any red flags. At the door he asked the cop, "When do you think I can get back in for good?"

"I'd give it a few hours," the officer said. "Probably around two."

"Great." Wes lifted the shirt. "Thanks again."

"You're welcome."

Wes walked over to the Triumph and stuck the shirt and the pages into the storage compartment behind the seat, then hopped on. There was every chance Detective Andrews would see him on it, but he didn't care. Not today.

As he pulled onto China Lake Boulevard his mind was so focused on his concern about Anna he almost didn't notice the sedan that pulled out of the Desert Rose parking lot a few seconds after he did. It was dark blue and, except for the color, looked very much like one of the cars that had cornered Lars the night before.

Wes decreased his speed a little to see if the sedan would pass him, but it also slowed, and kept pace about ten car lengths back.

Wes could feel his anger growing. Forman again. Watching him. He was sure of it. But as much as he would have liked to confront the driver, he needed to know what was in Lars's papers more.

He eyed the road ahead, all the while keeping tabs on the sedan.

Then, at the last possible second, he took a sharp right, and hit the accelerator. He checked his mirror again and grimaced. The sedan had made the turn behind him.

If he had any doubts he was being followed, they were gone now.

But the driver of the sedan had made a mistake. He was hanging too far back.

Wes took a left, then sped to the end of the block, and turned left again before the sedan had even made the first turn. Two intersections on, he turned right and knew he'd lost his pursuer. Just to be sure, though, he made several more random turns.

The sedan made no reappearance.

A couple minutes later he spotted the old Carl's Jr. where Lars had worked in high school. It was as good a choice as anywhere else, so he turned into the lot and parked. He grabbed the papers out of the storage compartment and headed inside.

After he got a soda, he took a seat in a booth near the back, set his drink out of the way, and placed the papers on the table.

The top page was some sort of personnel information sheet. In the upper right corner was a black-and-white photograph of Lieutenant Adair. It was the same photo the newspaper had run. To the left was the kind of information you would expect: name, birth date, height, weight, education. Oddly, the line for current address was blank. Under "Family" was written: "Wife—Stacey. Children—Darla, Rachel." Each name had a corresponding birth date.

Below that was a list of military postings. Most were configurations of numbers and letters that Wes didn't recognize. Fleets designations? Maybe squadrons?

There were several more sections. "Rank History." "Commendations." "Special Training." Most contained few entries or none at all.

By the lack of information, Wes would have assumed Lieutenant Adair had been only an average officer at best. But there was no such thing as an average fighter pilot.

More confused now than he'd been when he'd started reading, he set the sheet to the side and looked at the second page. Printed on it was a description of a weapons system the F-18 had been equipped with during its ill-fated flight, called SCORCH. Wes didn't understand most of the technical jargon, but what he did understand was that the SCORCH system had been integrated into the operating system of the plane itself.

The third page, as far as he could tell, had nothing to do with Adair at all. It concerned something known as Project Pastiche.

PROJECT PASTICHE

Project Pastiche is based at the Pentagon. All inquires concerning the project should be made through Admiral Nolan Barker in Naval Operations. All further information is classified.

PP-214

The only other information was an initiation date of two years previous. Why Lars had thought it was important was lost on Wes.

He started to set the page down, then stopped and looked at it again.

PP-214.

He picked up the personnel sheet, then looked at the list of Adair's previous postings. There it was at the bottom. Adair's very first posting: PP-214.

Did that mean Adair had been part of Project Pastiche?

He looked back at the project sheet, specifically at the initiation date, and frowned. The dates didn't line up. Adair's service in PP-214 was listed as occurring prior to when Project Pastiche had been in existence.

Maybe the designation was used for more than one thing? That didn't sound very organized, and if the Navy was one thing, it was organized.

Not sure how the pieces fit together, he put the pages to the side and took a look at the last sheet. On it were two lists.

PP-214 Personnel

Barker, Nolan	Admiral	
Lorang, Kyle	Commander	Operations
Butler, Thomas	Lieutenant	Computer Technician
Karner, Kenneth	Lieutenant	Computer Technician
West, Thomas	Lieutenant	Computer Technician

PP-214 Pool 7B

Lemon, Theodore	Lieutenant	Complete
Faith, Brian	assign	Available
Briley, Donnel	Lieutenant	Complete
Adair, Lawrence	Lieutenant	Complete
Bruce, Cameron	assign	Available

So Adair *was* tied to Project Pastiche. But what did "Pool 7B" mean? And how were those in it different from those listed under "Personnel"?

As Wes was trying to make sense of everything, his gaze strayed over to the papers he'd already examined. Something on the second sheet caught Wes's attention. It was near the top. A short, almost invisible crease.

No, not quite a crease.

He flipped the page over. On the back was a word

written in blue ink. With everything that had happened, Wes had forgotten Lars had taken the sheet back and written something on it. He had said it was "the key."

The word was "Jamieson." It meant nothing to Wes. Sure, it was a name. But was it a first or last? Or even the name of a place? Perhaps it was a project designation.

Whatever the case, it was just one more piece of the puzzle, and try as Wes might, there wasn't enough in any of the papers for him to get a grasp of what it all meant.

He needed a computer, but not just any computer. It had to be one that wouldn't bring Commander Forman straight to him while he was using it.

Unless . . .

He stared out the window, thinking for a moment, then nodded to himself.

Casey.

He started to grab his cellphone, then stopped. After Lars's paranoia the night before had proven justified, Wes didn't know if he could trust his phone to make the call. What he needed was a landline no one could tie him to.

It only took him a couple seconds to come up with a solution for that, too.

CHAPTER
60

THE MAN IN THE SEDAN WAS ALREADY EXITING the Desert Rose parking lot when he saw Stewart race out ahead of him on his motorcycle. The watcher didn't let that stop him, though. He had things to do, and Stewart wasn't his concern for the moment. Still, he kept his pace slow so that he wasn't accidentally spotted.

He was surprised when Stewart made the same turn off China Lake Boulevard he needed to make, but decided not to change his plans, so he made the turn, too.

It was when Stewart increased his speed and took a sudden turn to the left that the man realized that Stewart had indeed seen him. It was an annoyance more than a problem. The distance between them was too great for Stewart to have seen the man's face.

Laughing as he passed the street Stewart had disappeared on, the man continued on his way west, beyond the city limits. When he reached the familiar dirt road, he turned left, automatically slowing to a near crawl to keep the washboard surface from rattling his car into a pile of useless scrap.

The lots in this area were each two and a half acres,

though many had been joined together to create five-acre desert kingdoms. The driveway the man turned down led onto one of these larger parcels.

Near the rear of the property was a light gray one-story house. It hadn't always been that color. When the man had painted it twenty-five years earlier, it had been light blue, but the desert sun had burned most of the tint out. He could have repainted it, but that would have been too much work for a place he seldom visited anymore.

He swung the sedan around, then backed it up so that the trailer hitch on the rear was only a few feet from the empty horse trailer parked underneath the attached carport. When the time came, it would only take him a couple minutes to hook them together.

Once inside, he headed straight for the kitchen, pulled a bottle of Gatorade out of the ancient refrigerator, then made his way to the bedroom that had once been his as a child.

On the floor was the duffel bag containing his clothes. He changed shirts, then glanced at the uncomfortable blow-up mattress in the corner. He was tired, sure, but not quite that tired yet. God, he couldn't wait until he was back in his cozy bed at home, his wife beside him. But there was work still to be done, so that little pleasure would have to wait.

Standing, he stretched, then walked back to the master suite. This had been his parents' room when they'd still been alive, but they wouldn't have recognized it now. All their 1950s-era furniture was gone, replaced by stacks of banker boxes full of newspapers and bills and files containing God knew what—all stuff his wife didn't want to get rid of but also didn't want at their house.

He turned on the light. Recently he'd covered the windows with plywood sheeting, creating a dark, cavelike

atmosphere. He kind of liked it, and thought he'd probably end up leaving them in place when he was done.

The woman was exactly where he'd left her, lying on
the small air mattress in the center of the room. Her
wrists and ankles were still tied, but there was no chance
she was going anywhere. The intravenous drip hooked
to her right arm, 0.5 percent Beta-Somnol in saline, took
care of that. She was in dreamland, and would be until
he decided otherwise.

He'd been surprised at how easy getting her into his
car at the motel had been.

"Miss Mendes?" he had said after she'd answered the
knock on the door to Stewart's room.

"Yes?"

"I'm Detective Thompson. I understand you're a
friend of Wesley Stewart?"

"Yes," she said. The concern on her face was both
sudden and predictable. "Is something wrong?"

The man had hesitated just enough to sell the lie.
"There's been an accident."

"An accident? Is Wes all right?"

"I'm afraid he's going into surgery. But before they
put him under, he asked for you. I was sent here to drive
you over."

"Yes. Yes, please." She moved back into the room,
slipped on her shoes, then grabbed a purse off the dresser
and joined him outside.

"I should let Dione know," she said. "Our boss."

"Do you just want to call her from the hospital once
you know a little more?"

She nodded. "Yeah. Good idea. I'll do that."

He stuck the needle in her leg before he even started
the car, and she was out a few seconds later. No scream,
no fuss. The only physical work he'd had to undertake

was carrying her into his parents' place once they got there.

The man checked her pulse, then turned off the light and closed the door.

Now he could take that nap.

CHAPTER
61

WES DROVE ACROSS TOWN, WORKING HIS WAY through neighborhoods he hadn't visited since he was a teenager, avoiding the main drags completely. Twice he turned down side streets when sedans pulled onto the road behind him. And twice he watched the sedans drive by without a glance in his direction.

Nerves on edge, he continued toward Downs Avenue. As he got closer his thoughts turned from worrying about being followed to worrying that the pay phone he was heading toward might not be there any longer. They were a dying breed, after all.

As he turned into the 7-Eleven at the corner of Downs and Inyokern Road, he allowed himself a small grin in relief. It *was* still there, right where he remembered it, next to a waist-high concrete wall that lined the edge of the parking lot.

He parked the bike so that it was facing outward, ready to move, then picked up the phone, deposited some change, and dialed his friend's number.

"Hello?" Casey said.

"It's Wes."

"If you're calling about that picture, I haven't been able to find any information yet."

Wes had forgotten he'd sent his friend the picture he'd found on the Web.

"Not the picture. Something else I need you to check on."

"I'm just about to head out to lunch. Whatever it is, I'll help you when I—"

"I'm in trouble," Wes said quickly.

There was dead air for a moment. "What kind of trouble?"

"Bad trouble."

"Hold on."

There was a click, and a prerecorded promo for the Quest Network's "Strange History Week" let Wes know he was on hold. Thirty seconds later, another click and Casey was back.

"Judy just went to lunch," he said. "More privacy in her office. Now, what do you mean you're in trouble?"

Wes quickly told his friend what had been going on.

"A cover-up?" Casey said.

"That's what I think."

"And they've taken Anna and this Tony guy?" His tone bespoke his disbelief.

"I know, it sounds nuts. But I don't see any other ex- planation. The police are investigating, but I highly doubt they're going to find them. And even if I tell them all this, they won't listen to me. I need more proof. Something that will force them to believe me."

"What can I do to help?"

"You ready to take some notes?" Wes asked.

"Absolutely."

CHAPTER
62

CASEY TOLD WES TO GIVE HIM THIRTY MINUTES and he'd call back. Wes moved into the shade in front of the store, but still close enough to hear the phone if it rang.

He knew this was all his fault. Nothing would have happened at all if he'd just stayed in L.A. His dad had told him not to come back. Had insisted, actually. And for seventeen years Wes had stayed away.

He ran a hand through his hair, the desert breeze blowing around him. Then, like now . . . if he'd only walked away.

Sometimes the right thing isn't the easy thing. His father's voice, often silent, but always there.

Gee, thanks, Dad.

But the voice was right. He could never have walked away. Not now, and certainly not then.

CHAPTER
63

WES PARKED THE VAN ALONG THE SIDE OF THE dirt road where all the other cars had parked, then he, Lars, and Mandy piled out.

In the distance, they could hear music. U2, "Even Better Than the Real Thing."

They'd gone only a dozen feet when Wes looked back at Lars. "Beer?"

His friend cringed, then ran back to the van and retrieved the six-pack he'd left on the floor.

As they reached the head of the trail leading to the Rocks, Michael Dillman stepped out of the shadows and blocked their way. "Evening, children. This is a party for grown-ups tonight. You bring any beer?"

Dillman was huge for a high school kid, at least six foot four, and had to be over two hundred and fifty pounds. All of which made him the perfect defensive lineman for the high school football team. It also made him the perfect candidate for party enforcer.

Lars held up the six-pack of Budweiser he'd liberated from his father's refrigerator.

"Cool," Dillman said, his whole body nodding with his head. "Have fun."

Wes, Lars, and Mandy walked past the human roadblock and started up the path.

Growing up in the desert had some very distinct advantages. The first, and maybe the most important, was that with all that space, a teenager could get into and out of trouble without anyone in authority ever knowing about it: off-roading, hiking, and, of course, partying.

There were a lot of places in the hills outside of Ridgecrest where the high school kids could party. Wagon Wheel, the Ravine, the Wash, and the Drama Rocks—the last the location of the party that night. The Drama Rocks got its name because it'd first been "discovered" by members of the high school drama club back in the 1970s. In the years after, its use had grown to encompass a larger cross section of the school, but the name had stuck.

The Rocks were located high in the hills southeast of town. To one side you could see the faint glow of lights from Ridgecrest and China Lake, and to the other the Trona Pinnacles on Searles Lake.

The main feature of the Rocks was a massive, teardrop-shaped boulder that had been sheered away on one side, creating the perfect windbreak for a bonfire. Even better, it was positioned so that it was impossible for anyone—law enforcement, parents—on the distant highway to see the flames.

Around this there were other rocks, thousands of them. Some piled on top of one another, creating little alcoves where those looking for a little one-on-one time could find some privacy. Others jutted outward, creating unseen drop-offs of ten or twenty or even thirty feet.

More than one drunken teenager had taken a wrong step and found themselves with a broken leg or dislocated shoulder. But no matter what happened up there, no one ever gave away its location. It was a sanctuary that remained known only to those who needed the freedom it represented.

While Wes and Lars *were* more experienced with the Rocks than Mandy, it wasn't by much. On their first visit they'd left after only an hour when they got bored waiting for anyone they knew to show up. Their second trip up had actually been during the day, when no one else was around. They'd wanted to see what it looked like in the sunlight, but had been disappointed by all the garbage and graffiti created by decades of drunken teenagers. They'd ended up enjoying the hike they'd taken in the area around the Rocks more, finding a couple of abandoned mines cut into the side of the hills and a few rusted soup cans that must have been over fifty years old. They had kept the cans, but had avoided going into the mines because often not very far inside there were deep holes dug straight down through the floor that were hard to see before you were already stepping into them.

This party was their third trip.

But since Mandy was a Rocks virgin, everything was new and exciting to her. She found out about the party from her older sister, who offered to act as guide, but had gotten sick the day before and couldn't go. Mandy had then begged Wes and Lars to come with her instead.

Music wafted down the path—R.E.M., Springsteen, Nirvana—growing louder and louder the closer they got. They passed a group of stoners who were laughing at some unknown joke and sharing a joint, and three guys Wes recognized from history class, drinking beer and throwing rocks at the stars.

"Slow down a little," Lars said. He'd fallen behind, already winded.

"Come on, Pudge," Wes said, channeling his father. "Pick it up."

"Don't call me that!"

A few moments later a voice off to the side said, "What are you looking at?"

Wes turned and saw two people tucked into a nook. It was too dark there to see their faces, but he could tell one was a girl, her shirt opened to her waist.

"Nothing," Lars said quickly.

"Pervert," she sneered, then turned back to her friend.

Lars double-timed it up to Wes and Anna. "Well, this should be fun."

The path narrowed, forcing them to shuffle through single file. Then the miniature canyon opened onto the clearing. At the far end, flames shot upward against the backdrop of the tear-shaped boulder. Surrounding the bonfire on the remaining three sides had to be over a hundred teenagers—drinking and laughing and talking, and some even dancing to the blaring music.

"There's more people here than I thought there'd be," Mandy said.

"Definitely bigger than the last party we were at," Lars said.

They stood where they were for a moment, suddenly intimidated.

"Come on," Wes finally said, taking a step forward.

As they neared the fire a voice called out, "Wes Stewart?"

A tall, thin teenager pulled himself out of the crowd at the flames. In his hand was a bottle of Jack Daniel's.

"Hey, Dodson," Wes said.

Slightly unstable, Gary Dodson negotiated his way over to them. "Never thought I'd see you at one of these."

"It's not my first time," Wes said defensively.

Gary thrust the bottle of Jack forward. "Drink?"

"No, thanks."

Gary offered it to Lars and Mandy; both declined.

"Ain't no fun if you're going to stand around sober all night," he said.

Lars held up the six-pack of beer. "Not planning on it."

Gary laughed. "Splitting that between the three of you, you won't even get buzzed." He stumbled off, chuckling to himself.

They soon found themselves standing near the fire, each holding a beer. Occasionally a partygoer would fall down, but since it was relatively early, most were still sober enough to get back up again.

Two beers and a few boring hours later, Wes walked out into the desert to relieve himself. As he was heading back to the fire, Carly Jones, a girl from his journalism class, cornered him. "Have a joint?"

"Uh . . . no," Wes said. "Sorry."

"No problem. I have one." She pulled a half-smoked roach out of her pocket and held it near her mouth. "Please tell me you have a light at least."

Wes shrugged apologetically. "I don't."

"Damn." She took a step closer, crossing into his personal space. "How are you going to make it up to me?"

He countered with a step back. "See if someone has a lighter?"

She reached out and touched him on the chest, her finger slipping through the gap between buttons and

touching his skin. "That's not what I was hoping for."
Carly had never been shy about making her interest in
him clear. It was a one-way infatuation.

Wes half moved, half slapped her hand away. "Let me
get that match." He flashed a smile and dodged past her.

Back at the fire, he found Lars in nearly the same spot
where he left him, and immediately said, "I think I see a
shooting star."

Lars shot a look at the sky. "Where?"

"No, moron. I think I see a *shooting star*," Wes repeated their exit code phrase.

"Oh, *right*." Lars nodded. "Thank God. I've been
ready to leave for thirty minutes."

"Why didn't you say something before?"

"I thought you were having fun."

Wes rolled his eyes. "Where's Mandy?"

"I . . . uh . . . thought she was right here."

"That's just great."

They couldn't leave without her, so Wes began asking
people if they knew where she was, but got nothing better than shrugs in response. Finally a girl named Cheri
Knight pointed into the darkness to the east. "Think I
saw her go that way. Probably taking a pee."

They found a spot against one of the rocks and waited.
But when Mandy didn't show up after several minutes,
Wes got restless. "I'll go check and see if she's really out
there. You stay here in case I miss her."

Wes turned down the path and began calling out her
name. But the only thing he heard in response was the
music and the rumble of the party behind him.

He kept walking. "Mandy?"

Still nothing.

He figured she couldn't have gone much farther than

he already was, so he was beginning to think Cheri had been wrong.

Somewhere ahead he heard a noise. It had been brief, so he wasn't sure if it had been a voice or just the breeze through the bushes.

He hesitated a moment, and was about to turn back to the party when he heard it again. Only longer this time. A cry. At least he thought it was a cry.

Wes began to run toward it. Ahead, there was a small ridge lined with boulders along the crest. As he neared the top he heard another sound. Different this time. Definitely a voice, but deeper than the first.

Then the original voice screamed.

Wes raced to the top, pulling himself quickly over the rocks to see what was happening. But the deep darkness of the desert hid more than it revealed.

A grunt, and a muffled cry, both from somewhere below and to the left.

Wes looked around, trying to find a way down the hill. He spotted a narrow trail about ten feet to his left and leapt toward it. Going faster than he knew he should, he all but stumbled down the hill. As he neared the bottom he threw his hands out toward a boulder to slow his progress, and barely avoided tumbling to the ground.

He paused for a second, took a deep breath, then pushed himself around a pile of rocks.

Mandy was lying on the ground ten feet away, terrified. One arm was trying to cover her exposed breasts, while the other was pulling down what was left of her shirt toward her bare waist. Her pants were lying on the ground off to the side.

And she wasn't alone.

Jack Rice was kneeling between her legs, his pants

pulled down. "Turn over and get on your knees. We're not done."

"What the hell's going on?" Wes said.

Jack whipped around. "Get out of here, Stewart."

Wes took a couple steps forward. "Mandy, are you okay?"

"She's fine," Jack said. "Now leave us alone, ass-hole."

Mandy turned away from Wes and began to sob.

"What did you do to her?" Wes demanded.

Jack got to his feet and pulled his pants up. "I said get out of here!" Mandy started to push herself up and away from Jack. But as soon as she was on her feet, he grabbed her and pulled her against him. "Where you going, baby?"

"Let her go!" Wes said.

Jack sneered. "We're having some alone time, Stewart. So this is none of your goddamn business."

Wes took another step forward, his hands clenching into fists at his side. "Let! Her! Go!"

Jack had a good four inches on Wes, and at least fifty pounds. But Wes wasn't thinking about any of that. The only thing on his mind was Mandy.

"Leave right now, Stewart," Jack said, "and maybe I won't beat the crap out of you."

Wes held his ground. "Right now, Jack!"

Mandy let out a loud cry as Jack tightened his grip. Looking at Wes, he said, "You're not very smart, are you?"

"I'm not leaving," Wes said.

"Your choice." Jack pushed Mandy to the ground, then glared at her. "You move and you're dead."

She pulled her legs to her chest and tried to curl up into a ball.

"What did you do to her?" Wes said.

Jack laughed, his alcohol-infused breath reaching Wes a second later. "*Do* to her? You think she didn't want it? Hell, she was begging me for more just before you got here."

"Begging you? That's not what it looked like to me!"

Jack lunged at Wes, telegraphing his move a half second before he stepped. Wes easily jumped out of Jack's line of fire, but what he didn't anticipate was Jack's arm flailing out as he passed by.

A meaty fist caught Wes just above his hip. Pain reverberated in an electric shock across his pelvis as he spun backward, tripped, and fell into a sage bush.

Wes tried to push himself up as Jack swung back in his direction. But he was unable to get to his feet before Jack was on him.

"You're screwed now!" Jack yelled in Wes's ear.

Blows began landing against Wes's sides and arms. Wild blows, made sloppy by beer and rage.

Wes did his best to absorb the onslaught, twisting and turning each time he was struck, but even unfocused, Jack was strong, and each hit was more and more painful.

Thwap.

Jack yelled out, one of his hands grabbing the side of his face as blood trickled down his cheek.

Not wasting the opportunity, Wes pushed up on Jack's chest, then slid to the left as Jack tumbled over and hit the ground. Freed, Wes scrambled to his feet again. He aimed a kick at Jack's ribs, but Jack twisted to the side and regained his footing. Wes braced himself to be rushed again, but Jack, his palm pressed against his bloody face, stared past him at something else.

"You bitch!" he yelled.

Wes glanced over his shoulder.

Mandy was standing a dozen feet away. She had pulled her pants back on, and was holding a rock in her hand. The sound he'd heard must have been a similar stone connecting with Jack's face.

"Run, Mandy! Get out of here!" Wes yelled.

She hesitated a moment, then sprinted into the brush. Wes pivoted to follow her, but Jack slammed a fist into Wes's back, knocking him sideways, then took off after Mandy.

Wes knew he couldn't give in to the pain. He forced himself forward, slowly for a few steps, but soon gained speed.

He couldn't see Mandy, but he could see Jack's silhouette moving up the slope between rocks and brush. He tried to close the gap, but the terrain made it difficult.

As he neared the top he heard Mandy scream, "Leave me alone!"

Wes scaled a boulder like it wasn't even there, then spotted Mandy and Jack just off to the left on top of a flat slab of stone. Jack was standing a few feet in front of Mandy, his back to Wes. As scared as she must have been, she was still holding on to her stone, ready to throw.

"Put the goddamn rock down," Jack ordered.

She raised the rock a few inches. "Get away from me!"

"I said put it down!"

Wes moved as quietly as he could across the rocks, staying out of Jack's line of sight.

"You don't want to mess with me," Jack told Mandy. "Put it down and I'll let you go back to the party."

She shook her head.

"Drop the rock, or I swear I'll—"

Wes, head lowered, raced forward and slammed into Jack's back. A loud expulsion of air escaped Jack's mouth as he was knocked off his feet.

Mandy leapt to her right, just barely getting out of his way.

As soon as Jack got back up, he whirled around, his eyes wild with rage.

But this time Wes was ready. As Jack made a run at him, Wes dodged to the side, then swung a fist as hard as he could into Jack's ear.

Jack cried out in pain and grabbed the side of his head. "You're dead, Stewart!"

He took a step toward Wes and swung with a right. Wes leaned back enough so that the blow glanced off his arm, then he moved in, landing two quick jabs to Jack's stomach. He immediately stepped back out of range as Jack's next swing caught only air.

Jack roared in frustration. He swung and missed again.

Wes attempted another blow, but this time Jack threw his arm up, blocking it, then hit Wes hard in the gut.

Staggering backward, Wes tried to get out of the way of the next punch, but was only partially successful as the blow meant for his chin found his shoulder instead. He winced as pain shot across his chest. When he was able to focus again, Jack was standing in front of him, grinning as if the fight was over and he'd won.

"Once I'm done with you, I'm going to make sure your girlfriend never forgets me," Jack said, sneering.

A ball of heat deep inside Wes's chest began to pulsate. A heat that remembered Jack the bully hitting kids in junior high for no reason, remembered Jack and his buddies throwing milkshakes at Wes's friends during lunch, remembered Jack groping Mandy's chest, her shirt in tatters.

The sound that came out of Wes's mouth began as a rumble and turned into a roar as he lunged toward Jack and began swinging.

Stomach.

Arm.

Face.

Arm.

Chest.

Face.

Stomach.

He kept throwing punches as fast as he could. Jack first tried to counter, but quickly moved his arms up to protect himself.

More blows, one after another after another.

Jack tried to move back out of range, but Wes matched him step for step.

"Watch out!" Mandy yelled.

Wes wasn't listening. He continued to hit Jack, oblivious to everything else.

"What the hell's going on?"

Lars's voice. Nearby, but unimportant.

Shoulder.

Face.

Ribs.

"Wes, the edge!" Mandy called.

"Stop! Goddammit! Stop!" Jack yelled. "I give. All right? I give."

That got through.

Wes dropped his arms to the side, panting. He realized that he had backed Jack up to within inches of the rock's edge. Beyond was a drop of at least two dozen feet.

"What the hell's wrong with you?" Jack asked moving his arms away from his face.

Wes breathed deeply several times. "You should have . . . never . . . touched her."

"Yeah?" Jack cocked his head. "Well, to hell with you." His hand snapped out and grabbed Wes's arm. He jerked Wes toward him, his intent clear. He wanted to send Wes over the drop.

Wes jammed his legs down, trying to stop, but his feet slipped across the boulder.

"Wes!" Mandy yelled.

Wes twisted wildly, trying to dislodge Jack's grip on his wrist with his other hand, but Jack held tight.

I'm going to die, Wes thought.

Then he felt someone grab his other hand and start to pull him in the other direction. "Let him go!" Lars yelled as he tried to yank Wes back.

Jack started to give Wes's arm another jerk, but just as he did, Wes shoved his arm downward. The unexpected movement broke Jack's grip, and the momentum that had been pulling Wes toward the edge transferred back to Jack.

Jack's eyes went wide as his arms began pinwheeling. In a desperate lunge, he reached out and caught hold of Wes's wrist, his fingers digging into Wes's skin. "Help me!"

Wes could feel Jack's palm grow slick with sweat, but he didn't move.

"I'm slipping," Jack said, panicked.

Another memory: Jack sticking his foot out in the lunchroom and tripping Kenny Morgan, one of the special-needs kids. Kenny's food splattering on the floor, his glass landing underneath him, breaking in two. "Dumbass," Jack had said.

And one final one: Jack kneeling between Mandy's legs, laughing at what he'd just done.

Some people didn't deserve the air they consumed.

"Help me!" Jack screamed.

His fingers were beginning to lose their grip. Wes stared at him for a second, then twisted his wrist ninety degrees.

One second Jack Rice was standing in front of him. Then the next he wasn't.

CHAPTER 64

WES, LARS, AND MANDY—NOW WEARING LARS'S hoodie—climbed down the slope to Jack Rice's body at the base of the rock.

"I think he's dead," Lars said.

Wes knelt down and checked Jack's pulse just to make sure. Lars was right. The son of a bitch wouldn't cause anyone grief anymore.

"We'll have to call the police," Wes said finally.

Mandy tensed. "Are you sure? I mean, do we really have to?"

"He's dead, Mandy. We don't have a choice."

They stood silently beside one another, looking down at the body. In the distance they could hear music from the party, faint, almost indistinguishable from the breeze.

"I don't know, Wes," Lars said. "Maybe Mandy has a point."

"What are you talking about?"

Lars looked at Mandy. "Did anyone see you with him?"

She shook her head. "He was out here when I came

looking for a place to go to the bathroom. Said he'd be my lookout if anyone else came. I didn't think he'd . . . I didn't think . . . thought he was my friend."

Wes put an arm around her shoulder. She started to pull away, but then stopped.

"It's okay," he said. "Don't think about it."

"So no one saw us with him," Lars said. "And there's no way anyone at the party could have heard anything. So . . . maybe we just don't tell anyone."

"Are you crazy?" Wes said, hardly believing what his friend had just suggested.

"It's not worth ruining our lives for that son of a bitch," Lars told him. "Think about it. You just killed someone. You want to ruin your life over that asshole?"

Wes's mom had often joked that teenagers treated every crisis like it was the end of the world. Only this time, Wes and his friends knew it would be. Once the police got involved, their lives would never be the same.

But to not tell anyone?

"Okay," Lars continued. "If you don't want to think about yourself, think about Mandy. What's her life going to be like once everything comes out? She's going to have to tell the police what Jack did to her. And she's not going to have to just tell it once. She'll have to do it over and over. And then she'll have to tell it again at your trial, in front of the public and reporters. Do you really want her to go through that?"

Wes glanced at Mandy. He could see the effect Lars's words had on her, the fear that what he was saying might come true. "So you're suggesting we just leave him here?" he asked, then, in a voice less confident than before, added, "We can't do that."

Lars looked out toward Searles Lake, then shook his head. "No. You're right. That's not a good idea. He's got your blood on him. If someone finds the body, the police will question everyone who was at the party. When they see that you're bruised up from a fight, it won't be hard for them to put two and two together. We can't let them find the body, not while you look like that. We have to put him someplace where no one will find him."

"Lars," Wes said, "even when he's reported missing, the police will still question everyone who was at the party."

"Sure," Lars said. "But they're not going to be looking for someone who's been beat up. In fact, we can tell them that you and I got into a fight if we have to. Hell, you should punch me right now."

"I'm not going to punch you."

"Fine, but you see my point, right?"

Wes stared past his friend, then put his head in his hands as the full weight of what had happened finally hit him. "Oh, God. I should have grabbed him."

"Are you kidding? He would have taken you both over. You wouldn't have been able to stop."

"We don't know that," Wes said.

"We do know that," Lars said. "He was going over with or without you. Look, the longer we wait, the more chance someone will wander out here and see us."

Everything was swimming through Wes's mind. The fight. The fall. What Jack had done to Mandy. Her screams. The police. His parents.

He couldn't focus.

Lars shook Wes's shoulder. "Hey! Did you hear me?"

Wes slowly nodded. "What are you suggesting we do?"

Lars looked around, then pointed to the east. "Didn't we find an old mine over that next ridge?"

Wes couldn't remember what he said after that, but he did remember him and Lars struggling to carry Jack across the side of the hill. And he did remember finding the mine with a hole ten yards in that went straight down for God knew how far. Lars didn't even give Wes a chance to second-guess their actions. He just rolled the body over the edge.

CHAPTER
65

WES HAD ACTUALLY BROKEN THE PROMISE HE'D made to Lars and Mandy not to tell anyone about that night. But he had never mentioned their names, only his own involvement. Of course, his father wasn't dumb, and though he didn't say anything to Wes, he would have known who else was involved.

They had sat in silence after Wes had finished telling him what had happened. Wes was sure his dad was going to force him to go to the cops and confess.

"This girl, you're positive he raped her?"

"One hundred percent."

Wes's dad drew in a deep breath, then exhaled loudly through his nose. "There are times we're faced with near-impossible situations. Ones where no matter which choice we make, neither direction feels like a good one. But most times, even in these circumstances, while there might not be a good choice, there's always a right one. And I'd say you made the right one."

His father didn't make him go to the police. He saw things in much the same way Lars had seen them. "I'll take care of this."

Two weeks later his parents sat him down in the living room and told him they were splitting up. Wes was to move to San Diego with his mother, while his dad would be staying in Ridgecrest. Wes had known things were bad between them, but it was still a shock. Several hours later his father found him in his room.

"Two things you need to know," his father said. "First, you had absolutely nothing to do with the problems your mother and I are having. It is what it is, and what we talked about tonight has been a long time coming. The second thing, and I want you to listen to me very carefully, once you get to San Diego you are never, ever to come back here again."

"Never? But when will—"

"No," Wes's dad said. "There's no questioning this." He paused. "I went out last week to the mine near . . . what did you call it? The Rocks?"

Wes stared at his dad, too surprised to confirm.

"I found some timbers farther back in the shaft and tossed them in the hole. The chance that somebody will find what's down there is almost zero. But if they do, I want you away from here. There's nothing there that's going to tie you to the body."

"My blood is on him."

"I took care of it. Your job is to just stay away."

In that instant Wes realized what his father had really done. He had gone to the mine, left footprints there, touched items that were now down the shaft with Jack's body. If the body was found, his father was going to take the blame.

"I can't ask you to—"

"No, you can't," his dad said. "I don't want to hear any more about it. This subject is closed."

CHAPTER
66

WES PICKED UP THE PHONE ON THE FIRST RING.

"Casey?"

No voice, just a faint double beep.

"Casey, can you hear me?"

Nothing for several moments, then a click, and the line went dead.

Confused, Wes started to hang the phone up. Suddenly he heard the sound of tires screeching on asphalt. He looked back toward the street.

Two dark sedans, the same military issue Lars had been driving, had just made the turn off Inyokern Road onto Downs, and were making a beeline for the convenience store parking lot.

"No," Wes whispered to himself.

He dropped the phone and jumped on the Triumph.

There was no time to do anything with Lars's papers, so he squeezed them between his hand and the grip as he kick-started the bike to life.

The lead car adjusted its course to intercept him, so Wes turned hard as he hit the gas, and raced past the near side of the sedan, then turned again and headed for the exit. But before he could get there, the second car skidded to a halt across the ramp, blocking the way.

Wes angled to his left, shot across the sidewalk, and flew off the curb. The tires shimmied as they hit the road, but sheer willpower kept the Triumph upright.

As Wes glanced over he got a quick glimpse of the second car's driver. It was Lieutenant Jenks.

Cursing under his breath, he took off down the street. Someone must have found out what Casey was doing, and discovered the call to the pay phone at the 7-Eleven. It was the only explanation.

Back at the store, the sedans sped out of the lot and took up the chase. They were faster than he'd expected. With every block, they got a little closer. If he was going to lose them, it wasn't speed that was going to do it for him.

He took a quick right, his turn going wide and taking him into the path of an approaching panel van. He swerved toward the sidewalk, barely missing the vehicle.

"Sorry," he shouted reflexively.

He checked behind him again. The sedans were there, but the turn had slowed them down.

Two blocks ahead the housing tracks fell away. Beyond was an area of large lots and open desert. Now he was the one with the advantage.

The driver of the lead sedan started coming on fast, but it was already too late. Wes spotted what he'd hoped for just ahead on the left. He took one more glance at the sedans following him, then veered across the road and onto the dirt motorcycle path that cut through an open field.

Behind him, the first sedan slowed for a moment, then continued down the street to the next intersection and turned left. Jenks's sedan, on the other hand, was far enough behind that it was able to turn left at the intersection before the open field. It sped forward, paralleling Wes for a moment, then raced past his position.

Their goal would be the next intersecting street, with the hope of cutting him off. At least that's what Wes was counting on. As he continued along the trail, he could see that the first sedan was now almost even with him. Wes slowed just enough to let it get ahead. The other sedan had already reached the intersecting road and was just pulling up to the spot where the motorcycle trail crossed. A door flew open and Jenks got out.

Wes let the bike ease back a little more, then, as soon as the first sedan had made its turn onto the intersecting road, he whipped the bike around in a one-eighty and took off back the way he'd come.

Five minutes later, after reentering the city and using the residential streets to mask his movements, he pulled in to the parking lot of the Church of Christ on Norma Street. Since it was still relatively early on a Monday, the lot was empty. He slowed the bike and eased it behind the A-frame building, out of sight from the road, then cut the engine.

His next problem was communications. If they could track down the pay phone he'd been using, they could easily pinpoint his position if he made a call on his cell. Unfortunately, he didn't have much of a choice.

He pulled the phone out and started to call Casey at his desk, then remembered Casey had gone into his boss's office.

"Judy Thomas, please," he told the Quest Network operator as soon as she answered.

"One moment," the woman said.

Another promotional audio took over while the call

was transferred. Ironically, it was an ad for *Close to Home,* hyping the upcoming Chicago episode.

"Wes?" Casey said.

"Are you all right?" Wes said.

"Where the hell are you? I've been trying to call that number you gave me, but all I get is a notice it's been disconnected."

"You've got to get out of the building."

"You won't believe what I— Wait. What?"

"Get out now! They know what you're doing."

"How do you know that?" There was the hint of fear in Casey's voice.

"They traced your call back to the pay phone I was using, and nearly grabbed me there. The only way they could have done that was through you. These are the same people who took Anna and Tony. You need to leave now. Don't tell anyone."

"Are . . . are *you* all right?"

"Don't worry about me. Just go!"

There was a pause. "Okay. But . . . I think you need to know what I found out."

Wes desperately wanted to hear what it was, but he said, "Later. Right now just get out of there. I'll call you on your cell at exactly one-fifteen, okay?"

Silence, then, "All right."

"Be safe," Wes said.

"You too."

If only it were that easy.

CHAPTER 67

LARS SPENT THE NIGHT IN A ROOM THAT WASN'T one of the normal military holding cells used by Naval Criminal Investigative Services, or NCIS. It was more like a windowless office where the desk had been replaced by a cot. Anytime he needed to use the head, he had to wait until one of the guards checked on him, and then he was escorted down the hall.

The guards weren't NCIS, either. They also weren't members of the contracted federal police force that handled the day-to-day law enforcement on the base. Rather, they were a group of naval personnel under Jenks's and Wasserman's command. Or, more accurately, under Forman's.

When he'd first woken up, he'd made a request to see someone from his office. The guard he had talked to had listened but made no promises. So far, no one had shown up.

Well, not *no one*.

At just after 7:30 a.m., as Lars had been eating breakfast, the door had opened and Commander Forman had entered.

Lars got slowly to his feet and, after a brief pause, saluted. If the commander read any disrespect in the delay, he didn't acknowledge it.

"Don't let me stop you eating," Forman said.

Lars sat back down, but didn't touch the food.

Forman leaned against the wall near the door and regarded Lars for a moment. "I trust you've been treated well."

"Well enough."

The commander moved the ends of his mouth up in an imitation of a smile. "Lieutenant Commander Andersen, were my orders unclear?"

"No, sir."

"Could you repeat them back to me, please?"

Lars chose to remain silent.

Frowning, the commander said, "Your little excursion last night. What was that all about?"

"There are duties I have that don't fall under your command." A beat, then, "Sir."

The ridge along Forman's cheek began to redden. "You are in a hell of a lot of trouble, you know that?"

Lars locked eyes with Forman. "Commander, if there is any trouble here, that would belong to you."

"And what the hell does that mean?"

"It means I've learned just how deep this cover-up of yours goes. Figured out your little arrangement with Laredyne. Oh, and I found out about Jamieson, too."

Forman froze just long enough for Lars to know he'd been right. Smiling to himself, Lars picked up his fork and started in on his breakfast again.

"Lieutenant Commander, I'm disappointed. I really thought you understood." Forman paused. "I'm going to do everything in my power to see that you are destroyed. And I'll tell you another thing, since you weren't able to finish the job on your friend, Stewart, I'm going to finish it for you."

Lars cut one of the sausages with his fork and put a piece in his mouth, chewing it several times before swallowing. "Commander Forman. You can go to hell."

Forman glared at him, then pounded twice on the door. When it opened, he looked back at Lars. "You have just ruined more than your career."

Lars kept his expression unchanged, making sure Forman got the message that he didn't care what the commander thought.

After Forman left, he put the fork back down and pushed the plate away. The truth was, he was worried. Not about his career, but about his own life. Affixing the blame to him would be so much easier if he were dead.

Several hours later, after his unfinished breakfast had been removed, and the lunch he had no desire to eat had been delivered, the door opened again. This time it looked like his request to speak to someone had been granted, as his new visitor was Lieutenant Commander Meyers.

"Janice?" Lars said.

"Lieutenant Commander Andersen." She looked at the untouched tray of food sitting on his cot. "Is there something the matter with your lunch?"

"Just not hungry," he said, confused by her formality.

"I see. Is there anything you need?"

"I'm fine."

She positioned herself between him and the door.

"Water? A bathroom break?" Her voice dropped. "Are you okay?"

"Pen," he mouthed. "I said I'm fine."

She gave him a nearly imperceptible nod. "Would you like me to take your tray for you?"

"Yes. Thank you. I'd appreciate that."

She walked over to the cot. As she bent down, she slipped a hand into her pocket, pulled out a pen, and dropped it on the bed.

"No," he whispered.

She hesitated, confused.

"On second thought," he said in a normal voice, "can I eat the fruit first?"

"Of course."

She backed off and Lars sat down next to the tray. When she was once again blocking him from the door, he scribbled a message on the napkin.

"How did you get in here?" he whispered as he wrote.

"When you didn't show up this morning, Commander Knudsen found out you were being held here. He sent me to check on you. They didn't want to let me in, but they didn't have much choice. What happened?"

So his request for a meeting *hadn't* been passed on. "No time," he said as he finished the note. He tapped the napkin. "Promise me you'll do what it says."

"You can count on me."

He smiled, then quickly ate the cup of fruit.

"Thank you, Lieutenant Commander," he said.

"You're welcome."

As she leaned down to get the tray, she crumpled the napkin into her hand, then shoved it in her pocket and turned for the door.

"If you need me for anything, please let one of your guards know. I'll instruct them they are to contact me immediately."

Once she was gone, he lay down on the cot. He'd

learned early on in his Navy career to take advantage of opportunities as they presented themselves. Janice had been an opportunity, quite possibly the only one he was going to get. Now all he could do was sit tight and see if it paid off.

CHAPTER
68

WES HAD SEEN ENOUGH MOVIES AND WORKED on enough crime documentaries to know that even when a cellphone wasn't being used, it could be tracked. As soon as he finished talking to Casey, he removed the battery, then went in search of another pay phone.

He found one in the park just east of the police station. It was a bit more exposed than the one at the 7-Eleven, but it did provide him with nearly unlimited avenues of escape.

Casey picked up on the first ring.

"Where are you now?" Wes said.

"I went down to—"

"Wait," Wes cut him off. "I shouldn't have asked. Don't tell me. We can't talk too long. And as soon as we're done, take the battery out of your phone and go someplace else."

Casey hesitated. "Uh, all right. But how will I know it's okay to go back home?"

"Digger," Wes said, using Casey's brother's nickname. "When things have settled down, I'll call Digger with the all clear. Check in with . . . them, just not too often. Wait until at least tomorrow morning to start."

"Jesus, Wes. What have you gotten into?"

"Don't worry. It'll be okay," Wes said. "Now tell me what you found."

"Right. Okay," Casey said. There was the sound of paper flipping. "SCORCH first. It was developed by a company called Laredyne Industries. Apparently they have been pushing very hard for the Navy to adopt it. If I'd had more time, I could have probably dug up more details, but what I did learn is that there's been a pretty vigorous debate about it in both the military and in Congress, with those opposed to the Laredyne system supporting a slightly different one developed by Nickerson Avionics."

"Okay, so the SCORCH backers won. So what?"

"They didn't exactly win," Casey said. "Not yet, anyway. Technically it's still in the testing phase. Funding for fleet-wide activation is part of an appropriations bill up for a vote in Congress next week. But I'm told several reps and a few senators aren't fans of the system. So there's a good chance that the bill won't get passed unless SCORCH is removed."

"Interesting," Wes said, still unsure how it fit in with what was happening. "Anything else?"

Casey paused. "The next thing I looked into was Project Pastiche. Do you have that list of names you read off to me?"

"Hold on." Wes found the page. "Okay. Got it."

"Skip the personnel section; I hadn't been able to find out much there before you told me to leave. Look at the names under 'Pool 7B.'"

"Looking at them now."

"I was able to identify Lieutenants Lemon, Briley,

and, of course, Adair. What do you think they have in common?"

"I assume they were all assigned to this PP-214 division at some point."

"They've all been reported as dead."

"Seriously?"

"Yeah," Casey said. "Briley was killed while on duty in the Pacific during a training exercise near Australia. His body was never recovered."

"When did this occur?"

"Thirteen months ago. Lemon was assigned to a ship in the Persian Gulf, but was killed while on a mission in Iraq. The report I found claimed there was little left of the body, and he had to be identified by DNA."

"That's odd."

"It gets odder. The two other names on that list, Brian Faith and Cameron Bruce?"

"The ones marked 'Available,' " Wes said.

"Right. As far as I can tell, neither man is serving in the military."

"That doesn't necessarily mean anything."

"I realize that. So I did down-and-dirty checks on all five men. Know what I found?"

"Just tell me."

"The three men who died? Their histories are remarkably similar. All were from small Midwest towns, but had no family living there anymore. All had similar educational backgrounds and credit histories. And, this is interesting, each had been in the service approximately the same amount of time before they died."

"I don't understand."

"Oh, one more thing. None of them ever existed."

Silence.

"I think you need to tell me that again," Wes said.

"Lieutenants Adair, Lemon, and Briley are not real people."

As crazy as things had gotten, what Casey had just claimed took things to a whole new level. "But I met Adair's children. They were at Commander Forman's house."

"Whoever's kids they were, they weren't Lieutenant Adair's."

Could they have just been *props*? "How do you know about Adair for sure?"

"This is what I do, remember?" Casey said. "I look at this kind of information all the time. I know what it should look like. People's lives are messy, even the most organized ones. These guys have backgrounds that are just too perfect. Sure, there are flaws on their records, but the flaws are perfect, too."

"And you're sure?" Wes asked, still finding it hard to believe.

"If it had been only one of them, I might not have picked up on it. But when I looked at all three, the patterns were obvious."

"What about the other two? Faith and Bruce?"

"Since I didn't have as much to go on with them, and the names are not entirely unusual, I wasn't able to track them down. But I'd be willing to bet, given time, I could uncover a history for each man that mirrored the others."

Wes stared at the horizon, stunned.

"Are you there?" Casey asked.

"Yes. Sorry," Wes said. "Why would they say Adair died in the crash, then?"

"My only guess would be that it had something to do with SCORCH. Maybe there was a problem with it that caused the crash. Given the upcoming vote, maybe that commander you talked to decided it was necessary to hide what happened." He paused. "I don't know. It's the best I could come up with."

"No," Wes said. "That's good. There's something there, but we're missing pieces."

"Like who was really flying the plane."

"That, for sure. What about that name I gave you? Jamieson?"

"I only had a little time for that. Not the most common name in the world, but certainly not that unusual, either. There are over thirty in the Navy alone."

"I was afraid of that," Wes said.

"There are also three professional baseball players, several dozen doctors on the West Coast alone, the CEO of a telecom company. . . ." Wes could hear pages flipping. "There's also a Senator Jamieson from somewhere back East."

"A senator?"

"Yeah. That one definitely stands out. I could find an Internet café and check him out if you want."

"No," Wes said, not wanting to get his friend any more involved than he already was. "You've done plenty. Find someplace to lay low, and don't show your head until you get my message."

"If you're sure."

"I'm sure."

CHAPTER
69

THE RIDGECREST PUBLIC LIBRARY WAS JUST A stone's throw from the park. Wes skipped the Internet terminals for the time being. If it turned out he needed to get on the Web, he'd save that for last.

Instead, he found a dedicated computer containing the library's catalog and began his search there. Not surprisingly, there were hundreds of references to the senator in the library database. Wes made note of the latest guide to the U.S. Congress, three magazine articles, and the obligatory, ghost-written autobiography.

He located the guide first. The page on the senator was mostly a recap of his voting record through the guide's publication date, short descriptions of bills he had sponsored, and a three-paragraph biography.

Senator Sean Jamieson was sixty-one, widowed, and the father of three children. He'd started out in Washington as a member of the House of Representatives when he was only thirty-three. Eight years later he won the Senate seat of a retiring lawmaker, and had remained in that office since then. Over the years, he'd been a member of many different committees, including Transportation, Finance, and Governmental Affairs. According to the bio, for the last two terms he had served on the Armed Services Committee and the Appropriations Committee.

That caused Wes to pause. Appropriations. The bill that included funding for SCORCH was up for a vote with them. If the system had been the reason the test flight had gone down, it could cripple the bill's chances. He read further, trying to discern how the senator might vote on the measure, but there was no clear indication.

He returned to the computerized index and looked for anything pertaining to the bill, then cross-referenced entries for both the bill and the senator. There were several, all news articles. According to the index, most of the articles had been digitized and were available on one of the library terminals.

Wes hesitated. If he didn't get on the Internet, he would be okay, right? He decided to chance it, and found an empty terminal close to an emergency exit.

The first five articles only mentioned the senator in passing. In the sixth article it became clear the senator had some doubts. But it was the seventh that contained a direct hit.

"There are many questions remaining about several of the programs covered in this bill," Senator Jamieson said during the Appropriations Committee hearing today. While he didn't point out any particular program, he has previously voiced his concerns with projects such as SCORCH, which he believes has not yet proven itself reliable.

Jamieson, a former Army Ranger with a long family history in the military, has continued to advocate for not only a strong military, but a smart one. One, as he says, that "doesn't waste money on projects that will not serve our modern military needs."

Jamieson *and* SCORCH.

But so what? Wes thought.

All right. The senator wasn't the biggest fan of the system. And potentially he was one of the on-the-fence votes. But why would Lars have written his name on the paper? It had to be something else, didn't it?

Wes reread the article, then an unexpected thought hit him. He grabbed the piece of paper where he'd written down the locations of the references for the senator, then headed into the stacks. Thankfully, the book he was looking for wasn't checked out. He pulled it down and began thumbing through it.

On page 229 he stopped.

Slowly he looked from side to side, sure that someone had to be standing nearby ready to grab him. But the aisle was empty.

As he looked down at the book again and confirmed what he'd already seen, a chill ran up his spine.

Quickly, before someone showed up, he peeled off the security tag, then slipped the book behind his back and under his shirt, tucking it into the waistband of his pants.

CHAPTER 70

WES APPROACHED THE DESERT ROSE MOTEL from the back, parking the Triumph against the building, out of sight, then walked around the side to a passageway that led into the courtyard.

He was relieved to see that the police were no longer stationed outside Tony's room. Now there was only crime scene tape stretched across the door.

What he was looking for was a motel phone. He was hoping he might find an open room. But before he got very far, he spotted a phone mounted on the wall of a small shed near the swimming pool. It was a little more exposed than he liked, but it would do.

He walked over, picked it up, and dialed Alison's room.

"Hello?"

"Are you alone?" he said.

"Wes? What's going on? Have they found them?"

"No. Not that I know of. Is there anyone there with you?"

"No. Why?" she asked, a bit of caution seeping into her voice.

He hesitated, then said, "Look, I know you're mad at me, but I just—"

"Who said I was mad at you?"

"I can hear it in your voice."

"I can't help it if you're hearing things."

"Alison, please. I just need your help."

A brief silence. "Ask Danny."

"Please."

"This whole thing's gotten me shaken up. I just don't feel up to doing anything."

He paused, then said, "I'm sorry."

"It's fine. I'm sure Danny will be free."

"That's not what I mean."

Her voice was still cool. "What *do* you mean?"

"I haven't exactly been up front with you. I should have . . . I mean, it shouldn't have taken . . ."

When he didn't go on, she said, "You should have what?"

"I'm sorry. I should have told you about Anna and me a long time ago."

Silence, then, "Why didn't you?"

"I didn't want to hurt you. You and I have always been friends. And I didn't want to ruin it with her. You know me, I overthink things sometimes."

"Yeah, you do that, don't you?" she said, then, "You don't owe me anything."

"Yes, I do."

Neither of them said anything for several seconds.

"Thanks," Alison finally said. After another moment she added, "What do you need?"

Wes would have smiled if he could. "Find Danny, then I need the two of you to meet me at that place we ate last week. John's Pizza."

"What's going on?"

"I'll tell you when I see you. I promise."

A pause. "All right," she said, the coolness in her voice gone but annoyance starting to take its place. "What about Dione and Monroe?"

Truthfully, he would rather Alison brought Dione than Danny, but he didn't want to jeopardize Dione's position with the network. Unlike the rest of them—all freelancers—she was staff. If what he had in mind didn't work, it would hurt them less than it would hurt her. And as far as Monroe was concerned, she was useless and never a consideration.

"We need to keep this small for now," he said. "Be there in fifteen minutes and make sure no one's following you. That includes the police."

He knew she wouldn't be able to let that one go, so he hung up.

CHAPTER
71

WES HAD EXPECTED ALISON AND DANNY TO drive over in one of the two SUVs, but was surprised when they arrived with Dori in her Lincoln. His first instinct was to grab his two friends and tell Dori to come back for them later. But then he stopped himself. If she was willing to help, both she and her car could be useful. He got off the Triumph and climbed into the back of the car, next to Alison.

"What's so Jason Bourne that we had to sneak over here?" Danny asked.

When Wes didn't immediately reply, Alison asked, "Something happened, didn't it?"

"I need your help." He made sure to look at each of them. "All three of you."

"What's going on?" Danny asked.

"I . . . I think I know who has Anna and Tony."

To say the others were stunned would have been an understatement.

"Are you serious?" Dori asked.

"Yes."

Alison reached for her pocket. "We should call the police."

Placing a hand on her arm, Wes said, "We can't. Not yet."

"Why *not*?"

"The police already think I might have something to do with pretty much everything that's been happening. If I tell them what I figured out, they'll just—"

"Why would they think that?" Danny asked.

"The break-ins? The disappearances? I've been involved in all of them."

"As a *victim*," Alison pointed out.

Before Wes could say anything, Dori said, "They might not see it that way."

Wes nodded. "Exactly."

"It doesn't matter," Alison insisted. "They'd still have to check any lead you gave them, wouldn't they?" She paused. "What am I thinking? Tell *me* what you think happened, and *I'll* tell them."

"It's not that simple," Wes told her.

Alison looked like she was about to explode. "Why not?"

"Just listen to me." Wes gave her a moment to calm down. "Do you trust me?"

"Of course," Alison relented. "We all do."

Nods from the front seats.

"Are you willing to help me get the proof we need?" Wes asked.

"If it'll get Anna and Tony back, absolutely," Alison said.

"What do you need us to do?" Danny asked.

This was the moment of truth. Either Wes took them fully into his confidence, or he got out of the car and did what had to be done on his own. Which left him no

302 BRETT BATTLES

choice at all, really, because he was one hundred percent sure the second option would fail.

He took a deep breath. "I was right about the pilot from the crash."

It took him nearly ten minutes to get the whole story out. Then, as soon as he finished, he described the plan he'd come up with.

"We could definitely do that," Alison said, immediately on board. "It would take me thirty minutes to rig it, tops."

"It's all right if we use your car?" Wes asked Dori.

"Yes. Absolutely," she said. "If it'll help your friends, anything. I'll even drive. This Commander Forman has met all of you. He'll be less guarded if I drive up."

As much as he didn't want to put someone he didn't know well in potential danger, he knew she was right. "Okay. Thanks."

"I don't know," Danny said. "I'm not sure I buy the Navy kidnapping people."

"Not the Navy," Wes said. "An element with*in* the Navy. There's a difference. This is unsanctioned. It's illegal."

"Still . . ."

"Danny," Dori said, "I think Wes might be right. You don't live here. Some pretty crazy things have happened."

"You believe Forman could have done this?"

Dori nodded. "After hearing Wes out, yeah, I do."

"I believe it," Alison added in quick support.

"Even if it's not true," Dori said, "it's worth finding out, isn't it?"

"I guess," Danny said, still not sounding completely convinced.

"Is that a yes?" Wes asked.

Dori reached over and put a hand on Danny's thigh. When he looked at her, she smiled and nodded again.

"Okay. Fine," Danny said. "I'm in."

Wes felt a flood of relief. "Thanks. I can't tell you how much I appreciate this." He checked the time. "We should get a move on it. You all head back to the motel and get the car ready. I'll call Forman."

As Wes climbed out, Alison reached over and touched him on the arm. "We're going to get her back. This is going to be okay."

He nodded, and tried to smile.

I hope you're right.

CHAPTER
72

COMMANDER FORMAN STARED OUT THE WIN-
dow of his office over Armitage Field, fuming. It had
been a stupid idea from the beginning. He had told Laredyne as much. But they had been insistent, and in the
end, Forman had thought, What harm could it do? At
worst, they'd be right where they were before the flight,
and at best, they might have turned things solidly in
their favor.

What harm could it do? Forman shook his head in
disgust. The twisted pile of metal that had once been an
F-18 proved how faulty that line of thinking had been.

Pilot error. That's what he had put in the report, and
in a way it hadn't been a lie. If the pilot had followed
Andersen's protocols, he would have never tripped the
glitch in the software the engineers at Laredyne had yet
to find a fix for. The error then triggered a massive systems shutdown. That son-of-a-bitch pilot had decided
on his own that a test run meant trying everything out
instead of following the road map he'd been given.

And now Andersen himself was a problem. Forman
had thought he'd played the lieutenant commander per-

fectly, taking an interest in the man's career, promising a transfer to a Pentagon job, then using the influence that had gained him to guide Andersen when he wrote the protocols. Then, after the crash, Forman had moved quickly to solidify Andersen's culpability, creating what he thought was going to be the perfect scapegoat.

But the lieutenant commander hadn't stuck to his script. His task had been simple. Make sure Wes Stewart wasn't a problem. Forman had picked up early on that Andersen had some underlying resentment toward his old friend. But no, instead of shutting Stewart up, he had actually turned on the commander.

Still, it wasn't the end of the world yet. They just needed a few more days. Once the Senate Appropriations Committee vote was over, Forman could finish the mop-up operation and move on to more important things. Like discussing how his actions deserved an even cushier post-Navy job at Laredyne than the one he'd been promised.

And if things did take a bad turn, he had Andersen to throw into the fire.

His desk phone rang. He punched the speakerphone button.

"Yes?"

"Call for you, sir. Mr. Wesley Stewart."

Forman paused. Stewart. The other problem. The commander had yet to figure out if he really needed to do anything about him yet.

"Put it through." He picked up the handset. "What can I do for you, Mr. Stewart?"

"We need to talk."

"Talk? About what?"

"I want you to release my friends."

"Your friends? I'm sorry. I don't know what you're talking about."

"You don't? Well, how about this. Jamieson. Know what that means?"

Forman sat up. He *did* need to take care of this problem.

"Interested in talking now, Commander?" Stewart asked.

"I don't know what it is you think you know, but if it'll help clear things up I'll meet with you. Why don't you come to my office and we can—"

"I have a better idea. Be in the parking lot behind the La Sonora restaurant at seven-thirty tonight. Alone."

"Really. I don't think we need to . . ." Forman didn't finish the sentence.

The line was already dead.

CHAPTER 73

THE MAN WAS AWAKE, SHOWERED, DRESSED, and fed by the time his phone rang.

"Hello?" He nodded as he listened. "No. That makes sense to me. When the opportunity is there, you go for it. . . . Don't worry. Everything will be in place. I'll be at the rendezvous point waiting."

He hung up and allowed himself a smile. Finally it was going to be over. Tonight he'd be sleeping in his own bed, his wife curled up beside him.

He walked down the hall, opened the door to the master bedroom, and flicked on the light. As he'd expected, the girl hadn't moved. That drug was some good stuff.

Might have to try it myself when we're all done.

"We'll be leaving in a few minutes," he said to the unconscious woman. "If you need to use the can, say so now."

He paused.

Silence.

"Suit yourself."

CHAPTER 74

IMMEDIATELY AFTER HE GOT OFF THE PHONE
with Stewart, Forman called Lieutenant Jenks.

"I'll have a tracking chip," Forman told his man after
he'd brought him up to speed. "You and Wasserman
and a couple of men take a helicopter and follow us. If
it looks like I'm in any trouble, or the chip stops emit-
ting a signal, come in hard and fast. I don't care where
we are. But otherwise stay out of sight. I'm not supposed to meet him until seven-thirty, so that's when you
should get in the air. Understood?"

"Yes, sir."

CHAPTER
75

BY THE TIME FORMAN PULLED IN TO THE PARK-
ing lot behind La Sonora, darkness once more had
claimed the desert.

Wes checked the time. 7:28 p.m.

He and Danny were two hundred feet away, around
the back corner of a Rite Aid drugstore. Wes's Triumph
was parked in the shadows nearby. Another dozen feet
back, Dori waited inside her Lincoln, ready to move on
Wes's signal.

"Do you see anyone else?" Wes asked after Forman
got out of his car.

Though they had a clear view of the La Sonora parking lot, lighting was poor.

"No."

Forman scanned the small lot for a few moments,
then entered the restaurant.

"You want me to go check?" Danny asked.

Wes thought about it for a moment, then nodded.
"Good idea."

Keeping in a crouch, Danny jogged out from their
hiding place and headed toward Forman's car.

Groaning, Wes almost yelled, "Just act normal!" But he held his tongue and watched Danny approach the car and peer inside. After a few seconds, Danny turned and shook his head slowly side to side, then started sneaking his way back.

Wes pulled out his phone and texted Alison a single character:

?

She was stationed at the other end of the alley, hiding out next to the Spirit gas station and watching the road. Her reply came through quickly.

Clear.

Good. It looked like the commander had actually done as he'd been told.

Wes looked over his shoulder at Dori in the Lincoln.

"Okay," he said. "You're on."

She nodded, then started the engine and cut across the Rite Aid lot into the alley. A few seconds later she pulled to a stop behind Forman's sedan. As she did, Danny ducked back around the corner with Wes.

"Guess we'll see if this works," he said.

Wes kept his eyes focused on the rear of the restaurant. "It'll work."

"Where *is* he?" Danny said after a couple of minutes had passed.

Wes had been wondering the same thing.

Another minute.

"Do you think he might have gone out the front?" Danny asked. "Maybe someone picked him up out there?"

"Why would he do that?"

"I don't know. It was just an idea."

Thirty more seconds.

"I'm going to go check," Wes said.

"Wait. If he sees you—"

"If he sees me, he sees me."

Wes had barely made it ten feet toward the alley when Forman reemerged from the restaurant. Wes stopped moving, hoping the darkness would conceal him. But it was unnecessary. Forman headed straight for his car, not even glancing in Wes's direction. He didn't even seem to notice Dori until he reached the door of his sedan.

"Get in my car and I'll take you to Wes," she said, her voice carrying just enough for Wes to hear.

This was a critical moment. If Forman tried to make a phone call, or said he needed to get something from his car first, Dori would take off and leave him where he stood. The meeting would be scrubbed, and Wes would be forced to think of an alternate plan.

But there was no call. No return trip to the car. The commander got into the rear seat of the Lincoln, and Dori took off.

By the time Wes ran back behind Rite Aid, Danny was already waiting by the motorcycle.

"We're on?" he asked.

Wes nodded. "We're on."

CHAPTER
76

WES DROVE THE TRIUMPH WHILE DANNY HELD
on to him from behind. It wasn't long before they caught
up to the Lincoln.

Though they had spotted no one else at the restaurant,
Wes didn't want to take the chance that the commander
might have someone keeping tabs on things from a distance. So he kept a careful eye on all the cars behind the
Lincoln, looking for any that seemed suspicious.

When he felt sure they were in the clear, he brought
the motorcycle up right behind the Lincoln and flashed
his blinkers. Dori began to slow. At the next street she
turned left, then pulled to a stop on the dirt shoulder
half a block down.

Wes parked the bike behind her.

"Don't crash it," he said as he got off the Triumph
and Danny scooted forward to take control.

Danny revved the engine. "Don't worry about me."

Wes moved around the side of the Lincoln and climbed
into the backseat with Forman. "Commander."

"Okay, Mr. Stewart," Forman said. "Are you done
having fun?"

Wes glanced into the rearview mirror, making eye contact with Dori. He gave a little nod. He saw her shoulder move and knew she'd activated the recording system Alison had hastily installed.

As soon as they were back onto the road, Wes said, "Where are they?"

Forman's brow furrowed. "You're going to have to be a little more specific than that."

"You know exactly who I'm talking about."

"I'm afraid I don't."

"All right, let's try this a different way. I know what you've been doing, what you're trying to cover up, and why."

The commander shook his head. "You're seeing phantoms, Mr. Stewart, and claiming trouble where none exists."

"Really? I say one name, and you come running to talk to me."

"I didn't come running," Forman said. "I came to put a stop to this. It was my intention to try one last time to reason with you to drop this ridiculous accusation. Obviously that was a mistake. If you'll just let me—"

"Tell me about SCORCH."

A tic. Just a small one. But it was enough for Wes to know he'd surprised the commander.

"That was the weapons system that was on the F-18 that crashed, wasn't it?" Wes asked.

"We use many weapons systems."

"But SCORCH is one of them, right?"

"SCORCH is a proposed system. It's not in active use at this time. You could have found that out with a simple Google search."

"Oh, I did. I also found out it's coming up for a vote in Congress."

Another tic.

"Perhaps," the commander said. "That's not my area of concern."

"Shouldn't it be your concern that SCORCH was the cause of last week's crash?"

"I've had enough of this." The commander put his hand on the door. "Pull this goddamn car over!"

"Let me ask you about something else. What is Project Pastiche?"

Forman's hand nearly slipped off the handle. No tic this time, just flat-out surprise.

"That . . . doesn't mean anything to me," he said.

"Really? I would think one of the things you would have done was look at the lieutenant's service record, if nothing else than to just familiarize yourself with his history. Project Pastiche was his first posting. Shouldn't that have stood out to you?"

"It's your friend Andersen, isn't it? He's fed you lies to cover his own ass. But I have news for you. Your pal has been arrested. Soon, whatever you think has been going on will be exposed as a delusion." Forman looked up front at Dori. "Please pull over and let me out."

"Not until he says it's okay," Dori said, tilting her head toward Wes.

Forman glared at Wes. "We're done. Let me out."

"I know what SCORCH is, and I know what Project Pastiche is, Commander. Your Lieutenant Adair, the man you said was responsible for the crash, he doesn't exist. He never did exist. Project Pastiche created him."

Forman's glare had turned into a look of stunned surprise.

"That's what they do, don't they?" Wes asked. "They create identities of people who aren't real in case someone needs a fall guy. Someone like you."

"You're not even making sense." Those may have been the words out of the commander's mouth, but his eyes betrayed the truth, that Wes was hitting far too close to home.

"So your fictitious Lieutenant Adair crashed a very real F-18 while testing a new *proposed* weapons system called SCORCH. Is that about right?"

The glare was back in Forman's eyes.

"Wait, it isn't right, is it?" Wes said. "Not quite. It wasn't really a test flight, was it? More of a trying-to-get-the-pilot-on-board kind of thing, wouldn't you say? Only the system didn't cooperate, did it? Too bad, too. Since this was supposed to be the flight that guaranteed full funding for SCORCH."

Dori turned quickly, then sped up.

"Someone's following us," she said.

Wes swiveled around to look through the rear window, but could see nothing, not even Danny on the motorcycle.

Dori made a rapid series of turns, then said, "I think I might have lost them. But I'll mix it up a little more, just in case."

Wes nodded, then refocused on Forman. "One of your friends?"

The commander scoffed.

The car took another turn.

"So what do you think? Am I close so far?" Wes asked.

"You're crazy is what you are. No one's going to believe any of this."

Wes smiled. "I want to show you something."

From under the front seat he removed the book he'd taken from the library—*From Where I've Stood: The Autobiography of Senator Sean Jamieson*. He flipped it open to a dog-eared page and turned it so Forman could see.

"Take a look, Commander."

On the page was a picture of the senator and his family.

"I'm sure you must recognize Senator Jamieson. He's one of the potential roadblocks to passage of the appropriations bill SCORCH is included in, isn't he?"

Wes braced himself as the car took another turn, now barely noticing Dori's attempts at evasive driving.

"I believe he's the one you were hoping to win over with the flight last week," Wes said. "But that's not how it worked out, is it?"

Wes moved his finger a quarter inch to the senator's left.

"Do you know this person?"

Without moving his head, Forman looked at the picture, then at Wes.

"Good," Wes said. "I thought that maybe since this photo is several years old you might not recognize him. That's Lee Jamieson, the senator's youngest son. Or, as he was known, Lieutenant Lee Jamieson. The man who was strapped into the F-18 when I—"

"Stop," Forman whispered.

Now Wes knew for sure he had been right all along. Forman and the people he was associated with must have thought they had a secret weapon in their attempt to get Senator Jamieson on board. His son. Let Lieutenant Jamieson try out SCORCH and then have him give his father a glowing report.

"I want my friends back. If you do that, I won't say a word about what I know."

Forman glanced quickly at Dori.

"She won't say anything, either," Wes said. "That's the deal."

The commander looked away. "Okay," he finally said. "Lieutenant Commander Andersen will be released within the hour."

"That's great, and we'll take that. But he's not who I'm talking about."

Forman stared blankly at Wes. "Then who the hell *are* you talking about?"

"Let's not play stupid, Commander. Anna Mendes and Tony Hall? Those names ring a bell?"

Forman shook his head. "No. Not at all."

The car began to slow.

Wes looked up. There were no lights around, no city. Just the dark desert. He twisted around and glanced out the rear window. Ridgecrest glowed in the distance, but the road itself was empty.

"Is something wrong?" he asked Dori.

Then, with a jolt, the Lincoln came to a sudden stop.

CHAPTER
77

THE CALL HAD COME IN AT 6:55 P.M., 9:55 P.M. where it originated, in Washington, D.C.

Lars knew something was up when the guard who brought him the phone was one of the federal cops and not one of Forman's men.

"I was given a message that you have information about my son." There was power in the voice on the other end. Power that almost, but not quite, masked an underlying level of concern.

"That's correct, Senator."

"If it hadn't come to me the way it had, I would have probably ignored it," Senator Jamieson told him.

Lars wasn't sure how Janice had gone about getting the senator's attention, but whatever she had done had worked.

"Thank you for calling me, sir."

"I understand you are in detention."

"Also correct."

"Do you want to explain to me why?"

Lars knew he had to be careful here. "You're familiar with SCORCH?"

Silence for a moment. "If this is some sort of trick to get me to vote for funding the program, then this phone call is over right—"

"No, sir," Lars jumped in. "Not a trick. At least not by me."

"What's that supposed to mean?"

"Sir, as I'm sure you know, I'm stationed at China Lake in the Mojave Desert." After the senator grunted in acknowledgment, Lars went on. "And I also assume you are familiar with what we do here. Testing aircraft, weapons, and flight systems?"

"I'm familiar."

"Systems like SCORCH."

"What is the point?"

"Sir, last Wednesday an F-18 installed with the SCORCH system took off on a test flight. The purpose of that particular flight was not so much a test of the system as it was a demonstration. The demonstration was for an audience of two. The pilot was one."

When he didn't immediately elaborate, the senator asked, "Who was the other?"

"You, sir." With a deep breath, he said, "Senator, the pilot of that plane was your son."

"I'm sorry, Lieutenant Commander, but you're obviously mistaken. My son is attached to the Seventh Fleet. Not China Lake."

"Senator, I think if you check you'll find that Lieutenant Jamieson was flown here the day before the test flight." Lars paused. "Sir, did your son have a scar on his right arm?"

The senator hesitated, then said, "Yes. He got it waterskiing during high school. But I fail to see what that has to do with this."

"Sir," Lars said, "the test flight we're talking about is

the one that crashed here last week. The pilot's body had a three-inch scar on its right arm. I saw it myself."

There was silence for several seconds, then the senator said, "Hold the line."

When he came back on, he was joined by Admiral Hines from the Pentagon. Lars repeated his story, laying out what he thought had happened.

By 7:25 Lars had been released. He made one request, to be the one who informed Commander Forman that he was to be taken into custody.

"Your cooperation in this is appreciated, Lieutenant Commander," the admiral had said. "But that's NCIS's job. I don't, however, have any objections to you . . . observing them in action."

"Thank you, sir," Lars said.

The flaw in his plan didn't hit him until he stepped into the parking lot. That's when he remembered his truck had been impounded and was on the other side of the base. He was about to go back inside to use the phone when he saw Janice standing in the parking lot beside her Mustang.

"Thought you might need a lift," she said.

"How did you know I was getting out for sure?" he asked as they both climbed in.

"I figured you wouldn't have asked me to get ahold of a U.S. senator if you didn't have a very good reason. And if you did, he'd get you out." She started the engine. "So, where are we going?"

A mixed team of NCIS investigators and federal cops were waiting when Lars and Janice arrived at Forman's house. While Janice waited by the car, Lars joined the team as they walked up the steps to the commander's front door.

Unfortunately, the only one home was Forman's wife.

One of the team members took Mrs. Forman into a back room to question her, while the rest moved into the living room to wait. Lars paced near one of the windows for a moment, then walked over to the lead NCIS investigator.

"I can't stay," he said. As satisfying as it would have been to be present when Forman found out he was finished, there was a more important task that he needed to do.

"All right. But I've been told to inform you that although you're out of custody, you are still under investigation. So no leaving town."

"Of course," Lars said. He'd been told as much by Admiral Hines, so it wasn't a surprise.

He jogged back to the Mustang and got in.

"Well?" Janice asked.

"He wasn't home. Just his wife."

"So what are they going to do?"

"Wait until he gets back."

"You don't want to stay?"

He shook his head. "Can you drop me off at the Desert Rose Motel? You know, just the other side of the hospital?"

Ten minutes later he was standing in the motel parking lot, the taillights of Janice's Mustang quickly fading into the distance.

He got Wes's room number from the office, then proceeded there and knocked. When no one answered, he scanned the parking lot. Wes's motorcycle wasn't around.

Out, Lars realized. *Damn.*

He settled against the wall, his gaze drifting across the parking lot toward the northeast, toward the base. He could see the emptiness that had once contained base housing. He remembered riding through those streets with Wes on the dirt bicycles they'd put together themselves. His had been painted red, while Wes had gone for a combination of orange and black. The Halloween bike, some of the kids had called it.

Lars remembered one time when they had ridden all the way to the Shopping Basket grocery store next to the indoor pool. There they ran into a couple of other kids they knew from junior high. For some reason, Lars had allowed one of the kids to talk him into shoplifting a candy bar. Since it was the first—and last—time he'd ever done anything like that, it was no wonder he was nervous. That was undoubtedly why the store manager stopped him at the door and made him empty his pockets.

"What's your name?" the manager had asked. "I'm going to call your parents."

Lars was terrified. More of his father than of the store manager.

"If you won't tell me, I'll just have to call the police."

Lars tried to speak, but nothing came out.

"It's not his fault." It was Wes. He was standing a few feet away.

"Oh, really?" The manager held up the candy bar. "So this just jumped into his pocket?"

"No, sir," Wes said. "I put it there when he wasn't looking."

The manager stared at Wes.

"He didn't know," Wes went on. "It's my fault."

The manager turned back to Lars. "Is that true?"

Lars stole a glance at Wes. His friend gave him a tiny nod.

"Yes," Lars whispered, hating himself for it.

Unbelievably, the manager let Lars go, telling him he

was banned from the store for a month. Outside, the other boys, having seen what was going down, were long gone. Lars wanted to leave, too, but he waited by the bike rack for almost forty minutes until his friend joined him.

"Did he call your parents?" Lars asked as they rode away.

"Nah," Wes said. "He just took me back in the office and acted like he was going to. Then he told me I could leave."

"He ban you, too?"

"Six months."

"Whoa."

Wes shrugged. "What do we need to go in there for anyway?"

They rode between the baseball fields and Murray Junior High, heading home.

"Thanks," Lars finally said.

"Sure," Wes replied. And with that they settled the matter, in the way only boys of a certain age could do.

Why had he ever doubted Wes? Not about the pilot, but years ago, when he'd been angry at Wes for leaving town? Angry at him for not showing up to Mandy's funeral? Lars knew better. He'd just forgotten.

An SUV slowed, then turned in to the lot. Lars recognized the women inside as Wes's crewmates from the shoot in Red Rock Canyon.

Lars raised his hand and waved as they got out. "We met the other day," he said. "I'm Wes's friend."

"Yeah, we know," the tall one replied. What had her name been? Adrianne? Alyssa?

The shorter one—Dione, he recalled—shut her door and moved around the front of the SUV. "You're the one in the Navy."

"Right," he said. "Lars."

"What do you want?" the tall one asked.

He looked at the women, confused by their tone. "I'm just waiting for Wes."

"He's not here," Dione said. "Come on, Alison."

Lars stepped in front of them. "I see that. Any idea when he might be back?"

"No."

"Okay. Did he and Anna go to dinner or something?"

The women looked at him as if he'd suddenly gone crazy.

"What did I say?"

"Are you the backup?" Alison asked. "In case Wes didn't show up?"

"Show up for what?"

"You know what."

"No," Lars said. "I don't."

"You're working for Commander Forman, aren't you?"

Lars tensed. "Forman?"

"You should leave," Dione told him.

"You need to tell me what's going on," he said, now all business.

Without a word, the women started to walk away. Lars immediately took up pursuit. "What did you mean 'working for Commander Forman'?"

"Like you don't know," Alison said without turning around.

Lars reached out and grabbed her arm, stopping her. "No, I don't."

"Let go of me!" she yelled, trying to twist free.

"For God's sakes, Forman's had me locked up since last night. You've got to tell me what's going on."

Alison stopped struggling. "Locked up?"

Lars let go of her arm. "Last night, Wes went with me to get some information that would prove he was right about the pilot of the crash last week. I found what I could and gave it to him. Then some of the commander's men showed up and took me in. I wasn't released until less than an hour ago."

"That information came from you?"

"He told you about it?"

The women shared another look.

"So you're not working with Commander Forman?" Alison asked.

"I'm the one who just turned him in. Base security is looking for him right now. Please tell me what's going on."

Again the women glanced at each other. Finally Dione nodded, and Alison told him about Wes's plan.

"Once they'd left La Sonora, I called Dione to come pick me up," she said.

Dione frowned in annoyance. "I've been told they decided it was best I didn't know. So the first I heard about anything was from Alison just now on the ride back here."

"If we told you, you would have tried to stop us."

"Yes. I would have."

"Then we did the right thing."

"Wes thinks Forman has Anna and this Tony guy?" Lars said. "That doesn't make sense."

"But the stuff about the crash is true, isn't it?" Alison said. "That means he must have them."

Lars was impressed, but not necessarily surprised, that Wes had been able to put it all together from the scant information he'd given him the night before. But no matter what, this latest bit didn't fit.

"Yes, the crash stuff is true, but kidnapping? No way.

Huge risk, no reward. I don't even think it would have crossed the commander's mind."

A motorcycle pulled in to the parking lot. Lars felt relief that his friend was finally here, but when the rider hopped off the bike and removed his helmet, it wasn't Wes. It was the other guy, Danny.

"Shouldn't you be following Wes?" Alison asked.

Danny quickly glanced around the parking lot. "They didn't come back here?"

"No," Alison said. "Why would they do that?"

Danny looked puzzled. "I *was* following them, and I could see Wes in the backseat talking to that commander guy, but then all of a sudden Dori just took off. I got lost a few minutes later, so I thought they might have come back here."

"She lost you on purpose?" Dione asked.

"Of course not," Danny said. "I think she was trying to be cautious. I just couldn't keep up." He glanced down at the bike. "Only the second time I've ever driven one of these."

"Who's Dori?" Lars asked.

"Danny's girlfriend," Alison scoffed.

"I don't remember meeting her. Is she part of the crew?"

"She's a local," Dione said. "Danny met her at a bar."

Something in the back corner of Lars's mind began poking at him.

"Dori who?" he asked.

Danny took a step back. "What business is it of yours?"

"Tell him, Danny," Dione ordered.

"Fine, okay. It's Dillman. What's the big deal?"

Dori Dillman. Lars had heard the last name before,

but it had been years ago. And it was a guy, wasn't it? Mark or Mike or something like that.

"Do you know her?" Alison asked.

He started to shake his head, then . . .

He thrust his hand out at Danny. "Give me the bike keys."

"What?"

"Give them to me. Now!"

Danny jumped. "Okay, sure."

He'd barely got them out of his pocket when Lars grabbed them and jumped on the bike.

"What are you doing?" Danny asked.

Lars kicked the bike back to life, then looked at Alison. "Call the police," he said. "Tell them . . ." *What?* "Tell them I know who has your missing friends, and that I'll call them as soon as I know where they should go. Tell them they need to be ready to move."

Without waiting for a response, Lars raced out of the parking lot and into the night.

CHAPTER
78

AT 7:25 P.M., AS LARS WAS WALKING OUT OF THE building where he'd been held overnight, Lieutenants Jenks and Wasserman were climbing aboard the helicopter they'd commissioned and were strapping themselves in. Up front the pilot and copilot were going through a final check so that they'd be ready to lift off at 7:30 on the dot.

Wasserman was carrying the GPS tracker, already pretuned to the chip the commander was carrying in his shoe. According to the display, the commander had just arrived at the rendezvous point in town.

Both lieutenants watched the screen as the dot representing Commander Forman began to move at a much slower rate than it had been.

"He's on foot," Wasserman said.

Jenks checked his watch: 7:29 p.m. He touched a button and spoke to the pilot. "Let's go."

There was a momentary delay, then the engine began to ramp up. Jenks put a hand on the seat, anticipating the rise, but at the moment the engine reached the liftoff pitch, the rotors suddenly began to cycle down.

Jenks pushed the mic button again, "Why aren't we in the air?"

"You'll have to ask them," the pilot said, pointing outside. "We were ordered by the control tower to power down."

Three men were walking purposefully toward the helicopter.

"Who the hell are they?" Wasserman asked.

"I'll check," Jenks said.

He disconnected his restraint, opened the door, and hopped out.

"I don't know what you think you're doing," Jenks said, "but we have a mission that's supposed to have us in the air right this very minute."

"Are you Wasserman or Jenks?" one of the men said.

"I'm *Lieutenant* Jenks. What's going on?"

The two other men moved past Jenks to the open door of the helicopter.

"Sir, you'll come with me now," the first man said to Jenks.

"The hell I will."

"Sir, if you'd rather, I could place you under arrest right here."

"Arrest? Who do you think you are . . . ?" He was about to address the man by rank, but realized for the first time the man was not wearing a uniform.

"NCIS, Lieutenant. Turn around and put your hands behind your back."

CHAPTER 79

A LARGE MAN DRESSED IN BLACK STEPPED OUT of the darkness and into the headlights. He had to be almost six foot five, and a good two hundred and thirty pounds.

"Who is that?" Wes asked.

Dori remained silent as the man walked up to the front passenger door, opened it, and climbed in.

"Evening, gentlemen," he said.

"Who the hell are you?" Wes asked. "Dori, what's going on?"

Forman didn't give a damn who the man was. He grabbed the door handle and started to pull. But the door didn't budge.

Wes grabbed at the handle next to him, but his door didn't open, either.

Dori threw the car into drive, and the Lincoln pulled back onto the road, its speed increasing rapidly, pushing Wes and the commander back in their seats.

"Sorry about the child locks," Dori said. "But can't have you accidentally falling out while we're moving, can we? That certainly wouldn't be safe."

Wes started to lean forward, but as he did, the new passenger twisted in his seat, then swung his hand up and rested the barrel of a large pistol next to the head-rest.

"Just relax," Dori said, glancing into the rearview mirror and catching Wes's eye. "Won't be long now."

"Won't be long for what?"

"What are you trying to pull here, Stewart?" Forman said.

"I'm not trying to pull anything," Wes said.

Up front Dori laughed, then said something to the new passenger in a voice too low for Wes to hear. As soon as she finished, the man motioned at Wes and the commander with his gun. "Why don't you two give it a rest," he said. "We can talk more when we get there."

"Get where?" Wes asked.

The man simply grinned but said nothing.

Wes looked out his window. Though a half-moon was beginning to rise in the east, it was still too low to provide much illumination. Still, he was able to make out the bulky shape of B Mountain off to the left, and knew they must be on the highway to Trona, the same highway that ran by the Pinnacles, where the crash had occurred.

At first he thought that was where Dori was taking them, though he had no idea why. Unless, that was, she'd turned the tables and was actually working for Forman. But the commander seemed just as out of the loop as Wes felt. Then, just before the highway dipped down into a narrow, rocky canyon that would have taken them toward the Pinnacles, Dori turned onto a dirt road leading southeast into the wilderness.

Wes had been on this road back in high school, but where he'd been heading then and where they were heading now couldn't be the same, could they? That didn't make any sense.

Hell, *none* of it made sense, he thought.

Ahead the road forked. The fork to the right was wider and more traveled, leading to God knew where. The one to the left was in far worse shape and led up into some hills in the east. It was the left fork Wes had gone down last time. And, before she even turned the steering wheel, he knew that was the direction she was going to take this time, too.

The car bounced as it hit a rut, knocking Wes into the commander.

"Hang on, gentlemen," the man with the gun said.

Wes moved back to his side, then tried to anchor himself with one hand on the door and the other against the roof.

They were going to have to stop soon. The road only went so far. He just hoped when they got to the end there would be other cars, throwing off whatever plan it was Dori and the man with the gun had in mind.

When they took the final turn, Wes's hopes rose as he spotted something parked up where the road terminated. Maybe it was going to be all right. There *were* others.

But as the distance closed, his rising hope nosedived. The other vehicle wasn't a car at all. It was a . . .

. . . horse trailer.

The Lincoln lit it up as they drew near. It had been backed in so that its doors were on the far side, away from them. And though it showed signs of age, it wasn't falling apart, and therefore couldn't have been out here for very long.

As soon as Dori brought the Lincoln to a stop and

turned off the engine, a deathly quiet settled over everything.

Finally she turned so she could look at Wes and Commander Forman. "My friend here is going to get out.
He'll open the door next to you." She flashed a glance at
Wes. "I'll wait here while you both climb out. And in
case you're thinking of trying something . . ." She raised
her hand in the air. Like her friend, she was also holding
a gun, only hers seemed even larger. "Everyone understand?"

"You need to let me go right now," Forman said. "I'm
an officer in the U.S. Navy, and you do not want the
kind of trouble we will bring down on you."

"Have you looked outside, *Commander*?" Dori asked.
"We're at least twenty miles from the closest building.
Where do you think you would go?"

A superior smirk grew on the commander's lips. "You
don't think I would have met Mr. Stewart without any
backup, do you? I have a tracking chip. Within minutes
a naval helicopter full of Marines is going to land. And
when they do, if I'm not free, you will *not* survive."

"A helicopter full of Marines." Dori laughed, deep
and loud. "You're a liar, Commander. If that were true,
don't you think your rescue team would be hovering
above us right now?" She shook her head. "No. You
came alone, thinking you could shut Wes up, because
guess what? Turns out Wes was right. You make me
sick, Commander. You're just lucky Wes here sickens me
more."

"What are you talking about?" Wes asked. "I barely
even know you."

"Where's the chip?" Dori's partner asked the commander. When Forman didn't answer, the man leaned

over the seat and slammed the butt of the gun against the commander's cheek.

Forman grunted as he fell back against the seat. "In my shoe."

"It doesn't matter," Dori declared.

"I think we should check, anyway," her partner said.

She shrugged. "Why not? All right, Commander, toss 'em both up here."

"I will not!"

Dori aimed the barrel of her gun at his chest. "Fine with me. We'll just take them off you after you're dead."

The commander did nothing for a moment, then reached down and removed his shoes. "It doesn't matter. They already know where I am."

"Shut it," Dori's partner said as he grabbed the shoes.

He then climbed out of the car and dropped them on the ground. A few seconds later, there were two loud gunshots.

"What do you know?" The guy held a shoe in the doorway so Dori could see it. "There *was* something there."

Dori smiled at the commander. "They don't know where you are now."

"That's not how that works," the commander said. "They already know our position. And destroying the chip is their signal to land."

"If you say so," Dori said, still smiling.

Forman looked out at the sky, his eyes searching for something that didn't appear to be there.

The door beside Wes opened.

"Now, both of you, out," Dori said.

Wes climbed out first. The commander, feet clad only in socks, followed.

The half-moon dimly illuminated the desert in a gray-blue light.

"Stay right there," Dori's partner said, his gun trained on them.

Once Dori was out, she pointed her gun at the commander, then said, "Wes, you're going to help my friend here, then we're all going to go for a walk."

The man waved the end of his barrel toward the horse trailer. "Come on," he said. "Around to the doors."

Not seeing much of an option, Wes did as he was ordered.

"Open it," the man said once they'd reached the back.

Wes grabbed the handle, yanked it up and to the right, releasing the latch. Because of the angle, gravity held the doors in place. He pulled outward on the one covering the right half, then gave it a little push so it swung all the way out, then over, where it slammed against the outside of the trailer with a loud bang.

The interior was bathed in darkness.

"The other one," the man said.

Wes repeated the action, this time with the left side.

Now that both halves were out of the way, dull moonlight was able to penetrate a few feet into the trailer. With the exception of some debris jutting out of the edge of the darkness, the rest of what Wes could see was barren floor.

"Go on," the man said. "Inside."

"You're going to lock me in?" Wes asked. "Why? What have I done to you?"

"Inside," the man repeated.

Wes's eyes narrowed. This was ridiculous. Whatever game they were playing, he was done.

"No," he said.

The man raised his gun. "*In*side."

"No," Wes repeated.

"Fine."

Wes held his ground as the man sighted down his barrel at his chest.

"I would think you'd want to go inside," Dori said.

Wes jerked at the sound of her voice. She and the commander had moved around the trailer and were standing a few feet away.

"I don't care what you think."

"Fine," Dori said. She looked at her partner. "Come on. We'll just leave her in there."

Wes looked back at the trailer. "Leave who in there?"

Dori had already started to walk away. "What does it matter? You've made your choice."

Wes took a step toward the trailer opening. It took a couple of seconds, but he soon saw the debris he'd noticed earlier wasn't debris at all. It was a knee.

No longer even conscious of the guns behind him, he clambered into the back. The knee gave way to a leg, then a hip, and a torso.

Wes crouched down and gently turned the body toward him.

"Anna?"

CHAPTER 80

LARS'S FIRST INSTINCT WAS TO DRIVE OVER TO
the house he knew Dori had lived in years before, but he
only went a couple of blocks before he pulled over to the
side of the road and retrieved his phone. She *could* still
live there, but if she'd moved, he would be wasting time
he couldn't afford to waste.

"What city, please?" a recorded voice said.

"Ridgecrest, California."

"What listing, please?"

"Dori Dillman."

There was a pause. "I have no listing for that name. If
you would like to look up another listing, please say
yes."

"Yes," Lars said.

"What city, please?"

"Ridgecrest, California."

"What listing, please?"

Lars paused.

"What listing, please?"

He hesitated a moment longer, then it came to him.
"Doreen Dillman."

"One moment, please."

If Lars heard one more "please," he was going to—

The recording came back on and provided a phone number. When he asked for an address, it supplied that, too.

"Son of a bitch," he said under his breath as he started the motorcycle back up. Good thing he'd checked. Her current address put her about a mile west of the Desert Rose Motel, nowhere near the place he'd been headed to.

The first thing he noticed when he arrived was that there were no cars parked in the driveway or along the curb out front. There were also no lights on in any of the windows. He pounded on the front door, waited, then pounded again.

No response.

He tried the doorknob. Locked.

"Wes!" he yelled. "Wes!"

He tested the door again, not to see if it was still locked, but to get a sense of its sturdiness. As was the case with many older homes, what had once been a solid barrier had become simply adequate. He took a step back, raised his right foot, then kicked. The sole of his shoe landed flat against the door next to the knob, creating a satisfying *crack*.

He raised his foot again and gave it a second shot. This time the noise was even louder.

It was the fourth one that sent the door flying open. He was through and into the living room before it had stopped moving.

"Wes!" he yelled.

Kitchen. Dining room. Family room.

All empty.

He raced over to the hallway that led to the back of

the house. Halfway to the end was a bathroom. He stuck his head in. Nothing.

He counted three bedrooms. The first looked like it was serving as a home office —a desk against one wall, bookcases and filing cabinets along the others. Littered across the floor were stacks of papers and magazines and folders and boxes.

He moved down to the next bedroom. Empty. Completely. No furniture. No boxes. Everything empty, that is, except the closet. It was half full of clothes. Men's clothes. On the floor was an old green duffel bag, Army issue.

The last bedroom was the master. This had a bed, a dresser, and a stand with a TV on it. The closet here was a walk-in. It was stuffed with women's clothing. But the room, like everywhere else in the house, was unoccupied.

Dammit! He felt the urge to punch a wall, so he took a deep breath and tried to relax. *Okay. Okay. They're not here. But there's got to be something that might tell me where they are.*

He quickly opened all the drawers of the dresser, but only found more clothes. He moved down to the office and started searching. Barely a minute passed before he realized that if there was something there, it would take him too long to find it.

Desperate, he walked back into the main part of the house. The living room, nothing. The kitchen, nothing. The dining room—

He stopped.

Taped to the wall of the dining room were dozens of newspaper clippings. But one had been placed prominently in the center of all of them, with arrows scribbled across the page. It was also the most recent article, from just the previous week. It was the feature on the crash, of course.

All the inked arrows pointed at the same thing. A name circled in the text.

Wes Stewart.

Lars let out a breath. *This is how she must have known Wes was in town.*

Lars turned his attention to the other articles, examining them one by one. They were all much older, from back in Lars's and Wes's high school days. He was on the tenth one when he paused.

Of course, he thought.

He ran out of the house, not bothering to shut the door.

God, I hope I'm wrong.

But he knew he wasn't.

CHAPTER
81

"ANNA?"

Wes touched her check. Warm. And from her nose he could feel air moving in and out.

She was alive.

"Anna?"

Nothing. Not even a twitch.

"Pick her up," the man said. He was standing just outside the trailer.

Wes clenched his teeth. "What did you do to her?"

"Pick her up, or I shoot her where she lies."

Wes might have been willing to gamble with his own life, but not with Anna's. He worked his hands under her body, then lifted her into the air. She groaned, but it was low, too quiet for anyone but Wes to hear.

"Good," the man said. "Now bring her outside."

His back to the door of the trailer, Wes whispered, "Don't worry. I've got you now."

He thought he felt her stir, but her eyes remained closed.

"Come on," the man said. "Move it."

Wes carried Anna to the opening, then paused.

The man had moved back several paces. "I'm not giving you a hand. So try not to drop her."

Wes turned sideways, then stepped carefully to the ground.

"What did you do to her?" he asked again.

"Let's go," Dori said.

She motioned with her gun for Forman to start walking.

"No," Forman told her. "The only place I'm going is to town. Either you drive me, or you give me the keys to your car."

The gunshot was quick, and unexpected. Forman fell to his knees, his left hand gripping his right arm, just below the shoulder.

"Let's go," Dori repeated, her gun still pointed at the commander.

Forman clenched his teeth and staggered back to his feet.

"You bitch," he said.

"Watch your mouth, or I guarantee the next time I pull the trigger you don't get up," she said. "Now, that way." She motioned to the path that led up to the crest.

They formed a single-file line—Forman first, then Dori, then Wes cradling Anna, and finally Dori's partner—and began walking. The path was little changed from the last time Wes had been on it, a well-worn groove about two and a half feet wide with, at first, desert and scrub on either side, then more rocks and boulders the closer they got to the top.

As they approached the final, narrow segment that curved between two large boulders, Dori tapped the barrel of her gun against Forman's back. "Don't even think about trying something."

If he had been, the warning was enough to keep him in check.

The shape of the rocks forced Wes to lean back and turn sideways as he shuffle-stepped to get both Anna and himself through. He made it almost to the end before his hip banged into a pointed obstruction.

Grunting in pain, he nearly lost his grip. He leaned farther back and was able to get Anna balanced without banging her into anything.

"Keep it moving," the man behind him said.

"Wes?" It was Anna, her voice low and weak.

Wes quickly turned so the man would only see Wes's back.

"Keep your eyes closed," he whispered. "Pretend like you're still out."

"What?" she said.

"Please," he said. "Just act like you're still unconscious."

Wes wasn't sure whether she was following his directions or she had actually passed out again, but her eyes remained closed, and she was quiet.

Six more feet and the rocks fell away. Wes almost expected to hear music blaring and see dozens of half-drunk teenagers standing around a bonfire. But there was no music, no fire, and no one but them.

Tonight there was no party at the Drama Rocks.

Dori and Forman stopped twenty feet in front of the concave rock that had served as a backstop for decades' worth of bonfires. The rock was a little blacker than before, but otherwise unchanged.

"Remember this place?" Dori asked Wes.

Wes could feel Anna tense at the sound of Dori's voice. Not unconscious, then, he thought. Just doing as he'd asked.

"What are we doing here?" Wes asked.

"Here?" Dori looked around, then shrugged and shook her head. "We're just passing through. Where we're going is that way." She nodded to the east. "Keep walking, Commander."

Their little parade started up again. Every once in a while, Dori would let Forman know when he was getting off course by shoving him with the barrel of her gun. It took them ten minutes to reach the next ridge, then they followed the crest until they arrived at a rocky clearing about a quarter the size of the one at the Drama Rocks.

From this point the hills curved southward toward more ridges and more rocks. In the east a long slope descended into the waterless dirt bed of Searles Lake. Wes could see the shadowy forms of the Pinnacles off to the left and, across the lake bed straight out, the dark scar Lieutenant Lee Jamieson had created when he crash-landed his F-18.

"This is about right, isn't it, Wes?" Dori asked.

Wes said nothing. But it *was* right.

She looked to the southeast and pointed at the next ridge. "And that's where you took him." She turned back. "You don't remember me, do you?"

Wes remained silent.

"Come on. We met several times."

"This is ridiculous," Forman said. "Whatever's going on between the two of you, I'm not part of it."

"You're right. You're not." Dori pulled the trigger of her gun again.

This time, as promised, the commander did not get back up.

Wes edged a step backward. He had to get Anna

away. If he could get behind some of the rocks, he might have a chance.

"Where do you think you're going?" Dori's partner asked. He moved to the right, cutting off the gap in the boulders Wes had been angling toward.

Dori strode over, stopping just a few feet away.

"Who am I?" she asked.

Wes pressed his lips together.

"Who *am* I?"

"You're Dori. . . . You're . . . I'm sorry," Wes said. "I don't remember."

"You don't *remember*?" Dori raised her gun and pushed the barrel against Anna's head. "Do you remember now?"

"Please," Wes said. "I don't. That was a long time ago."

"But you remember my sister," Dori said. "Michael says you visited her grave."

Her partner nodded. "Yesterday afternoon."

Mandy? Her . . . sister?

Wes tried to remember back. Mandy *did* have a sister. Older than her by a few years, and hardly ever around when Wes was over. Her name had been—

"Doreen?" he said.

Dori smiled, then moved the gun away from Anna's head. "See, I knew you'd remember."

"But your last name is Dillman," Wes said, as if that would change everything.

"It's what happens when you get married, Wes," she told him as if he were a child. "You take the last name of your husband."

Michael snickered.

Michael . . . Michael Dillman.

Wes remembered him more than he remembered her.

This Michael Dillman, while still tall, had shed some of the pounds he'd used to go after quarterbacks during football season.

"Of course, I had planned on having an entirely different last name. Doreen Rice. Wife of Jack Rice. You remember him, don't you?"

Jack Rice. Jesus.

"But what about Danny? You've been sleeping with him for days."

The corner of her mouth rose in a smirk. "You think I'd really be interested in a moron like him? He was just a way to get closer to you."

"Him and I are gonna have a talk as soon as we're done here," Dillman said. "Remind him it's not nice to go after a married woman."

Wes felt his anger rise, but he knew he couldn't let it get the best of him. He was the only thing standing between these two psychos and Anna. "Let my friend go," Wes pleaded. "And you can do whatever you want to me."

Dillman smirked. "Don't think she's in any condition to go anywhere."

"Besides, you'll do what we want, anyway," Dori added.

"Anna doesn't have anything to do with this," Wes said. "Just let her—" He stopped himself. He'd been so focused on Anna since he'd found her in the trailer, he'd totally forgotten—"Tony? Where is he?"

Dillman squinted. "Is that your other friend? The guy?"

"Yes."

"Sorry," Dillman said.

"What do you mean 'sorry'?"

"He saw me putting that article on your bike. Couldn't have him hanging around knowing about that."

"Where are you keeping him?" Wes asked.

"He's with Jack," Dori said.

At first Wes didn't know what she meant. Then it hit him. "Oh, no. No, no, no!"

Anna's breath caught in her throat. She'd guessed Tony's ultimate fate. Wes squeezed her lightly with one of his hands, hoping to convey the need for her to remain calm.

"He shouldn't have been out that late," Dori said.

"The articles," Wes said. "The messages on the mirrors, too? The call to the police?"

Dori shrugged. "Sorry."

"Were you also the ones who stole my equipment?" he asked.

Dori laughed, then used her gun to point at the still form of Commander Forman. "I think you have him to thank for that."

"So what are you going to do now? Throw us down the mine shaft, too?"

"Your girlfriend, yes," Dori said. "But not you. See, first you forced me to drive you and the commander out here with a gun I didn't know you had. Then once both of you got out, I took off. But you made the commander hike to this place, and killed him." She smiled sadly. "Unfortunately, in your triumph you neglected to pay attention to where you were going, and walked off the edge of the rocks, pretty much where you got rid of Jack. How does that sound?"

"No one's going to believe that."

"Sure they will. I have you on tape interrogating the commander in the car."

"You also have everything that happened afterward."

Dori shook her head, then held up a hand and mimicked pushing a button. "Turned it off before my husband got in. Oops."

Wes looked at Dillman. "Look, I'm sorry about Jack. It was an accident. You should just let us go."

"Jack's been gone a long time," Dillman said. "I don't actually care what happened back then."

"You did all this for me, didn't you, baby?" Dori said. Michael grunted in confirmation.

"But Mandy was your sister," Wes said to her. "Jack Rice raped her."

Dori scoffed. "That's the same thing she tried telling me, but that's not what happened."

"What? I was there. I—"

She laughed dismissively. "You may have thought you knew my sister, but you didn't. I lived with her. I knew how her petty mind worked. Jack was *mine*. But she couldn't stand that. She hated the fact that I was in love. Every time he came to the house, she made sure to say hi to him and give him that ugly smile of hers. At the party she took advantage of the fact I was sick and couldn't go, so got him alone and spread her little legs for him."

Wes stared at her. "That's not how it was at all."

"He was mine," she went on, acting like she hadn't heard him. "He loved me. He was going to *marry* me." She locked eyes with Wes. "I was pregnant. Did you know that? It was Jack's baby. Our baby. We were going to get married in the spring, then move away after graduation. But that never happened. My own sister ripped that from me."

"What are you taking about? She was *raped*!"

"Whatever happened out there, she *wanted* it! She *asked* for it! Hell, she probably even *begged* for it!" Dori breathed heavily for several seconds, her chest heaving. Finally she seemed to calm down at bit. "I spent a whole month crying and worrying about Jack. Where had he gone? Why hadn't anyone found him? I guess with all that, it wasn't a surprise I lost my baby. Then I had nothing. I confided in Mandy. She hadn't known I'd been pregnant; I'd been keeping that a secret. I thought she'd be sympathetic. I thought she'd do what sisters are supposed to do. But instead she got angry. She told me her lies about what happened that night at the party. She called Jack a monster. She said that she was glad he was gone and *never coming back*. I don't think she even realized her mistake, but I caught it immediately."

"They weren't lies," Wes said.

"Of course that's what you'd say. I wouldn't expect anything less. You know how I got her to tell me what happened?"

Wes shook his head.

"I pretended like I believed her. I acted like I also thought Jack was this animal she was claiming him to be. She was eager to tell me everything. And when she was done, I knew she would have to pay."

Even if Wes wanted to move at that moment, he couldn't. He was riveted to the stone, shocked beyond anything he'd ever felt before. "So you killed her?"

"It was simple, really. I knew which day it needed to happen, the anniversary of Jack's death. So I made sure things worked out that she was home alone that afternoon. All I had to do was crush some of Mom's sleeping pills into a can of soda, then fill up the tub, and make sure Mandy stayed under. The only hard part was carrying her ass from the living room into the bathroom after she passed out." A pause, then a tilt of the head. "I helped her on her way. Like what you did with Jack."

She extended her arm, aiming the barrel of her gun at Wes's head. "Now put the girl down. No more wasting time."

Wes had to force himself to move. He turned and scanned the immediate area, looking for a good spot to set Anna down.

"Right there's fine," Dillman said, pointing at the ground directly behind Wes.

Wes pretended like the spot Dillman had indicated was a little farther back, so that Anna would be that much farther from whatever was about to happen.

"I said right there!" the man yelled.

"Okay, okay," Wes said.

As he knelt down he squeezed her again. Once she was on the ground, he bent over her to give her a kiss on the cheek. He whispered, "Count to one hundred, then get up quietly and get away. I'll distract them."

Again she tensed.

He knew she wanted to protest, so he added, "Just do it," then stood back up.

"Saying your goodbyes?" Dori asked.

"You could have killed me years ago. I would have been easy enough to find."

"But *I* wasn't around. See, Michael joined the Army when I married him. Got stationed on the East Coast. Then we spent some time in Germany and a few other fun places. Didn't come back here until he got out a couple years ago. By then I was willing to forget all about you. Besides, I didn't leave you completely unscarred."

"What do you mean?"

She snorted. "Let's just say killing you will be a lot easier than killing your dad."

Wes felt suddenly weak. It was all he could do to keep from falling to the ground. "What?"

"Mandy wasn't the only one unable to keep a promise. After she told me what happened, I used to go out to the mine to be close to Jack. One day your dad shows up, and I realized you had to have told him, too. He never saw me, though, but I saw him. So I started keeping a close eye on him. He came back several times. It finally dawned on me he was planning on moving Jack. I couldn't have that. So on the night it looked like he was going to do it, I followed him again, planning on stopping him in the act. He showed up with a truck full of gear, but instead of starting, he seemed to be waiting for someone. When whoever it was didn't show up, he left."

Lars, Wes realized. He would have been the only one his father could have trusted to help him. That's why "Pudge" had been on his schedule. But why move the body?

"I knew he'd try again, and there was no way I could watch him all the time. I couldn't wait any longer." She paused, a self-satisfied smile on her face. "So I knocked on your front door after he got home. I said I was your friend, and asked if I could use the phone because my car was giving me trouble. It was easy enough after that. Once he was knocked out, I drove his car out to Nine Mile Canyon, and Michael followed in mine. You know the rest. The next week Michael enlisted, and I went with him."

"You bitch," Wes said.

"I wasn't the one who started the killings. You were." She raised her gun. "Now move it. You know where I want you."

Yes. He did.

CHAPTER
82

LARS WAS DOING EIGHTY WITHOUT A HELMET as he passed the city limits east of town. It was another mile before he saw the flashing lights in his side-view mirror. But while the cop car was slowly gaining, it wasn't going fast enough to catch up anytime soon.

Lars eased off the throttle. The bike had more to give, but losing the cop was not something he wanted to do. If he was right about where Wes was, it would take the cops a good twenty minutes to get there after he called them. At least this way there would be one squad car with him already. The trick was to remain a tantalizing target. So far, so good.

The problem was he had never personally driven out to the Rocks. The few times he'd gone had all been back in high school, and on each trip Wes had been driving. So it wasn't surprising he almost overshot the turnoff. As it was, he ended up leaving a long skid mark on the highway to keep from missing it. Once he'd finished the turn, he stopped on the dirt road, engine idling.

Lars knew he had a decision to make. Guess, and chance being wrong, or wait until he was sure, and chance being too late. *Hell, I could already be too late.*

He pulled out his phone and saw that the reception indicator was down to two bars. If he went much farther, the signal would be gone altogether. It looked like he didn't have a choice, after all.

He was halfway through his phone call when the police cruiser pulled to a stop across the mouth of the road. There was only one man in the car. He immediately jumped out, his hand hovering above his gun.

"Step away from your vehicle!" the officer ordered.

"Have you got my location?" Lars said into the phone.

"Got it," Janice said.

"You know what to do," he said. "I've gotta go."

"Sir, I'll tell you only one more time," the cop said, stepping toward Lars.

Lars stuffed the phone in his pocket.

The cop was only ten feet away now. "Get off the motorcycle."

"No time," Lars said. "We've got to get out there." He pointed in the direction of the Rocks.

"Sir, keep your hands where I can see them," the cop ordered, his own hand now resting on the butt of his gun.

"Listen, Officer. My name is Lieutenant Commander Lars Andersen. There is a crime happening out—"

"I don't care who you are. Get off the motorcycle now!"

"Listen to me," Lars said. "There's been a kidnapping. There are people in serious trouble. I need you to follow me."

"Sir. Don't—"

"Call the station, they're already expecting to hear from me. Tell them to send everyone they can to the Drama Rocks."

Lars put the bike into gear and took off, not waiting to see what the cop decided to do.

CHAPTER
83

WES MOVED OUT ONTO THE FLATTOP ROCK where he and Jack had fought, and from where Jack had fallen to his death years before. It resembled a wide plank, and now it was his turn to walk it.

In his head he had been keeping count. He was up to forty-six. In less than sixty seconds, Anna should be making her move. He couldn't think about what had happened to Mandy, or Jack Rice, or, dear God, his father. He needed to keep Dori's and Michael's attention fully on him long enough for Anna to get away. Once she was safe, he'd be able to relax. It wouldn't matter what they did to him. At least Anna would have a chance.

"Move to the edge," Dori said.

Wes held his position.

"I said move." She raised her gun to emphasize her point.

"Shoot me and you ruin your whole I-killed-the-commander scenario," Wes said.

"I shoot you, it just looks like you guys got into a gunfight."

Fifty-nine.

Wes took a small step toward the drop-off. "You really think people are going to believe I did this?"

"You're already having problems with the cops. You told me that yourself."

Sixty-five.

"My friends will know it's not true. They won't let it go."

"Your friends will be back in Los Angeles before the end of the week. And in a month, they'll have forgotten all about you."

Michael Dillman was still too close to Anna.

Wes took a step in his direction. "You willing to go to jail for this?"

"Get back," Dori said.

Wes stared at Dori's husband. "Well?"

"She said get back," Dillman told him.

Wes didn't budge.

Eighty. Almost time.

Dillman moved the barrel of his gun a couple of inches back and forth.

"Is that supposed to scare me?" Wes asked.

"I don't care what it does."

Ninety-four.

"Now get back."

Then, to drive the point home, Dillman took three large steps toward Wes.

One hundred.

Wes held up his hands and moved back to where he'd been before. "Better?"

Behind Dillman, Anna stirred. First she turned her head a few inches and opened her eyes. Then she pushed up and got silently to her feet.

"So after I jump, then what?" Wes said.

"What then doesn't matter," Dori said. "Not to you."

Anna was leaning a little to the side, still unsteady from whatever she had been given.

Run, Wes thought. *Get out of here.*

She righted herself and looked like she was about to do just that.

"Two ways to do this," Dori said. "You jump or we shoot you. I'll let you choose."

Dillman smiled. "Bet we have to shoot him."

Anna had stopped.

Get out of here!

"I'll . . . I'll jump," Wes said.

A look of horror swept across Anna's face.

"You've got ten seconds, then we shoot," Dori said.

"I'll go, I'll go," Wes said, hoping Anna would get his hint to move it.

"I don't see you falling," Dori said.

Wes took a step back to the very edge of the rock.

"No!" Anna screamed.

Both Dori and Dillman whipped around.

Without thinking, Wes charged forward, crashing into Dillman. They fell to the ground, the man's head knocking against the surface of the boulder. Wes pushed Dillman hard, grinding his head into the stone.

Dori's attention had been on Anna, so she didn't react until she heard the two men hit the rock. Training her gun on Anna, she swiveled her head to see what had happened.

But by then Wes was already on his feet and headed her way.

Dori tried to bring the gun around, but he got there first, and he wrapped his arms around her, going for the weapon. The impact caused her finger to twitch. The gun fired, the sound near deafening at such a close range.

Dori screamed out in anger as Wes grabbed at her wrist, fighting for control of her pistol. She twisted and turned under his arms, trying to force him to let go, but he held on tight.

Another gunshot. Not quite as loud, and not quite as near.

Wes twisted around, looking in the direction of the noise.

Swaying slightly, face bloodied, Dillman was aiming his weapon at the rocks where Anna had been standing. For half a second Wes thought she'd been hit, but her body wasn't lying on the ground. In fact, he couldn't see her at all.

Dori took advantage of his distraction and slammed her shoulder into his chin. One of his hands slipped, and she rocked to her left, nearly freeing herself. But he quickly regained his grip and pulled her back against his chest.

"Michael, goddammit!" she yelled. "Help me!"

Dillman swiveled around and fired a shot.

Wes felt a hot, searing pain a split second before Dori winced. He knew instantly he'd been hit, the bullet entering through the fleshy part of his back on the lower left.

Dori moaned, then slipped downward.

Wes wrenched her back up, and twisted her around so that she was between him and Dillman, then easily ripped the gun out of her hand. It was then that he realized she'd been hit, too. The bullet must have passed all the way through him and into her.

A rock sailed out from behind some small boulders and clattered on the ground near Dillman's feet. The big man whipped around to see where it had come from.

Wes had never shot a weapon in his life, but as Dillman raised his pistol in Anna's direction, Wes squeezed the trigger of Dori's gun.

Thunder rocked the desert as flames licked out of the end of the barrel.

Dillman fell face-first onto the ground, his gun clattering across the stone surface, then flying off the edge into the darkness.

"Michael!" Dori screamed as she wiggled free of Wes's grasp. She staggered over to where Dillman lay, and fell to her knees. "Michael." She put a hand against his motionless face, then let out a wail.

"Dori," Wes yelled. "It's over."

Suddenly she was on her feet again, rushing at Wes, a scream of fury spilling from her mouth.

With one arm wrapped around her side, she used the other to take a swing at Wes. He tried to back out of her range, but she kept coming as blood began to soak her shirt.

"You bastard!" she yelled. "You killed him!"

"Dori, stop," he said.

"You killed him!"

"I had no choice," he said.

"You pushed him off, because my goddamn sister told you to. You killed my baby. You bastard!"

It wasn't Dillman she was talking about. It was Jack.

"Enough!" Wes yelled as another blow hit him on the arm. "Enou—"

A large hand clamped down on his shoulder and spun him around.

Dillman. He was a gut-shot mess, but alive. He pushed Wes into Dori, and made an awkward grab for the gun, but missed.

Wes whipped around and realized they were only a

few feet from the edge of the rock. One good shove from Dillman and he and Dori would go over the side.

He tried to duck around the bigger man, but Dillman reached out and grabbed him.

Twisting left and right and left again, he struggled to get out of the man's grasp. When he turned again, the butt of his gun knocked against Dillman's hip and popped out of his hand, smacking against the rock.

Dillman let go of him and made a grab for the weapon.

But it was Dori, not her husband, who came up with the gun. She pointed it at Wes.

"You goddamn son of a bitch," Dori spat. "It *is* over now."

She staggered slightly from her wound, then took a step backward for balance. But she had misjudged her position, and her foot landed half on, half off the rock.

Her eyes went wide and her arms flew out as she fought to keep from falling.

Dillman tried to grab her, but instead of connecting with her hand, he knocked into her arm, stealing what little balance she had left.

With a face clouded in disbelief, Dori vanished over the edge.

CHAPTER
84

DILLMAN FELL TO HIS KNEES, LOOKED OVER the drop, then collapsed to the ground.

"Dori!" he cried out. When he said her name again, his voice had weakened. There was no third time.

Wes knelt down and checked Dillman's pulse. He was still alive. Barely.

His own energy waning, he sat down on the rock.

"You're bleeding." It was Anna. Her hand touched the wound on his back, then found similar damage around front. "Oh, God."

"Went clean through," he told her, panting a little. "Is that good?"

"We need to get you to a hospital."

The thought of walking all the way back to the car was not an exciting one. He wasn't even sure he could do it, but he knew he was going to have to try. Then he remembered . . .

"Dori's got the car keys," he said. "One of us . . . is going to have to climb down and . . . get them."

"You stay here. I'll do it."

"Yeah. That's probably best," he said, trying to smile.

But before she could move, he touched her on the leg. "What about . . . Forman? Is he dead?"

"I didn't check."

She rushed over to where the commander lay. "He's still breathing. But there's no way we're going to be able to get him to the car."

"Keys first," Wes said. "We can worry about that . . . later."

Maybe there was some old wood around here they could use to make a travois. Worst case, once they were within cellphone range, they could call for help.

As Anna moved off into the darkness, he tried to track her progress, but soon he could hear nothing but his own breathing and the sounds of the breeze in the brush. He considered scooting over to Forman, but he knew he needed to conserve his strength, so the commander was going to have to just hang in there on his own.

A memory came to him, of him and his father camping up at Kennedy Meadows. Just the two of them sitting by the fire while a couple of trout cooked in a pan over the flames.

"What are we going to do tomorrow?" he had asked.

"Whatever you want," his father told him.

"I want to fish again."

"Then that's what we'll do."

"I love you, Dad." Not the Wes of the memory, but the Wes bleeding on the rocks said.

The sound of movement in the brush. It was off in the direction Anna had gone.

"Please tell me you found them," Wes said, his voice not nearly as strong as he'd thought it would be.

More steps.

"Anna?"

Someone moved into the leveled area. The shadowy form was too tall to be his girlfriend.

Wes looked around for Dori's pistol, unsure if it had gone over the side with her, but he didn't see it. Instead, the best he could do was a palm-size stone. He picked it up.

"You don't seriously think you could hit me with that, do you?"

"Lars?" Wes said.

The moonlight revealed the face of Wes's old friend.

"I thought you were . . . ? How did you . . . ?"

Lars was about to say something, then he glanced at Dillman's body.

"That who I think it is?"

"Michael Dillman. Remember him? He . . . was Dori's husband. Dori Dillman . . . Only Dori Dillman was—"

"I know," Lars said. "Mandy's sister."

"How did you know?"

"Later." Lars paused. "Where's Commander Forman?"

Wes nodded with his chin toward the dark form lying on the rock. "That's him. Anna checked him a few . . . minutes ago. He's alive."

Lars jogged over to the commander and did his own check. When he came back, he said, "What about you? Are you okay?"

Wes raised the hand that had been pressed against his wound. "I've been better. Anna went down . . . to get the keys so we could take Dori's car. Now that you're here . . . maybe we can get the commander out, too. Wait, if you have a car, we can just take that."

Lars shook his head. "I'm on your motorcycle."

Wes stared at him. "I don't even want to know how that happened."

"Where did you say Anna was?"

"Down . . . there." Wes looked toward the edge.

Lars walked out to the end of the rock, then knelt down and glanced over.

"No Anna. Unless she's that body lying down there."

"Dori," Wes said.

Sounds in the bushes again, only this time it was Anna who stepped out. She was dangling something in her hand. "Found them. Now let's get—"

She pulled up short as Lars stood up from where he'd been kneeling.

"Lars?" she said, then brightened. "Great. You can help me get him to the car."

"You're not going to need the car," Lars said.

"What are you talking about?" Wes asked.

Then he heard a noise in the distance, something familiar. It almost sounded like the breeze, but it was growing steadily louder.

It took Wes a moment, but as soon as he placed it he smiled.

Helicopters.

CHAPTER
85

WES SPENT TWO NIGHTS IN THE RIDGECREST Regional Hospital, before being airlifted—courtesy of the United States Navy—to the UCLA Medical Center in Los Angeles. Anna spent every moment she could with him, overstaying visiting hours and making the nurses force her to leave.

Dione and Alison came by a few times, each telling him he was looking good, and asking when he was going to come back to work.

"We've got a shoot lined up for New Orleans at the end of the month," Dione said one afternoon. "I expect you to be ready by then."

Wes had smiled and thanked her, but had not committed. He knew he was going to have to get back to work soon, but it wasn't something he wanted to think about yet.

Casey came by often, too—that is, after Wes remembered to call his brother and tell him to pass along the all-clear signal.

Danny visited only once. He looked like he'd aged ten years, and there was none of the humor he usually displayed. It was obvious he had taken Dori's deception hard.

"You can't blame yourself," Wes told him. "No way you could have known. Hell, I didn't even recognize her."

"Sure," Danny said without conviction, then left not long after, the cloud over his head as dark as it had been when he arrived.

Three days after Wes had been moved to Los Angeles, Lars showed up.

"Forman is still in intensive care but out of danger," he said after a few moments of small talk.

"What story is he telling?" Wes asked.

"The truth, actually."

"Really?" Wes was surprised.

"The investigators had pieced most of it together by the time he regained consciousness. And when they told him they'd already rounded up the two other commanders and a rear admiral who'd been involved with him, he knew he had no choice."

They were silent for a moment. "What about you?" Wes asked. Lars had admitted his own part in Forman's plan while they had waited for the helicopters to land at the Drama Rocks.

"My involvement is still under investigation."

"I'm sorry, Lars. If you want me to talk to somebody, I will."

Lars smiled. "It's okay. I'll be fine . . . well, maybe not fine, but I'll make out all right. Senator Jamieson has been very helpful."

"Oh, I see. You have friends more important than me now."

"Something like that."

They both laughed.

"So why didn't Lieutenant Jamieson just follow your script? None of this would have ever happened if he had."

"No, you're wrong," Lars said. "It would have. Maybe not with him, but with somebody else if SCORCH had been approved. Don't get me wrong. I wish he hadn't died, but exposing the flaws and those who were pushing for a defective product may have actually saved dozens of lives. So it was a good thing that the lieutenant was a straight shooter, and felt compelled to give SCORCH a full workout before giving his father his report."

"Funny I haven't seen any of this on the news."

In fact, the only news that had come out had been a local story in Ridgecrest about the accidental death of longtime resident Doreen Dillman.

"The parties involved have agreed a more sanitized version is better for all concerned."

Wes raised an eyebrow. "And Senator Jamieson?"

"He's also on board. In a few days his son will be reported killed in a training exercise at sea. The group who was responsible for his actual death will be dealt with appropriately by the Navy."

Wes looked skeptical.

"I gave them my word you and your friends would go along with it, too," Lars said.

"You seriously think they'll all go along with it?"

"I've already talked to them."

"Even Dione?"

"She was tough, I'll give you that. But she said yes."

Wes frowned. "Swept under the rug nice and neat."

"Dealt with nice and neat, that's all. I admit it's not exactly right, but some good has come out of it. Project Pastiche has been shut down, Forman and his people have been rounded up, and SCORCH has been officially canceled."

They were silent for a moment.

"What about Tony?" Wes asked.

"His body was retrieved two days ago." Lars paused. "They found fiber evidence linking Dillman to the body. Couple that with Dillman's confession to you, and as far as the police are concerned the case is closed."

Dillman had never regained consciousness, and had died the day after his wife.

"And the other body?" Wes asked.

"There was no other body," Lars said, his tone indicating that no matter what had really been found, officially the mine was empty.

So that was it. The incident with Jack was over. Wes was . . . free.

"Then you're here just to make sure I play along?"

"I'm here to check on my friend," Lars said. "If you don't want to play along, I can't stop you."

The corner of Wes's lip rose. "Your Navy friends wouldn't be too happy about that."

Lars shrugged. "Too bad."

"I have to ask you something else."

"Sure. What?"

"About my father. You were supposed to meet him that night, weren't you? You were going to help him move Jack."

Lars was silent for several seconds. "Yes."

"What I don't understand is why Dad wanted to move him."

"That was Dori's doing, I think. He saw signs that someone was nosing around the mine on several different occasions. He was afraid the body would be discovered. He asked me to help him. But . . . but I chickened out. I'm so sorry, Wes. I should have been there. Maybe if I was, he'd still be alive."

Wes shook his head. "No. What would have happened is that Dori would have realized you were involved, too, and you would have been killed years ago."

Lars gave him a small smile. "Thanks."

They talked for a few more minutes, then the door opened and Anna came in.

"Sorry," she said when she saw Lars. "You guys need a little time?"

"No," Lars said. "Not at all. I need to leave, anyway. Got to drive back up this afternoon." He looked at Wes. "Let's not let it go another seventeen years."

Wes shook his hand. "Yeah. Let's not."

Lars gave Anna a hug and then was gone.

Alone with Anna again, Wes felt that maybe, just maybe, life was going to be okay.

"Move in with me," he said, knowing it was partially the drugs talking, but also knowing it was the truth.

She looked around. "This room isn't big enough for both of us."

"Very funny." He shut his eyes for a moment, then popped them open as he realized he'd started to drift off. "I'm . . . serious."

She leaned over and kissed him. "I know you are. Now sleep. I'm not going anywhere." He smiled, not sure if she'd just said yes, but knowing even if she hadn't, she'd get there.

As soon as his eyes shut, an image flashed in his mind. Trees and the coast and Anna's arms wrapped around his waist as they rode on his father's old motorcycle.

The bike, his father, the trees . . .

. . . A memory. No, not so much a memory as a promise unable to be fulfilled. A trip his father was going to take him on. A camping trip on motorcycles to Redwood National Park near the California-Oregon border. A trip that had never happened.

As sleep began to overtake him, he knew that as soon as he was out, he and Anna would take that trip.

For his father.

And for himself.

It would be the right thing to do.

ACKNOWLEDGMENTS

THE SAYING IS: YOU CAN'T GO HOME AGAIN. Well, I hope I've proved that wrong. While I've manipulated and added things to aid in the telling of this story, Ridgecrest and China Lake are very real places, ones that have played important parts in my life. I won't spell out what's real and what I've invented (though those who have lived there will easily pick those out). The one exception I will say is that the Drama Rocks do exist, though if they are still called that these days I have no idea. And, with apologies to many old friends, I've also taken the liberty of moving them several miles to the east.

There are several people whose help has been invaluable in the writing of *No Return*. My friend and fellow novelist Bill Cameron's comments and suggestions were invaluable, as was the support of Robert Gregory Browne, Sophie Littlefield, Tasha Alexander, and Tim Hallinan. Which reminds me, a big thank-you to the folks at the Novel Café for the food, the table, and the friendly smiles.

A big thank-you, also, to childhood friend and retired

Naval Commander Richard Evert, and two other friends from those early days, Ted Lemon and Karen Mendonca. Motorcycle tips came from Chris Franklin (thanks, Chris!), but any mistakes I've made would be mine alone. Thank you to Sue Ann Jaffarian for pointing me toward Jonathan Hayes on drug matters, and to Jonathan for helping me find what I needed . . . not for me personally, but for the story.

Finally, stories are often sparked by something an author has heard or experienced. In August of 1979, Lieutenant Commander Theodore Faller had just taken off from China Lake in a QF-86 Sabre when his engine failed. Below him were the homes and businesses of Ridgecrest. Fighting with his controls, he managed to crash land in an empty field just beyond the fence of an elementary school that now bears his name. While he survived the crash, he did not survive the fire that consumed the plane once he was on the ground.

I remember the smoke that day, rising above the town, me and my friends wondering what had happened. The story came out in the days that followed, and we all knew that Lieutenant Commander Faller died a hero.

His story has stayed with me all these years, and my intention in using a similar event in *No Return* is intended as a way for me to honor what he did so many years ago.